THE CASE OF
THE FIERY FINGERS

Poker-faced Nellie Conway, who nurses bed-ridden Elizabeth Bain, brings trouble when she calls on Perry Mason with a glass phial containing four pills which she suspects are poison. Her employer, Nathan Bain, she says, had promised her money to give them to his wife. Perry Mason has them analysed and finds they consist of good old-fashioned aspirin! But when Bain accuses Nellie of theft and provides proof by ultra-violet light, the case which began like a hoax becomes suddenly sinister, and Perry is in it up to the neck.

by ERLE STANLEY GARDNER

THE PERRY MASON CASES

The Case of

The Case of
The Fiery Fingers

by

ERLE STANLEY GARDNER

THE THRILLER BOOK CLUB
121 CHARING CROSS ROAD
LONDON, W.C.2

THIS EDITION 1958

PRINTED IN GREAT BRITAIN
AT THE WINDMILL PRESS
KINGSWOOD, SURREY

Foreword

In all the earth there is probably no mental occupation quite as fascinating as that of finding clues and then accounting for them, which is all that detective work really is and about all that astronomy really is.

A detective, for instance, finds the head of an unburnt match broken off and lying by itself on the floor at the scene of a murder. Is it a clue or is it just one more bit of trivia?

Perhaps he will deduce that the murderer was given to the habit of snapping matches into flame with his thumbnail, that this particular match was slightly defective and therefore the head broke off in place of snapping into flame.

Then when the murderer is apprehended the detective will find out that the man simply wanted a small stick with which he could push a key out of the lock in a door, and had broken the head off a match and used the matchstick to fulfil his purpose.

And so it goes. Whenever a man feels that he has an explanation to account for some physical clue he is only too likely to find that his conclusions, while brilliant and logical, are completely incorrect.

But if these clues happen to have been discovered by an officer of the Massachusetts State Police there isn't much possibility of a brilliant but erroneous deduction.

Because such clues are sent to the laboratory of Doctor Joseph T. Walker, scientist, toxicologist and general all-around technical detective, who has an uncanny ability to separate mental wheat from imaginative chaff, the answers given are the right ones.

Let a discarded coat be picked up along one of the Massachusetts highways by a casual pedestrian who happens to notice what seems to be a bloodstain, and watch what happens.

Doctor Walker's piercing eyes make an examination which is different from the ordinary examination because he knows of a dozen things to look for, things that never would occur to the ordinary man.

That little hole, for instance, may seem to be of minor significance until by photographing it in infra-red light he brings out powder stains proving that it is a bullet hole. By using soft X-rays he will find bits of metallic fragments in the garment, and by a spectro-analysis of those fragments will name the manufacturer of the bullet in question.

Or perhaps that peculiar imprint which is visible only under a certain angle of transverse lighting will, when properly photographed, assume the form of a perfect circle indicating that the wearer of the coat may have been struck by a hit-and-run driver. The headlight of the offending automobile left its circular imprint in the garment, whereupon a microscopic examination is quite likely to bring out little slivers of glass, some of which may be distinctive enough to furnish an important clue.

A further microscopic examination of the threads of the garment may disclose a flake-like substance no bigger than the head of a pin, which Doctor Walker will turn on edge, and examine under a powerful microscope. He will then announce that this is a small chip or flake of paint peeled off from an automobile driven by the hit-and-run culprit. The automobile, he will announce, was first painted a robin's-egg blue when it came from the factory, it was next painted a conservative black, then covered with a neutral tan and is now a vivid red.

I have watched Doctor Walker at work in his laboratory. I have peered over his shoulder while he has discovered things that the average man would never even look for, and then has translated those things into clues which, properly evaluated, have on countless occasions led to the apprehension and conviction of a criminal.

I first became acquainted with Doctor Walker at one of Captain Frances G. Lee's seminars on homicide investigation at the Harvard Medical School. I have since had occasion to drop into his laboratory several times. Every time I do so, I find him engaged in some fascinating crime problem where his common sense, his uncanny keenness of mind and his marvellous technical training bring forth logical but unexpected conclusions, just as a magician reaches into an unpromising silk hat and brings forth a very live, very convincing, and very substantial rabbit.

Of course, the rabbit was there all the time, and from the viewpoint of the magician the silk hat was the logical place to look for it.

I know of many cases where Doctor Walker's mind, following physical clues as a bloodhound follows scent, has brought murderers to justice, and I know of some cases where the same mental qualities have been used to prevent innocent men from being unjustly convicted.

Quietly, modestly, unobtrusively, Doctor Walker goes to his work day after day, dedicating his life to the cause of practical justice.

Society needs more men like Doctor Joseph T. Walker. The time and money, spent in the highly technical training such men must have to become thoroughly competent, represents a profitable investment on the part of organised society.

But there is more than mere technical training that

makes Joe Walker the man that he is. He has an un-swerving loyalty to his ideals, a quiet courage, an inherent faith.

And so I dedicate this book to a competent scientist, a true friend, and a man whose pattern of life is a source of inspiration to those who are familiar with it,

DOCTOR JOSEPH T. WALKER.

Erle Stanley Gardner

1

PERRY MASON had just returned to the office after a long day in court.

Della Street, his secretary, pushed a stack of half a dozen letters on his desk and said, "These are ready for you to sign, and before you go home there's one client in the office whom you should see. I told her I thought you'd see her if she'd wait."

"How long's she been waiting?" Mason asked, picking up the desk pen and starting to skim through the letters which Della Street had typed out for his signature.

"Over an hour."

"What's her name?"

"Nellie Conway."

Mason signed the first letter, Della Street efficiently blotted the signature, picked the letter up, folded it and slipped it in the envelope.

"What does she want?" Mason asked.

"She won't tell me, but she says it's an urgent matter."

Mason frowned, signed the second letter, and said, "It's late, Della. I've been in court all day and . . ."

"This girl's in trouble," Della Street said with quiet insistence.

Mason signed the next letter. "What does she look like?"

"Thirty-two or thirty-three, slender, dark hair, grey eyes, and the most perfect poker face you have ever seen."

"No expression?"

"Wooden."

"How do you know she's in trouble?"

"Just the way she acts. There's a peculiar tension about her and yet her face doesn't show it."

"Any signs of nervousness?"

"Nothing outward. She drops into a chair, sits in one position without moving her hands or her feet, her face is absolutely expressionless, her eyes move a little bit, but that's all. She doesn't read, she just sits there."

"But not relaxed?" Mason asked.

"Just like a cat sitting at a gopher hole waiting for the gopher to come out. Not a move that you can see, but you have the feeling of inner tension—waiting."

"You interest me," Mason said.

"I thought I would," Della Street said demurely.

Mason abruptly signed the rest of the letters in the pile of mail without even bothering to glance at them.

"All right, Della, let's get her in. I'll have a look at her."

Della Street took the mail, nodded, stepped out into the outer office and returned shortly with the client.

"Nellie Conway, Mr. Mason," she said crisply.

Mason motioned the woman to a seat in the soft, comfortable chair which he had installed in the office so that by lulling clients into complete physical relaxation he might relieve their emotional tension and so loosen their tongues.

Nellie Conway disregarded the motion and took one of the less comfortable wooden chairs, moving with a gliding silence as though she had trained herself to make no unnecessary sound.

"Good afternoon, Mr. Mason. Thank you for seeing me. I've heard a lot about you. I was hoping you'd get in earlier. I'm going to have to hurry because I have to be on duty at six o'clock."

"You work nights?"

"I'm a nurse."

"A trained nurse?"

"A practical nurse. I work on cases where the people can't afford hospitalisation or trained nurses. We work longer hours and, of course, we do things a trained nurse won't do, and we get less money."

Mason nodded.

Nellie Conway turned to fasten steady grey eyes on Della Street.

Mason said, "Miss Street is my confidential secretary. She will sit through the interview and make notes, if you don't mind. She has to know as much about my business as I do in order to keep things co-ordinated here in the office. Now, what did you want to see me about?"

Nellie Conway folded gloved hands, turned her triangular face towards Perry Mason and, without the faintest flicker of expression in voice or eyes, said, "Mr. Mason, how does one go about preventing a murder from being committed?"

Mason frowned. "I wouldn't know."

"I'm serious."

Mason regarded her with searching eyes, then said, "All right. This is out of my line. I specialise in defending people who are accused of crime and I try to see that my clients at least get an even break, but if you *really* want to know how to go about preventing a murder I would say there are four ways."

"What are they?"

Mason held up his hand and checked off the four ways on his fingers. "One," he said, "you remove the victim, or the potential victim, from the danger zone."

She nodded.

"Two," Mason said, "you remove the murderer, or the potential murderer from the place where he can have any contact with the victim."

Again she nodded.

"Three," Mason said, "you remove all weapons of murder, which is pretty difficult to do."

"So far they've all been difficult," she said. "What's the fourth?"

"The fourth," Mason said, "is the easy one and the practical one."

"What is it?"

"You go to the police."

"I've been to the police."

"And what happened?"

"They laughed at me."

"Then why come to me?"

"I don't think you'll laugh."

Mason said, "I won't laugh, but I don't like abstractions. My time's valuable. Apparently you're in a hurry. I'm in a hurry. I don't like this business of having a client say, 'A wants to murder B.' Let's get down to brass tacks."

"How much are you going to charge me?"

Mason said, "That depends on how soon you quit beating about the bush."

"I'm a working woman. I don't make a great deal of money."

Mason said, "Therefore it's to your interest to have the charge as low as possible."

"That's right."

"So," Mason said, "you'd better tell me what this is all about, and talk fast."

"Then how much will you charge me?"

Mason regarded the wooden face across the desk. He glanced amusedly at Della Street. His eyes turned back to his client and softened into a smile. "One dollar," he said, "for advice, if you've told your story within the next four minutes."

There was not the faintest sign of surprise in her face. She repeated merely, "One dollar?"

"That's right."

"Isn't that unusually low?"

Mason winked at Della Street. "What's your standard of comparison?"

She opened her purse, her gloved hands took out a coin purse. She opened it, selected a folded dollar note, smoothed it out and put it on the desk.

Mason didn't touch it. His eyes kept regarding her with puzzled curiosity.

She closed the coin purse, put it back in her bag, snapped the bag shut, put the bag on her lap, folded her gloved hands on the bag and said, "I think Mr. Bain wants to murder his wife. I'd like to prevent it."

"Who's Mr. Bain?"

"Nathan Bain. He's in the produce business. You may know him."

"I don't. Who's his wife?"

"Elizabeth Bain."

"How do you know all this?"

"By using my powers of observation."

"You're living in the house?"

"Yes."

"Waiting on someone?"

"Yes. Mrs. Bain. Elizabeth Bain."

"What's the matter with her?"

"She was hurt in an automobile accident."

"Bad?"

"I'm afraid worse than she realises. There's been an injury to the spine."

"Can she walk?"

"No, and she isn't ever going to walk again."

"Go ahead," Mason said.

"That's all."

Mason's face showed annoyance. "No, that isn't all," he said. "You think that he wants to murder her. You aren't a mind reader, are you?"

"Sometimes," was the unexpected answer, delivered in a calm voice.

"And you're getting this from reading his mind?"

"Well, not exactly."

"There are other things?"

"Yes."

"What are they?"

She said, "Nathan Bain wants to marry someone else."

"How old is he?"

"Thirty-eight."

"How old's his wife?"

"Thirty-two."

"How old's the girl he wants to marry?"

"About twenty-five."

"Does she want to marry him?"

"I don't know."

"Who is she?"

"Some woman who has an apartment in the city. I don't know exactly where."

"What's her name?"

"Her first name's Charlotte. I don't know the last name."

Mason said irritably, "I'm having to draw it out of you like pulling teeth. How do you know he wants to get married?"

"Because he's in love with this woman."

"How do you know?"

"They correspond. He met her at a convention. He loves her."

"All right," Mason said, "so what? Lots of healthy men thirty-eight years of age have restless eyes and a roving disposition. It's a dangerous age. They come back home if you leave them alone. Sometimes they don't. There are lots of divorces, but there aren't many murders."

Nellie Conway opened her purse. "Mr. Bain offered me five hundred dollars if I would give his wife some medicine."

Mason cocked a quizzical and somewhat sceptical eyebrow. "You're certain of what you're saying, Miss Conway?"

"Absolutely certain. I have the medicine here."

"Why did he say he wanted you to give it to his wife?"

"He didn't say. He just said that he thought that this medicine would be good for her. He doesn't like his wife's doctor."

"Why not?"

"The doctor was an old friend of Elizabeth's."

"You mean Bain is jealous?"

"I think so."

"Look," Mason said irritably, "all of this doesn't make sense. If Bain wants his wife out of the way he'd much rather have her divorce him and marry the doctor than to try and get rid of her by giving her poison. If he wanted to—let's take a look at this 'medicine'."

Without a word she handed him a small glass tube which contained four tablets about the size of a standard five-grain aspirin tablet.

"Were you to give these to her all at once?"

"Yes, at bedtime—when she was being quieted for the night."

"Did he pay you the money?"

"He said he'd pay me the money when I'd given her the medicine."

"How was he going to know if you gave it to her?"

"I don't know. I guess he trusts me. I wouldn't lie."

"Not to him?"

"Not to anyone. I don't believe in lying. It weakens your character."

"Why didn't *he* give her this medicine?"

"He can't go in the room with her."

"Why not?"

"The doctor has said he couldn't."

"You mean a doctor tells a husband he can't go in the room where . . . ?"

"Elizabeth hates the sight of him. She gets upset, almost hysterical every time she sees his face. We're forbidden even to mention his name."

"Why does she feel that way?"

"I think she really knows she'll never walk again. Mr. Bain was driving the car when the accident happened. She thinks it was avoidable."

"You mean that he deliberately tried to . . . ?"

"Don't put words in my mouth, Mr. Mason. I said she thinks the accident was avoidable."

Mason's facial expression was a combination of exasperation and curiosity.

"I gather you don't like Mr. Bain?"

"He's a very strong, fascinating man. I do like him, very much."

"Does he like you?"

"I'm afraid not."

"So," Mason said, "he comes to you and offers to pay you five hundred dollars to give his wife poison, thereby putting himself entirely in your power, leaving a witness who could testify in case anything did happen to his wife. . . . It doesn't make sense. . . . How do you know it's poison?"

"I just *feel* that it is."

"You don't know what the medicine is?"

"No."

"Did he tell you what it was?"

"No, just that it was medicine."

"Why did he tell you he wanted you to give it to his wife?"

"He said he thought it would make her feel better towards him."

"This whole thing is screwy," Mason said.

She said nothing.

"And you went to the police?"

"Yes."

"To whom did you go?"

"I went to the police station and told them I wanted to see about a murder, and they sent me to a room that had a sign on the door saying 'Homicide'."

"And what did you do?" Mason asked curiously.

"I told someone my story and he laughed at me."

"Do you remember his name?"

"His name was Holcomb, he was a sergeant."

"Did you show him this bottle?"

"No."

"Why not?"

"I never got that far."

"What happened?"

"I told him, just as I've told you, that I thought Mr. Bain wanted to murder his wife, and I tried to tell Sergeant Holcomb why, but he laughed at me. He was in a big hurry. He had to go some place and he said . . . well, he said an unkind thing."

"What did he say?"

"He said I was neurotic, but I'm not."

"When did Mr. Bain give you this medicine?"

"Yesterday."

"Did you tell him you'd give it to his wife?"

"I made him think that I might."

"And you've been carrying that little bottle around in your purse ever since?"

"Yes."

"Taking it out from time to time when you wanted to get at something that was underneath?"

"I suppose so."

"In other words," Mason said, "there aren't any of his finger-prints left on that bottle by this time?"

"I don't suppose so."

Mason took the bottle, removed the cork, looked down at the contents, then spread out a sheet of paper and dumped all four of the tablets on the table. As far as the eye could determine, they were all identical. Mason picked out one of the tablets, returned the other three to the little tube.

He said, "Della, get me two plain envelopes, please."

Della Street opened the drawer of her secretarial desk, took out two envelopes and gave them to Mason.

Mason took the tablet he had taken from the tube, put it in an envelope, sealed the envelope, wrote his name across the flap, then took the tube containing the three tablets, placed it in the second envelope, sealed the flap, wrote his name across that flap and said to Nellie Conway, "Write your name across the flap so that part of the name is below the sealed flap and part of it is on the flap, just as I've done."

She took the pen and wrote the name as he had instructed.

"What's Bain's address?" Mason asked.

"Nineteen-twenty-five Monte Carlo Drive."

"You go on duty at six o'clock?"

"That's right."

"How late do you work?"

"Until eight in the morning."

"Then what happens?"

"A day nurse comes on."

"You have the longer shift?"

"Because the night nurse doesn't have so much to do."

"Why does she need a night nurse? Doesn't she sleep at night? In other words, couldn't the nurse be within call——"

"Mrs. Bain is a little difficult to manage at times."

"Why?"

"Well, her mind is upset. She's been worrying a lot, and . . . well, the fact she won't let her husband in the room . . . the doctor wants a nurse with her all the time. Expense doesn't mean anything to them."

"Who has the money?"

"She does."

"Bain is in the produce business?"

"He makes a living," she said, "but Mrs. Bain has the money. It's her separate property. She inherited it. She had it when she was married. That's why he married her."

"Does Mrs. Bain know about this other woman?" Mason asked.

"Of course. That's where I first got my information."

"From Mrs. Bain?"

"Yes."

"How long ago was this accident?"

"Somewhere around a month. She was at the hospital for ten days, then she came home."

"You've been working there ever since?"

"Yes."

"Who else is working there?"

"The day nurse."

"She's been on about as long as you have?"

"Yes."

"Who else?"

"A housekeeper."

"What's her name?"

"Imogene Ricker."

"How long's she been working there?"

h, she's been working there a long time. She's very
...ed to Mr. Bain."

"Does Mrs. Bain like her?"

"Oh, yes."

"And she goes into Mrs. Bain's room?"

"Certainly. Sometimes she takes spells for us nurses."

"How old is she?"

"Oh, I don't know. I'd say somewhere in the late thirties.
One of those peculiar, shadowy women who seems to be
everywhere and nowhere. You never know where she's
going to turn up. She gives me the creeps, Mr. Mason.
You've seen these cartoons of the haunted house with that
thin woman sitting there with the dark eyes and the inscrutable expression? Well, she's just like that."

"The point I'm getting at," Mason said impatiently, "is
whether Mr. Bain trusts her."

"Oh, I think Mr. Bain trusts her implicitly. She's been
working for him for years. She worked for his first wife,
and after his first wife died, well, then she kept right on as
Mr. Bain's housekeeper——"

"How long ago did his first wife die?"

"I don't know exactly. He's been married to Elizabeth
Bain a little over two years, I think, or right around two
years, and I guess he was a widower for three years. Well,
that would make his . . . I don't know, somewhere around
five or six years. Why?"

Mason said, "Has it ever impressed you as being exceedingly improbable, young lady, that with a housekeeper in
the house whom Mr. Bain had known for at least three
years, and perhaps considerably longer, he'd pick on you, a
total stranger, and out of a clear sky offer you five hundred
dollars to poison his wife?"

"Yes," she said. "It's occurred to me as being unusual."

"Unusual," Mason said, "is a very, very mild designation.
He gets along with the housekeeper all right?"

"Why, of course. They very seldom speak. She's quite taciturn."

"Any romantic attachment?"

"Heavens, no. She's angular, with deep-set, dark eyes——"

"So there's no reason for Mrs. Bain to be jealous of her?"

"Don't be silly, Mr. Mason. That housekeeper has no more sex than . . . than an angleworm."

"So the housekeeper could go into the room at any time and give Mrs. Bain medicine?"

"Why, certainly. I told you she helps out with the nursing when we want to get a few minutes off."

"Then why should Mr. Bain pick on you?"

"I don't know, Mr. Mason. I'm only telling you facts."

Mason shook his head. "It's all screwy. I'll get in touch with Sergeant Holcomb at Homicide and get his reaction. You keep the envelope with the medicine in it. I want to keep this one pill. I may get in touch with you later on. There's a telephone out there?"

"Yes."

"Is it all right to call you there?"

"Oh, yes."

"What's the number?"

"West 6-9841."

"Well," Mason said, "my advice to you is to keep those pills for evidence, not to commit yourself in talking with Mr. Bain, and let me talk with Sergeant Holcomb. If he wants to investigate, he can."

"He doesn't. He thinks I'm crazy."

"Your story has certain elements of improbability," Mason said dryly.

"Could I call you later on tonight?" she asked.

"Not very well."

"I have a feeling something may happen, Mr. Mason, when I go back there. Mr. Bain is going to ask me if I

gave his wife the medicine and . . . well, if I tell him I
didn't, he's going to get angry and suspicious."

"Then tell him you did."

"He'll know that I didn't."

"Why?"

"Because his wife is still alive."

Mason said, "I don't get this thing. It's a completely
cockeyed story, it doesn't make sense any way you look at
it. Yet somehow you seem to be completely convinced."

"Of course I am convinced, Mr. Mason."

Mason said, "I tell you what I'll do. I'll give you the
number of the Drake Detective Agency."

"What's that?"

"They have offices on this floor," Mason said. "They do
most of my detective work. I'll arrange to keep in touch
with the Drake Detective Agency, and if anything of importance should develop, you can call there. They'll know
where to reach me."

"Thank you, Mr. Mason."

Della Street wrote the number of the Drake Detective
Agency on a card, arose from her secretarial desk and
moved over to hand the card to Nellie Conway.

"Are they open at night?"

"Yes, they're open twenty-four hours a day," Della
Street said.

"And you'll speak to them about me, so that I——?"

"I'll speak to them about you," Mason said, and glanced
at his wrist watch.

"Thank you very much, Mr. Mason."

She arose from her chair, stopped and regarded the
dollar note on the desk. "Do I get a receipt?"

Suddenly Mason's eyes narrowed. "I wouldn't try to
charge you twice."

"I'd like a receipt. I'm very methodical in my book-
keeping."

Mason nodded to Della Street. "Make it for consultation, Della."

Della Street slipped a printed billhead into her typewriter, moved swift fingers over the keyboard, then handed the typewritten statement to Mason. Mason signed it, handed it across to Nellie Conway and said, "Here you are, Miss Conway, or is it Mrs. Conway?"

"Miss."

"All right. Here's your receipt. Now we have your dollar and you have the receipt and you will perhaps hear from me again."

"Thank you, Mr. Mason. Good-night to both of you."

She turned and walked with that strange gliding motion back across the office.

"You can go out this way," Della Street said, arising swiftly and escorting her out of the exit door that opened into the corridor.

When the door had clicked shut Della Street raised her eyebrows in a silent question at Perry Mason.

The lawyer was sitting at the desk, his face granite hard, his eyes level-lidded with thought.

"Well?" Della Street asked.

Mason said, "What a set-up! What a plan!"

"How do you mean?"

Mason said, "It was all right. I was just riding along, half-asleep at the switch, until she asked for the receipt. That did it."

"I'm afraid I don't get it. I . . . Whatever possessed you to only charge her a dollar, Chief?"

Mason laughed. "I knew she was sitting there expecting me to say ten dollars or twenty-five dollars, and then going to try to argue me into taking half of whatever figure I set, so I thought I'd trick some expression into her face by surprising her to death. I wish now I'd said a hundred dollars and got her out of here."

"Why?"

"Because I don't want to have anything to do with her," Mason said. "We're in a mess."

"I don't get it."

"Look," Mason said, "suppose something *does* happen to Mrs. Bain. See how the little minx has fixed things? Consider the position she's put us in. She's been to Homicide Squad. She's consulted me. She has my receipted bill to prove it. We all think she's a little screwy. We pass her off as one of these psychopathic screwballs and . . . Get me police headquarters. Let's see if we can get Sergeant Holcomb on the phone."

"You know he hates the ground you walk on, Chief."

"I don't feel too overly cordial toward him," Mason said, "but I want to try and verify that story, and I want to get myself on record as having tried to get Holcomb to do something. We'll steal a page from Nellie Conway's book and pass the buck."

"I get you," Della said, smiling. She moved over to the telephone, looked at her watch and said, "It's five-thirty. He's probably gone home."

"We'll try him anyway, and if he isn't there we'll talk to somebody in charge. Perhaps it would be better to get Lieutenant Tragg. Lieutenant Tragg has sense."

"Tragg likes you. He'd be more apt to listen. . . ."

"I don't care about whether anyone listens," Mason said, "I want to get my skirts clean. I don't like the smell of this. I don't like any part of it, and the more I think of it the less I like it."

Della Street tried for the outer switchboard and said, "I guess Gertie's gone home, Chief."

"Get him on my private line," Mason said.

Della dialled a number, then said, "I want Homicide Squad, please . . . Homicide Squad? This is Mr. Mason's office. Mr. Mason would like to talk with

Lieutenant Tragg if he's there, or with Sergeant Holcomb if he . . . Will you put him on, please? . . . Yes, Mr. Mason is right here . . . Yes, I'll put him on the line."

She handed the telephone to Mason, saying, "Sergeant Holcomb."

Mason put the phone to his ear. "Hello . . . Hello . . . Holcomb?"

Holcomb's voice was uncordial. "Hello, Mason, what is it this time? Got a corpse?"

"I don't know," Mason said. "Did a woman see you some time today? A Nellie Conway?"

"That nut!" Holcomb said.

"What did she want?"

"Hell, I don't know. She's nuts. She's talking about someone who wants to murder someone, and I asked her how she knew, and she said it was just an intuition or something of that sort, and I told her she was barking up the wrong tree, that she didn't have any evidence."

"What makes you think she didn't have any evidence?"

"She didn't, did she?"

"I don't think you heard her whole story."

"Hell, Mason, I haven't time to sit here all day and listen to a lot of psychos . . . Good Lord, I can show you a thousand screwball letters we get down here in the course of a month that——"

Mason said, "This woman is peculiar. That doesn't mean she——"

"The hell it doesn't!" Holcomb said. "She's crazy!"

"Well," Mason said, "she's been in here and tried to tell me her story. I thought I'd pass it on to you."

"Thanks," Holcomb said. "You've listened to her, you've telephoned me, you've passed the buck. Okay, so what?"

Mason said, "I just thought I'd tell you it's a situation I don't like."

Holcomb said, "There's lots of things we don't like. How do you feel about the income tax?"

"I love it," Mason said.

"Go to hell," Sergeant Holcomb told him.

"Now wait a minute," Mason cautioned. "This woman tells a peculiar story in a peculiar way. She says the husband of the woman she's nursing——"

"I know," Holcomb interrupted, "is in love with some other gal and wants his wife out of the way. So you ask her how she knows, and she says she's intuitive."

"And the husband wanted her to give his wife some medicine and——"

"Oh, nuts!" Holcomb interrupted. "I'll tell you what I think. I think this gal is trying to get the husband in bad because she wants to discredit him."

"That could be."

"I'll bet it is. Why should the husband give *her* medicine to give his wife?"

"She thinks it's poison."

"I see, so the husband calls in a nurse who doesn't like him and makes her a witness who can crucify him . . . Now I'll tell you something else. I know something about the background of that case. This guy she's working for is okay. The wife is hysterical, neurotic, and this little tramp of a nurse is . . ."

"Yes?" Mason prompted as Holcomb hesitated.

"Well, I don't think I should tell you *all* I know. She's been to you as a client?"

"Yes."

Holcomb laughed. "Well, Mason, I hope she makes you a profitable client—lots of business," and Holcomb roared with laughter.

"Well," Mason said, "I've reported to you."

"That's right. You've passed the buck. Go to hell and good-bye!"

Sergeant Holcomb, still laughing, banged up the phone.

Mason's face darkened as he dropped the telephone back into its cradle. "Damn Holcomb," he said. "He's getting smart. Now he accuses me of trying to pass the buck."

"Well, what were you doing?" Della Street asked, a mischievous twinkle in her eye.

Mason grinned. "Passing the buck. Why else would I call the guy?"

2

PAUL DRAKE, head of the Drake Detective Agency, moved with a shambling gait which to the casual observer seemed slow and tedious, but actually there was a double-jointed suppleness about the man that enabled him to perform a prodigious amount of work and cover a great deal of ground without seeming ever to be in a hurry.

Perry Mason at times likened him to a juggler who would drop a plate and then, when it was hardly more than three inches from the floor, reach down and catch it before it crashed, with a motion so perfectly timed that it seemed to be almost leisurely.

Drake jack-knifed himself into the overstuffed chair, swung his knees up over the arm, clasped his hands behind his head and eyed Mason with a bored indifference that was completely deceptive.

"What's the pitch, Perry?"

"I'm up against just about the goofiest problem I've ever encountered in my whole career."

"What is it?"

"A woman came in with a proposition that sounded entirely screwy. She wanted to know how much my advice was going to cost her and, just for the hell of it, I told her a dollar."

"What happened?"

"She paid the dollar."

"It's better to charge a dollar and get it in cash than to make a charge of a hundred dollars and get beat out of it." Drake said, grinning. "What's the trouble with her case?"

"I wish I'd never seen her."

"Why don't you give her her dollar back and tell her you can't do anything for her?"

"That's just the point, Paul. That's what I *think* she wants me to do."

"Well, what do you care what *she* wants? Just so you wash your hands and get out of it."

"There are some things you can't wash your hands of," Mason said. "It isn't that easy."

"Why not?"

"She comes to me with a completely cockeyed story about a wife being in danger, about a husband who's trying to get her to poison the wife——"

"That's easy," Drake said. "Advise her to go to the police."

"She's been to the police, Paul."

"What did the police do?"

"Laughed at her and kicked her out."

"That should make a precedent for you. What's the complete story?"

Mason told him.

When he had finished Drake said, "What do you want me to do, Perry?"

Mason handed Paul Drake the envelope containing the pill he had taken from the bottle Nellie Conway had shown him. "Let's find out what it is, Paul. It *might* be cyanide of potassium. Then I'd ring up my friend, Sergeant Holcomb, and have him jumping around like a cat on a piece of fly-paper."

Drake grinned.

"The point is," Mason went on, "we have only one tablet. If we use it up in an analysis——"

Drake said, "It's a cinch, Perry. I have a friend who

has access to a crime laboratory where they have one of these new X-ray defractors that uses X-rays and gets a graph from the molecular defraction of a substance. I don't know how it works. All I know is, it does the work. You can take an unknown powder and get a pretty good idea of what's in it in a very short time, and it only takes a microscopic amount of powder to do the job."

"Okay," Mason said. "I want to be sure and keep this tablet so there won't be any possibility of substitution or loss. I've had it in an envelope, sealed, and with my name on it. Now I'll give it to you. You put it in an envelope, seal it and put your name on it, keep it in your possession and——"

"And be prepared to swear that that's the tablet I got from you just as you can swear that's the tablet you got from Nellie Conway?"

"That's right. How much is it going to cost to have this thing given a quick test?" Mason asked.

Drake said, smiling, "Well, this man is broad-minded. He always takes into consideration the ability of a client to pay. I'll suggest to him that he wouldn't want to charge more than twenty-five per cent of the fee you're getting for the entire case, and that'll probably sound all right to him, and I guess two bits won't be too much for you to pay, eh, Perry?"

Mason made as if to throw a book at the detective and Drake dodged.

"Go on," Mason told him. "Get the hell out of here and go to work. How long will it take to tell what's in the pill?"

"I may be able to get it done in an hour."

"Tell you what we'll do, Paul. Della and I will go out and put on the nosebags, then we'll come back and look in on you and then I'll drive Della home."

"The way he talks," Della Street said, "you'd think a girl never had a date."

"I beg your pardon," Mason said. "What do you have on for this evening, Della?"

"Well," she said demurely, "now that you bring it up that way, I haven't anything that I can't cancel in favour of a nice thick steak done medium rare, a stuffed, baked Idaho potato with lots of butter, some toasted French bread, a bottle of Tipo Chianti and——"

"Stop it!" Drake said. "You're driving me nuts. I'm going to have to get by with a hamburger sandwich which I'll hold in one hand while I drink a cup of coffee with the other."

"Don't let it worry you, Paul," Mason said, grinning. "That's just what she *wants*. What she gets may be different. I'll take her to a Chinese place and get her a bowl of white rice. Come on, Della, let's eat."

Mason switched out the lights in the office and held the door open for Della. "Another day," he said.

Della Street held up the dollar note which Nellie Conway had given the lawyer, and said to Paul Drake, "*And* another dollar!"

3

An hour and a half later, Mason and Della Street, leaving the elevator, sauntered into Paul Drake's office, exchanged greetings with a girl at the night switchboard and then walked into Drake's private office.

"I haven't anything yet," Drake said. "I'm expecting something any moment."

"How much of the tablet did you use, Paul?"

"Not much. This guy had a smart idea. He had a hair-like drill and bored a little hole right in the centre so he could get a cross-section right straight through. He had some other stuff he had to find out about on a rush order so that's what's causing the delay. He . . ."

The telephone rang. Drake reached for the receiver and said, "This will probably be it."

Drake said, "Hello . . . Yes, this is Paul Drake . . . All right, go ahead."

Drake flashed Mason a warning glance, then said, "Well now, just a minute. Just hold the phone. I'll see if I have his number where he can be reached."

Drake pushed his hand against the mouthpiece and said, "This is your girl friend. She's all excited. She wants you right away. She says it's very, very important."

"Oh-oh!" Mason said. "This is it!"

"What do I do? Tell her . . . ?"

"No," Mason said. "Tell her I just came in, that you'll try to find me."

Drake said into the telephone, "Well, I don't know

where he is right at the moment. I have a number where I can reach him later on. If you could . . . Oh, wait a minute, there's somebody in the other office now. I think I hear Mason's voice . . . Oh, Mason! . . . Was that Mason who just came in? Well, tell him I want him . . . Yes, tell him there's a phone call for him."

Drake waited a couple of seconds, then said, "He just this moment came in. Just hold the line. I'll get him on the phone for you."

Drake nodded to Mason, who took the telephone from the detective and said, "Hello."

Nellie Conway's voice, sharp with excitement, reached his ears. "Oh, Mr. Mason, something terrible, absolutely terrible has happened! I must see you right away."

"Where?" Mason asked. "At my office?"

"No, no. I can't leave here. I'm not free to come. Please, can't you come out here right away? It's 1925 Monte Carlo Drive. I . . . oh . . . !"

With that sharp exclamation and with no word of goodbye, she dropped the receiver into place at the other end of the line, severing the connection.

Mason grinned at Paul Drake and said, "Well, I guess I was right, Paul."

"What?"

"It's a frame-up of some sort."

"So what do you do?" Drake asked.

"It isn't what *I* do," Mason said, "it's what *we* do. Come on, Della, you're going to drive out with us. We may call you in, in case we want to have someone make a statement."

"Don't you want me to wait for the call to find out what's in that tablet?" Drake asked.

"The tablet," Mason said, "will either be cyanide or arsenic. And in all probability Mrs. Bain has just died. Come on, Paul, we're going out and discover a corpse."

"And then what?"

"Then," Mason said, "I'll try to get myself extricated from a very nasty predicament. Nellie Conway will be proclaiming to all and sundry that she told me the whole story while Mrs. Bain was still alive. People will think I'm a hell of a lawyer."

"I don't get it," Drake said. "I simply can't see where all this is going to leave your client. It makes her look like . . . just what *is* her position, Perry?"

Mason said, "All this little byplay leaves Nellie Conway in a position where she can accuse the husband of having administered the poison while she had her back turned, since she had refused to help him. Don't you see, the girl's given herself a perfect alibi. She's gone to the police and tried to get them to prevent a murder that was about to be committed; she's come to me and tried to get me to try to prevent a murder that was about to be committed, and then the murder is committed. My poker-faced client has given herself a beautiful alibi, or at least she thinks she has."

"Perhaps she has at that," Drake said.

"By making a goat out of me," Mason said grimly. "Come on, let's go."

4

DELLA STREET whipped Mason's car around corners, swerved in and out of traffic, making fast time, seldom putting on the brake to slow down, seldom pushing down hard on the throttle, managing despite traffic to maintain a steady, even speed.

Paul Drake, in the back seat, shook his head lugubriously. "Sometimes I'd rather you'd drive, Perry."

"You kicking again, Paul?" Della Street asked over her shoulder.

"Not kicking, just commenting," Drake said.

Mason said, "Paul just isn't accustomed to good driving, Della. He even kicks when I drive."

"Can you imagine *that*?" Della Street exclaimed.

"Just like a taxicab in Paris," Mason said. "At first I used to think they went like hell. They don't. They just hit one speed and stay there. The French driver knows that if he puts his foot on the brake it's going to cut down on his gasoline mileage, and the same holds true if he puts his foot on the throttle, so he just goes about thirty miles an hour steady, no matter what's in front of him."

"And you think I'm doing the same thing?" Della Street asked.

"Heaven forbid!" Drake interposed. "You're hitting fifty and not giving a damn about anything."

Della Street slowed. "Well, I get you there in less time, so you don't suffer so long, Paul. Monte Carlo Drive should be along here somewhere. It's within the next . . ."

"Here it is," Mason said.

Della Street swung the car to the right, still going fast enough so that the tyres screamed as she whipped around the corner.

Paul Drake made an exaggerated gesture of putting his hands over his eyes.

Della Street slid up to the big two-and-a-half-storey white house, with its lawn, hedge and wide verandas giving it the appearance of a country estate despite the fact that it was within thirty minutes of the centre of town.

"Do you want me to come in with you and bring a book?" she asked.

Mason said, "No, Drake will be with me. We'll declare ourselves. How is it they say it, Paul?"

"In no uncertain terms," Drake said.

"That's the stuff," Mason told him. "You wait here, Della. Keep the motor running. We may want to go places in a hurry."

"Regular cops and robbers," Della Street said, smiling. "Don't let anybody sell you boys a bill of goods."

"We'll try not to," Mason promised, and, with Paul Drake trailing behind him, hurried up the cement walk, ran up the steps to the porch and pressed the bell button by the side of the door.

The porch light clicked on almost as soon as the chimes sounded, and the door swung open.

A short man, who seemed to be bursting from the seams, said, "Well, it certainly didn't take you long to get here."

Mason said cautiously, "We didn't violate any speed laws. What seems to be the trouble?"

"Step right this way, please," the man said.

He turned and led the way across a reception hall into a big living-room.

Mason studied the man's back. The coat was well-tailored but tight. The man's heels pounded the floor with the quick, energetic steps of impatience. Like many short, heavy men he seemed buzzing around in a continual atmosphere of hectic futility, trying to pound time into oblivion by sheer nervous hurry.

"Right in here," he called over his shoulder. "Right this way, please."

He didn't even look back as he pushed his way through curtains and into a sumptuous living-room where everything seemed to have been carefully and systematically planned, a room which radiated the touch of an interior decorator. Each chair was in its proper place so that it balanced the mass and colour design of the room. The curtains had been pulled across the windows, but it was quite evident that the view was on the east, where the huge picture window was in the centre of the room with easy chairs and ottomans on each side.

Nellie Conway was standing near one corner, her eyes widened slightly. Aside from that her face held no trace of expression.

A tall, slender man, whose face had deep lines and who might have been fighting ulcers, was standing behind one of the overstuffed chairs, his forearms resting across the back of the chair, a cigarette dangling from the corner of his mouth. He seemed to be detached from the life in the room, wrapped only in the gloom of selfish dejection.

A woman of uncertain age, tall, gaunt, grim-faced, stood well back in the room. The room seemed to fit her exactly. It could have been her methodical, mathematical mind that had arranged the furniture with such careful precision and kept it so arranged.

She looked at Mason and for a moment her dark,

inscrutable eyes locked with his, then she moved silently over to where Nellie Conway was sitting, placed a reassuring hand on her shoulder. "I think it's going to come out all right, dear," she said. "Don't be frightened." She gave Nellie a little pat, then turned and walked from the room.

"Mr. Mason," Nellie Conway said.

"Eh? How's that?" the fat man asked.

"This is Mr. Bain, my employer," she said.

"Eh? What's that? Who the hell is this?" Bain asked.

Nellie Conway went on talking to Mason without paying the slightest attention to Nathan Bain.

"Mr. Bain is my employer," she explained. "He has just had the temerity to accuse me of theft. This *gentleman* on the right is a private detective who seems to have been working on my case for some little time without doing me the courtesy of letting me know anything about it, and the police, I believe, are on their way."

"How's this?" Bain asked, whirling to Perry Mason. "Aren't you the police?"

The man Nellie Conway had described as a private detective said, dispiritedly, without moving the cigarette from its position, "Perry Mason, the famous criminal lawyer. That's Paul Drake with him, head of the Drake Detective Agency. Does most of Mason's work. Hello, Drake."

Drake said, "I don't think I place you."

"Jim Hallock."

"Oh yes. I place you now," Drake said without cordiality.

"What seems to be the trouble?" Mason asked.

"What the devil are you doing here?" Bain demanded. "I called the police."

"Thought I'd drop in and see what the trouble was."

"Well, where do you fit into the picture?"

Mason said, "Miss Conway asked me to call."

"Nellie?"

"That's right."

"You mean Nellie Conway asked you to call here?"

"That's right."

"For heaven's sake, why?"

"Because," Nellie Conway said, "I'm tired of being pushed around. You're trying to frame a crime on me and I don't propose to be framed. Mr. Mason is my attorney."

"Well, I'll be damned!" Bain said, and sat down abruptly in one of the occasional chairs, looking at Mason with gimlet eyes that had been pushed back into his head by the layers of fat that had grown around them.

Jim Hallock shifted his position enough to remove the cigarette and shake ashes from it casually on the expensive carpet. "She must have phoned Mason when she said she wanted to run upstairs and see how her patient was getting along," he explained to Bain.

"Mason! Perry Mason, employed by a cheap crook like this!" Bain said. "I can't believe it. It's preposterous."

"It's nothing to me," Hallock said to Bain. "You're the one who's doing it, but I think I'd qualify that 'cheap crook' business. We haven't proved anything yet and . . ."

"The hell we haven't proved anything yet. We've caught the thief. We've caught her red-handed."

Hallock shrugged his shoulders and said, "That's what I *thought*."

"Well, it's so, isn't it?"

Hallock said nothing, merely stood there, leaning over the back of the big, overstuffed reading chair, as though smiling inwardly at some joke which appealed to him very much indeed. "I guess you've never seen Mason in court," he said.

"I don't get this," Bain said.

"I think," Mason told him, "that if someone will explain, we may clarify the situation."

"Are you representing Nellie Conway?" Bain demanded.

"Not yet," Mason told him.

"Why, yes, you are too, Mr. Mason. I paid you a retainer. I have your receipt."

"That was in another matter," Mason said dryly. "What seems to be the trouble here?"

Hallock said to Bain, "You don't need to talk if you don't want to. The police are coming here. They'll take charge."

Bain sputtered angrily, "I'll tell the whole story if I want to. All of a sudden, I seem to be the one that's on the defensive. I haven't anything to hide. My wife is sick, Mr. Mason. Nellie is the night nurse. She's not a trained nurse, just a practical nurse. Lately we've been losing jewellery and some cash. Personally, I suspected Nellie right from the first. But before I did anything I consulted Mr. Hallock, employed him as a detective. I wanted to get proof. I was only too well aware that any false accusation on my part might expose me to a suit for damages. A certain type of individual goes around looking for openings like that."

"I think that's unfair," Nellie Conway said.

Bain paid no attention, but went on, "Hallock had some very practical suggestions. We removed most of the really valuable pieces from my wife's jewel box and substituted imitations. Then we dusted the jewel box with a fluorescent powder so that if anyone touched that box some of the fluorescent powder would adhere to the fingers. Then we took pains to take the jewel box out of my wife's desk and leave it on top of the desk as though we'd overlooked putting it back. We made a complete inventory of the contents of the jewel box, Mr. Mason. All of the jewels were imitations but it was such an expensive jewel case no one would ever have thought the jewels were other than genuine.

"This afternoon Hallock and I again made an inventory of the contents of the jewel box. Nothing was missing. Tonight, when the day nurse went off duty, we once more checked the contents of the jewel box. Everything was in its place.

"About half an hour ago, when Nellie came down here to fix some hot malted milk for my wife, she was gone quite a long time. We purposely gave her an opportunity to be alone and undisturbed. Then we entered the room after she'd taken the hot malted milk upstairs, and inventoried the contents of the box. A diamond pendant was missing, so we called Nellie down here, turned off the lights and switched on some ultra-violet light. The results were all that anyone could have asked.

"I don't know how that stuff got on my fingers," Nellie said.

"Was there fluorescent powder on your fingers?" Mason asked.

Bain said, "See for yourself," and, with the self-importance of a showman who is putting on a good act, he marched over to the light switch and jabbed it with his thumb. Instantly the room was plunged in darkness. Then he pushed another switch. There was a buzzing noise and after a second the room was filled with ultra-violet light.

"Show the gentleman your hands, Nellie," Bain said with sarcasm.

Nellie Conway held up her hands. The finger-tips were flaming with iridescent light that had a peculiar bluish-green tinge and was exceedingly brilliant.

"There you are," Bain said. "Try and laugh *that* off."

He switched the ultra-violet light off and the room lights back on.

Nellie Conway turned pleadingly to Perry Mason. "Can't you see," she said, "this is all a—a part of that thing I was telling you about."

Nathan Bain said, "Let's get this straight, please. You're here representing Nellie. Is that right, Mr. Mason?"

"She asked me to come."

"And this gentleman with you is . . . ?"

"Mason's detective," Jim Hallock interposed. "I warned you, Bain."

"I see no reason why either of you gentlemen have any right to intrude upon these premises," Bain said. "I'm going to ask you to leave."

Mason said, "I'm a little dubious about whether Miss Conway is a client, Bain, but I'm not particularly impressed with your attitude."

"You don't have to be impressed with my attitude. This woman is a thief and . . ."

"Just a minute," Jim Hallock interrupted. "Let's not jump at conclusions, Mr. Bain, if you don't mind. There has been a series of jewel thefts. We're asking the police to investigate. There's certain evidence that Miss Conway will be called on to explain."

"That's it," Bain interposed hastily. "I'm not convicting her before she's tried. I've simply set a trap for her and she's . . . she's got that stuff all over her fingers."

Hallock smiled sceptically. "That's better, but it's too late to do any good."

Bain turned to Nellie Conway. "I don't see what you think you have to gain, Nellie. After all, I could bring myself to be lenient with you if you would make restitution, and . . ."

He broke off as the door-bell rang, and, saying to Hallock, "Keep an eye on them, Jim," he ran to the door, his short legs working like pistons. A moment later he called, "Well, here are the police. Now we'll see who's running this show."

The police needed no introductions. Bain, having made a brief explanation in the reception corridor, ushered the two uniformed radio officers into the room, and they immediately made their presence felt.

"Okay," one of the men said. "We'll dispense with the attorney and his stooge and see what this girl has to say for herself."

Mason said to Nellie Conway, "If that's the way they want it, don't say a word. That fluorescent powder is nice stuff but it doesn't actually prove anything. It's used in cases of petty crimes to trap a person and fill him with dismay at the idea of being caught with the evidence clinging to his fingers. A person usually becomes tearfully repentant under such circumstances and confesses."

"Shut up," one of the officers said to Mason. "Bain wants you to go home. It's his house."

"If it's an attempt to frame an innocent person it won't stand up in front of a jury," Mason went on, still talking to Nellie Conway. "Now mind what I'm telling you, the case won't stand up and . . ."

"That's enough," the officer said, moving belligerently forward.

Mason turned his eyes to the officer. "I'm advising a client," he said.

"I want them out," Mr. Bain said. "They have no business being here."

"You heard what the man said. Out!"

Mason said, "Right at the moment I'm trying to advise my client."

"Well, you can advise her some place else."

"And," Mason said, turning back to Nellie Conway, "don't let them kid you into believing that this is any serious crime. The most they can charge you with is petty larceny."

"What do you mean, petty larceny?" Bain sputtered. "Why, my wife's diamond pendant was worth five thousand dollars. It's . . ."

"Sure," Mason said, "but you outsmarted yourself. You put cheap imitations in the jewel box. It's the imitation that's missing. How much is that worth?"

"Why . . . I . . . How do you know it isn't the real pendant?"

"Don't get in an argument with him," one of the officers said. "Come on, Mason, on your way. You can advise your client after she's booked at police headquarters."

"Can you keep quiet?" Mason asked Nellie Conway.

"If you tell me to."

The officers grabbed Mason and Paul Drake, pushed them out of the door.

"Don't say a word," Mason cautioned over his shoulder.

"Come on, buddy. Make it snappy," the officer said.

"Not even about . . . about that other matter?" Nellie Conway called after him.

"Don't talk, period," Mason shouted back as the officer propelled him out of the front door.

"Well?" Della Street asked, as Drake and Mason approached the car. "It looked as though you went out on your ear."

"That made me mad," Mason said. "Just for that I am going to represent Nellie Conway, and Bain will wish he had never ordered those cops to give us the bum's rush."

"What happened?" Della asked. "Who was murdered? The wife?"

"No murder," Mason said, "just a case of petty theft, and some smart private detective has been using fluorescent powder. I think I'm going to have to teach that pair a lesson."

"Specifically what are we going to do?" Della Street asked.

"Specifically," Mason said, "we're going to follow that police car. When they take Nellie Conway to jail we're going to bail her out."

"And then what?"

"And then," Mason said, "Paul Drake is going to telephone his chemist friend. We're going to find out just what particular brand of poison Nathan Bain was trying to get Nellie to administer to his sick wife. From that point on there's going to be hell to pay."

"You mean you'll call the police?"

Mason smiled and said, "No. I'll represent Nellie Conway in a petty larceny case just for the pleasure it will give me to cross-examine Mr. Nathan Bain."

"Will they bring her right out?" Della Street asked.

"If she follows my advice and refuses to talk, they're pretty sure to bring her right out. If they can get her talking, or trying to explain things, the situation may be a little different."

Paul Drake said, "We don't really need to follow that police car, Perry. We could just go on to headquarters and wait for them there."

"And have her taken to some outlying precinct where we wouldn't know where she was," Mason said. "I've had 'em do that before."

"In murder cases," Paul Drake said.

"They may do it in *this* case."

"Nuts. You've never monkeyed with this small stuff, Perry. They may not even charge her."

"Big oaks grow from tiny acorns," Mason said cryptically.

"Meaning what?" Drake asked.

"Meaning Nellie planted something," Mason told him. "I can feel it sprouting."

They were silent for a few minutes.

"We can't follow that police car without getting into trouble," Drake pointed out. "They'll use their siren and——"

"We'll make a stab at it," Mason told him. "Somehow I don't think they'll burn up the road. They may try to get nice and friendly with Nellie on the way to jail so that she'll talk. If she——"

"Here they come now," Della Street interrupted.

"Move over," Mason told her. "Let me get behind that wheel, Della. This may be the kind of driving that Paul really likes."

"Have a heart, Perry," Drake pleaded.

The officers escorted Nellie Conway down to the radio car. One of the officers walked over to where Mason's car was parked and said, "No need for you to stick around, Mason. Bain is going to follow us in his car and sign a complaint. He doesn't want to talk with you and we don't want you to talk with him. Get smart and go home."

"I am smart," Mason said.

"All right. On your way then."

Mason looked around at the kerb and said, "I don't see it."

"Don't see what?"

"The fire-plug."

"What fire-plug?"

"The way you were ordering me away I thought that I must have parked in front of a fire-plug. However, I don't see it and there seems to be no parking limit in this——"

"Okay, wise guy. See where it gets you," the officer said, and walked back to his car.

A few moments later a car came rolling out of the driveway and blinked its lights. The officers started their car and drove down the street. Bain's car fell in behind and Mason tagged on behind Bain.

Forty minutes later Nellie Conway was out on a two-thousand-dollar bail bond furnished by Perry Mason.

Then the lawyer walked upstairs and into the office of Homicide to encounter Sergeant Holcomb.

"I think you overlooked a bet on that Conway woman," Mason said.

"You usually do feel that way." Sergeant Holcomb seemed to be chortling inwardly.

"I'm warning you that you'd better look into it."

"I've already looked into it," Holcomb said, grinning. "In fact, I happen to know all about it. Bain and I have met, and when he began to suspect Nellie Conway of stealing cash and jewellery, he phoned me for advice.

"I'm the one who told him to get Jim Hallock and use fluorescent powder, and catch her red-handed—and that's just what he did.

"She evidently got wise. Bain had her under suspicion and she decided she'd plant an alibi by accusing him of trying to murder his wife. In that way he wouldn't dare to prosecute her.

"And you, the smart lawyer, walked right into the trap!"

Holcomb threw back his head and laughed. "For a man who's supposed to have been around, you do the damnedest things. You fell for that little tramp's story. Ha-ha-ha!"

Mason said, "Don't be too sure. The shoe may be on the other foot. When Bain knew she wasn't going to give the poison to his wife, he decided to discredit her."

"Oh, nuts," Sergeant Holcomb said. "When Nellie knew he was getting on to her, she went and cooked up this story and got some tablets she claimed Bain was trying to get her to administer to his wife. I'd personally be willing to bet even money they're just props to back up her story, and that she grabbed 'em out of the first bottle she found in the bathroom. Nine chances out of ten they're aspirin tablets. That's what they looked like to me.

"Hell, Mason, figure it out. Would Bain be so dumb, even if he wanted his wife to have pills, to give them to a woman he was about to arrest for theft, and put himself in her power?"

And Holcomb once more threw back his head and roared with laughter. At length he calmed enough to say, "Don't let that little minx hypnotise you with a yarn that will arouse your sympathies, Mason. If you're going to be her lawyer, get your fee in advance, and in cash."

"Thank you so much," Mason said, and walked out.

Holcomb's booming laughter followed him down the hallway.

Mason rejoined Della Street and drove back to Drake's office.

Paul Drake, who had gone back by taxicab, was waiting for them. He handed Mason a graph some eighteen inches long, consisting of a long period of wavy lines running up into high peaks, down into troughs.

"What's that?" Mason asked.

"That's the way these X-ray defractors do their analysis. Here's the note from the chemist. He says:

" 'Dear Paul:

" 'The graph is very distinctive. There's no question on earth but what the tablet you gave me consists of acetylsalicylic acid. I'm returning the tablet herewith, with a little hole drilled in the centre.' "

"Acetylsalicylic acid!" Della Street exclaimed. "What's that?"

"That," Mason said, "is exactly what Sergeant Holcomb said was in it."

"Well, what *is* it?" Della Street asked impatiently.

"Acetylsalicylic acid," Drake said, "is the chemical name for the active ingredient in good old-fashioned aspirin."

"Come on," Mason said. "Let's go home. We're all washed up—I can't withdraw from that Conway case now. I'll have to defend her. One thing, Paul, slap a subpœna on that housekeeper as a witness for the defence. That'll give Bain something to worry about. This has been the sort of day I *don't* like."

"Better take this pill along with you, Perry," Drake observed, grinning. "It's swell for headaches!"

5

HARRY SAYBROOK, the deputy District Attorney, seemed definitely annoyed that an ordinary petty larceny case had been turned into a jury trial, and his annoyance manifested itself in everything that he said and did.

Perry Mason, on the other hand, was urbane, fair, logical, and smilingly frank to the jury.

Judge Peabody from time to time cocked a quizzical eyebrow in Mason's direction as the noted criminal lawyer sat calmly complacent while James Hallock, private detective, testified that he had been employed by Mr. Nathan Bain, that he had understood generally a whole series of small thefts had been taking place at Nathan Bain's house, and that as a result the witness had secured a neutral coloured powder which would fluoresce to a vivid blue-green colour when exposed to ultra-violet light. He had placed this powder all over a jewel box in which certain articles of jewellery were being kept.

The witness further testified that he had been in the house when the defendant, who was employed as a practical nurse, had come to work on the evening of the tenth. He had, he explained, been introduced to the defendant as a business acquaintance who was selling Mr. Bain some mining property.

The witness further testified that in company with Mr. Bain he had previously made an inventory of articles contained in the jewel case. The articles, so far as he had seen, were pieces of jewellery. He had made no attempt to ascertain their value. Later on he had been given to understand that they were pieces of costume jewellery. However, at the time of his first examination the witness had contented himself with making a rough pencilled sketch of each article of jewellery and general description of the article.

At the time the defendant had come to work on the evening of the tenth he had examined the jewel case and had found every article which he had inventoried to be intact. Two hours later, at the request of Mr. Bain, he had made another inventory of the jewel box and had found that one of the articles, a diamond and pearl pendant, was missing. That thereupon, at the suggestion of Mr. Bain, they called the defendant into the living-room; that at a pre-arranged signal the ordinary incandescent bulbs had been switched off and the room had been flooded with powerful ultra-violet light; that under the influence of this light the fingers of the defendant showed as a fiery bluish-green.

Harry Saybrook turned to the jury and nodded, as much as to say, "So you see, it's as simple as that."

When Saybrook had assured himself that the jurors had fully realised the damning nature of Hallock's testimony, he turned to Perry Mason with something of a challenge and said, "You may cross-examine, Mr. Mason."

On the witness stand, Jim Hallock braced himself for the abusive cross-examination which attorneys for accused persons usually heaped upon the head of a private detective.

"Why," Mason said, apparently with some surprise, "I have no questions," and then, turning to the jury, added with the utmost candour, "I think this man is telling the truth."

"What?" Saybrook exclaimed in surprise.

"I think he's telling the simple truth," Mason said. "What's so surprising about that, Counsellor?"

"Nothing, nothing," Saybrook blurted. "I'll call my next witness, Nathan Bain."

Nathan Bain marched to the witness stand and under Saybrook's questions told his story. His wife was sick. It had been necessary to employ a day nurse and a night nurse. The case did not require trained nurses working in eight-hour shifts since there was a housekeeper to lend a hand on occasion, so Bain had hired two practical nurses, a day nurse and a night nurse. The defendant had been the night nurse.

Shortly after the nurses had started work certain things began to disappear around the house, small sums of cash, liquor, items of jewellery. Bain made a point of stating that he couldn't be certain that it was more than a co-incidence, so far as the defendant was concerned. But he decided to set a trap. He had taken his wife's jewel case from the desk where it was usually kept, and had purchased articles of costume jewellery which had then been placed in the jewel box. The witness had then consulted James Hallock, the witness who had just testified. At Hallock's suggestion a fluorescent powder had been placed upon the box. The box had then been left on the writing desk as though someone had inadvertently neglected to return it to the interior of the desk.

Then Bain went on to describe the events of the evening of the tenth with particular detail.

Perry Mason yawned.

"Do you wish to cross-examine *this* witness?" Saybrook asked.

Mason hesitated just long enough so that Bain, feeling he was to escape without question, started to arise from the witness chair, then Mason said, "Just a moment, Mr. Bain, I do have one or two questions I want to ask you."

"Yes, sir," Mr. Bain said.

"When was this fluorescent powder placed upon the jewel case, Mr. Bain?"

"On the tenth."

"At what time?"

"About nine o'clock in the morning."

"The day nurse then was already on the job?"

"Yes, sir."

"Who placed the powder on the box?"

"Mr. Hallock did."

"And you stood by and watched him?"

"I did. Yes, sir."

"And previously you had placed these articles of costume jewellery in the jewel case?"

"Yes, sir."

"What type of jewel case was that, Mr. Bain?"

"It was a casket made in the form of an ancient trunk, covered with leather and studded with silver nails, with leather handles on each side."

"About what were the dimensions?"

"It was rather a large jewel case. I would say about fifteen inches by ten inches by ten inches."

"It was the property of your wife?"

"Yes, I'd given it to her for Christmas a year ago."

"And prior to the time the fluorescent powder was dusted on this jewel case, you had taken an inventory of the contents in company with Mr. Hallock?"

"Yes, sir. We did that together."

"Then the costume jewellery, or the imitation jewellery, was replaced in the casket, and then the casket was dusted with powder. Is that right?"

"That's right. Yes, sir."

"Now, did you have occasion to investigate that jewel box or casket during the day in order to see if the day nurse had taken something.

"I did. Yes, sir."

"How many times?"

"Twice."

"When?"

"About two o'clock in the afternoon and then at six o'clock, shortly before the day nurse went off duty."

"And then you investigated it again in the evening?"

"Yes, sir."

"How many times?"

"Twice."

"When?"

"Immediately after the defendant came on duty so that we knew nothing was missing at that time, and then again about two hours later—which was when we found that one of the articles of jewellery was missing."

"Who made the examination?"

"Mr. Hallock and I."

"Who opened the jewel case, Mr. Bain?"

"I did."

"Do you mean that you left this jewel case lying around in plain sight with no lock?"

"No, sir, it was locked."

"And it was kept locked?"

"Yes, sir."

"Then how could anything have been missing?"

"The thief either had a duplicate key, which was not an impossibility, or the lock was picked, which would not have been difficult."

"I see. Mr. Hallock didn't have a key to the jewel case?"

"No, sir."

"You had a key?"

"Yes, sir."

"And your wife had a key?"

"Yes, sir."

"You weren't using your wife's key then?"

"No, sir."

"How did you happen to have a key to your wife's jewel box?"

"It was simply a matter of precaution, Mr. Mason."

"I'm afraid I don't understand."

"Women are always losing things," Bain said, rather self-righteously, "so as a matter of precaution against having my wife lose the key to her jewel box, I only gave her one key when I gave her the box. I retained one key in a safe place."

"Oh, I see," Mason said, with a swift glance at the five women who were on the jury. "You felt that that reserve key would be safe in your possession and would guard against your wife's negligence?"

"Yes, sir."

"That your wife would naturally be inclined to lose her key?"

"Well, I thought she might."

"As you expressed it, I believe, you have rather a contempt for the ability of women to keep things?"

"Just a moment, Your Honour," Saybrook shouted and jumped to his feet. "The witness didn't say that at all."

"I certainly understood him to say that," Mason said. "Perhaps not in those words, Counsellor, but——"

"If you're going to cross-examine the witness use his own words," Saybrook said.

Mason smiled and shook his head. "I know of no rule of law that requires me to do that, Mr. Saybrook. I simply ask the witness questions on cross-examination. The witness can correct me if I'm wrong. I certainly understood his testimony to be that he was rather contemptuous of the ability of women to be trusted with responsibilities, and I think the jury will bear me out in that."

And Mason flashed a quick glance at the jury.

"The witness didn't say any such thing," Saybrook said.

"Well, now," Mason said magnanimously, "I'm going to be the first to apologise if I misunderstood him. It's only a few pages back in the record, Counsellor, and I'm going to ask the court reporter to read back exactly what the witness said."

Saybrook, suddenly realising that Mason's tactics had been in the nature of a bait which had caused him to make an issue of what otherwise might have been passed over, and was now serving to emphasise it to the jury, said, "Oh well, there's no use wasting all that time. I'll withdraw the objection. The jurors will remember what the witness said and I know they're not going to let you put words in the witness's mouth or——"

"Not at all, not at all," Mason said. "I'm now interested in knowing exactly what the witness did say and I'm going to apologise to him if I've misunderstood what he said."

"Well, I didn't mean that," Bain interposed uncomfortably.

"You didn't mean what?" Mason asked.

"That women weren't to be trusted with things."

"I thought that was what you said."

"I didn't say anything of the sort."

"Well, now," Mason said, "let's have the record read by the court reporter."

Judge Peabody said, "All right, gentlemen, if you'll just keep quiet now so the court reporter can search back in his notes, he'll find the testimony in question."

There was a tense silence in the court-room. Saybrook found outlet for his nervous energy by running his hand through his thick black hair. He didn't like the turn that events were taking.

Bain sat self-righteously erect on the witness stand, waiting to be vindicated.

Mason settled back easily in his chair, waiting with the

respectfully attentive attitude of the man who feels that the information which is about to be forthcoming is of the greatest importance.

The court reporter said, "Here it is. I'll read the question and answer:

> '*Mr. Mason:* How did you happen to have a key to your wife's jewel box?
>
> ANSWER: It was simply a matter of precaution, Mr. Mason.
>
> QUESTION: I'm afraid I don't understand.
>
> ANSWER: Women are always losing things, so as a matter of precaution against having my wife lose the key to her jewel box, I only gave her one key when I gave her the box. I retained one key in a safe place.
>
> QUESTION: Oh, I see. You felt that that reserve key would be safe in your possession and would guard against your wife's negligence?
>
> ANSWER: Yes, sir.
>
> QUESTION: That your wife would naturally be inclined to lose her key?
>
> ANSWER: Well, I thought she might.
>
> QUESTION: As you expressed it, I believe, you have rather a contempt for the ability of women to keep things?' "

Bain squirmed uncomfortably on the witness stand as the court reporter finished reading.

"I thought that's what you said," Mason observed. "It was, wasn't it?"

"Well, it wasn't what I meant," Bain snapped.

"Oh, then you said something you didn't mean?"

"Yes, sir."

"Under oath?"

"Well, it was a slip of the tongue."

"What do you mean by a slip of the tongue, Mr. Bain? Did you say something that wasn't true?"

"Well, I said something that . . . I said it without thinking."

"Without thinking of what?"

"Well, I was only trying to say that my wife has a habit of losing things and . . ."

"And you did generalise by stating that that was a trait that women had generally?"

"Oh, Your Honour," Saybrook said, making his voice weary with exasperation. "Surely this is a minor matter. Good Lord, we've been over it time and time and time again. The question is already asked and answered in the record *ad nauseam*."

"I don't think so," Mason said. "I think that it's rather important to find out what attitude this witness may have, not only toward women generally, because my client is a woman, but also I'm particularly interested in finding out what's in the back of his mind when he states on cross-examination that he made statements he didn't mean. I'd like to find out how many *other* things in his testimony may have been incorrect."

"Nothing in his testimony is incorrect," Saybrook shouted.

"You mean then the witness really does feel that women are not to be trusted with responsibility?" Mason asked.

A few of the scattered spectators in the court-room laughed. Judge Peabody smiled and said, "Well, Mr. Mason, I think you've made your point."

"But I certainly desire to cross-examine this witness as to just what he means by what he says, Your Honour."

"Go ahead," Judge Peabody said.

"Is that the only thing in your testimony that is incorrect?" Mason asked.

"That isn't incorrect."

"Oh, you meant every word you said then?"

"Yes, I meant it," Bain shouted.

"I thought you did," Mason said, smiling. "Now let's be frank, Mr. Bain. After you realised that your statement might offend some of the women on the jury you tried to change it, but actually you meant it. Isn't that a fact?"

"Your Honour, I object," Saybrook shouted. "That's not proper cross-examination, and——"

"It goes to show the biased attitude of the witness," Mason said, "and is a reflection on his credibility."

"The objection is overruled. The witness may answer," Judge Peabody said.

"Isn't that it?" Mason asked.

"All right, if that's the way you want it, have it that way," Bain snapped angrily.

"Come, come," Mason said, soothingly. "It's not the way I want it, Mr. Bain. I'm simply trying to find out something about your mental processes. Isn't it a fact that you made this statement rather heedlessly without considering its possible effect and . . . ?"

"All right, I did. So what?"

"Nothing, nothing," Mason said, "I'm simply trying to get your frame of mind, your attitude. You meant what you said and you said what you meant, but when you realised the remark might have been impolite you tried to pass it off as a slip of the tongue. Is that right?"

"That's right."

"So it really wasn't a slip of the tongue, it was the truth. Is *that* right?"

"That's right."

"So you were stating an untruth when you said it *was* a slip of the tongue?"

"Call it a slip of the mind," Bain snapped.

"Thank you," Mason said, "now let's get back to the facts in the case."

"It's about time," Saybrook commented, his tone showing extreme weariness.

Mason smiled at him. "I'm sorry if I've bored you, Counsellor."

"That will do," Judge Peabody announced. "There will be no interchange between counsel. Confine your remarks to the court and your questions to the witness, Mr. Mason."

"Very well, Your Honour," Mason said cheerfully. "Now you want the jury to understand, Mr. Bain, that you yourself opened this jewel casket to look in it shortly after the defendant came on duty that night."

"I did. Yes, sir."

"You had your key?"

"Yes, sir."

"By the way, did you tell your wife that you had an extra key?"

"No, sir. I did not."

"Indeed," Mason said. "Why not?"

"Objected to as incompetent, irrelevant, and immaterial, and not proper cross-examination," Saybrook said.

"The objection is sustained," Judge Peabody ruled.

"But," Mason said, "you *did* have a key to your wife's jewel casket and you carefully kept that information from her. Isn't that right?"

"That isn't right," Saybrook shouted. "Your Honour, Counsel is deliberately distorting the testimony of this witness. He never said any such thing."

"I'm asking him now," Mason said. "He can answer that question yes or no."

"The objection is overruled," Judge Peabody said. "I'll permit an answer to that one question. I think we've gone over the matter several times but nevertheless I will permit the witness to answer this one question."

Bain hesitated.

"Yes or no?" Mason asked. "Is it a fact or isn't it?"

"Well, I didn't carefully keep the information from her."

"You kept it from her?" Mason suggested.

"Yes, I did," Bain snapped.

"You want the jury to understand that you kept it from her carelessly and negligently, that you simply overlooked mentioning it to her?"

"Well, I . . . I just wanted to have the extra key, then I'd surprise her in case she lost her key and couldn't find it. I . . ."

"But she never did lose her key, did she, Mr. Bain?"

"Not that I know of, no."

"And you feel that you would have known of it if she had lost it?"

"I suppose so."

"Then," Mason said, smiling, "you have to admit that your comments as to your wife's inefficiency in such matters were not well-founded."

"Objection," Saybrook shouted. "That's——"

"Sustained," Judge Peabody said. "I think we've gone into this matter far enough, Mr. Mason."

"Very well, Your Honour," Mason said. "I have just a couple more questions."

Mason shifted his position in the swivel chair at the counsel table and, catching the eye of one of the women members of the jury, let his face soften into a half smile.

The woman promptly smiled back.

Mason said, "Now, let's see, Mr. Bain. You opened that jewel case and I understand that when you did Mr. Hallock was there with you?"

"Yes, sir."

"And you pointed out that something was missing?"

"Yes, sir."

"And Mr. Hallock compared the contents of the jewel box with his list?"

"Yes, sir."

"Now, how was Mr. Hallock able to do that without touching the jewel box?"

"I never said he did it without touching the jewel box," Bain said. "Don't put words in my mouth!"

"Oh, then he *did* touch the jewel box?"

"I suppose so. He naturally would have. I didn't say he did, and I didn't say he didn't."

"But your best recollection now is that he did?"

"He may have."

"Do you know whether he did or not?"

"I assume that he did."

"So," Mason said, "after the fluorescent powder had been placed on the jewel box *you* touched the jewel box and *Mr. Hallock* touched the jewel box."

"Yes."

"So presumably at that time you and Mr. Hallock both had fluorescent powder on your fingers."

"I assume so. Yes."

"There were three people in the downstairs part of that house. All three of you had fluorescent powder on your finger-tips. You, Mr. Hallock and the defendant. Is that right?"

"Hallock and I had a right to have the fluorescent powder on our finger-tips. The defendant didn't."

"What do you mean, you had a right to?"

"We had a right to go to the jewel box."

"Certainly," Mason said, "but if you are going to rely on the assumption that the fluorescent powder on a person's finger-tips meant that a piece of imitation jewellery had been stolen, you could say that since Mr. Hallock had the fluorescent powder on his finger-tips that he had taken the piece of jewellery."

"Certainly not."

"Why not?"

"Because he wouldn't have."

"How do you know he wouldn't?"

"He was there for the purpose of preventing the theft."

"Oh, come, come," Mason said. "Not for the purpose of preventing the theft. You put the imitation jewellery in there because you felt some was going to be stolen. You left the jewel casket in a place where it was plainly obvious. In other words, you were baiting a trap. You *wanted* some of the jewellery to be stolen, didn't you?"

"Well, I thought we could catch the thief that way."

"Exactly," Mason said. "So, for all you know, Hallock may have gone to the jewel box and taken out that piece of jewellery."

"He didn't have a key to it."

"Neither did the defendant, did she?"

"I suppose she must have."

"Simply because you assume that she took the article of jewellery?"

"Well, she must have got into it in some way."

"And you had a key?" Mason said.

"I've told you I did a dozen times."

"And you might have gone to the jewel box and taken out that article of jewellery."

"I didn't."

"I'm not suggesting that you did," Mason said. "I am simply saying that you might have done so. You had the opportunity."

"Yes."

"And," Mason said, "you didn't put the fluorescent powder on the *inside* of that jewel box? You put it on the outside?"

"That's right."

"So that if the defendant had simply moved the jewel

case for the purpose of getting at something that was behind it, or if she had inadvertently touched it, she would have had this powder on her fingers."

"Well, she had it on her fingers."

"I understand," Mason said, "but she could have got that on her fingers simply by touching the outside of the jewel case in an attempt to reach for something back of the jewel case—perhaps to pick up a magazine or——"

"There weren't any magazines around it."

"Just where was it, by the way?" Mason asked.

"Out on top of the writing desk."

"Was that where your wife usually left it?"

"No."

"Where did she usually leave it?"

"It was usually kept inside the writing desk."

"And the desk was kept locked?"

"I believe my wife kept it locked. Yes, sir."

"And did you have a key to that desk?"

The witness hesitated.

"Yes or no?" Mason snapped.

"Yes."

"Did you give that desk to your wife for Christmas?"

"No, sir."

"That desk was bought some time ago as part of the household furniture?"

"That's right."

"Your wife had a key to it?"

"Yes."

"And you had a duplicate key?"

"Yes."

"Did your wife know you had that duplicate key?"

"I don't know."

"You had retained a duplicate key to the desk without telling your wife that you had it?"

"I never said I didn't tell my wife."

"You said that you didn't know whether she knew that you had a key."

"Well, I can't remember whether I told her or not."

"I see," Mason said, smiling. "You made it a point to keep a key to your wife's writing desk, and then when you wanted to, shall we say, find some method of discharging the defendant in disgrace, you took the jewel case out of the desk and placed it on top of the desk in an inviting position?"

"Well, I wanted to get the thing cleared up one way or another."

"That jewel case was rather unusual in appearance, wasn't it?"

"Yes, sir."

"A woman would naturally want to look at it?"

"Well . . . Nellie Conway wouldn't have any business doing it."

"A woman who was living in the house, who was there, seeing this rather beautiful jewel case on top of a desk might not have had occasion to look at it?"

"Well, she wouldn't have had occasion to touch it."

"But if she had touched it, just to have felt the leather," Mason said, "she would have got this fluorescent powder on her fingers?"

"Yes."

"Now, when the defendant was arrested, you went to headquarters to sign a complaint?"

"Yes."

"So the defendant was taken from the house, and you went from the house. Did that leave your wife there all alone?"

"No, sir. I called the housekeeper, Mrs. Ricker, and asked her to sit with my wife until I could get back and get a relief nurse."

"Did you explain to Mrs. Ricker the reason it was necessary to call her?"

"Yes."

"Tell her you had had Miss Conway arrested?"

"Words to that effect."

"And she was willing to take on this extra work?"

"She certainly was. She was glad we'd caught the thief. She told me she'd been wondering all day why that jewel case had been left out of the desk. She said she'd tried to put it back in the desk twice, but the desk had been locked."

"Oh, *she'd* tried to put it back?"

"So she said."

"Then *she* must have picked it up after the fluorescent powder had been put on it?"

"Objected to," Saybrook snapped, "argumentative, calling for a conclusion of the witness, not proper cross-examination."

"Sustained," the judge said.

Mason smiled at Bain. "But you didn't examine the housekeeper's hands under ultra-violet light?"

"No."

"In the name of reason," Mason said, "why didn't you put that fluorescent powder on the inside of the jewel case so that——?"

"I don't know," Bain blurted. "That was all Hallock's idea. He handled that part of it."

"But you assisted him, didn't you?"

"I watched him."

"You were there and saw him do it?"

"Yes."

"And you were his employer? If you had told him that you wanted the fluorescent powder on the inside he would necessarily have had to follow your instructions."

"I don't know."

"But you were paying him?"

"Yes."

"By the day?"

"Well, I offered him a bonus."

"Oh," Mason said, "you offered him a bonus. What was the bonus for, Mr. Bain?"

"Well, I agreed to pay him so much a day and then if he cleared the job up satisfactorily I'd pay him a bonus."

"You'd pay him a bonus. How interesting. How much of a bonus?"

"A hundred dollars."

"So," Mason said, smiling, "if a piece of relatively inexpensive costume jewellery was missing from that jewel case and there was evidence that would link the defendant with that missing bit of jewellery, Mr. Hallock was to get a hundred dollars. Is that right?"

"I don't like the way you express it," Bain said.

"Well, express it in your own way."

"It was a bonus for completing the job."

"The job was to have been completed when Miss Conway was arrested?"

"When we caught the thief, whoever it was."

"How many people in that house?"

"My wife, Mrs. Ricker, Mr. Hallock, Nellie Conway and I."

"You didn't examine Mrs. Ricker's hands, notwithstanding you knew she'd handled the jewel box?"

"No. She's been with us for years."

"And everyone else in that house, except your wife, *did* have fluorescent powder on the fingers?"

"Well . . . yes."

"Yet you picked Miss Conway as the thief?"

"Yes. It had to be her or nobody."

"It had to be her?"

"Yes."

"So your bonus to Mr. Hallock was to get this one person arrested and convicted?"

"To get the thief."

"Have you paid the reward yet?"

"No."

"Why not?"

"The defendant hasn't been convicted. It was to be paid when the job was finished."

"I see, then you *do* have a doubt in your own mind as to whether this jury should or would convict the defendant?"

"Objection, argumentative."

"Sustained."

Mason smiled and said, "I have no further questions, Mr. Bain. Thank you."

Saybrook said angrily, "You didn't tell Hallock that he was to get a hundred dollars in case he got evidence that would convict this defendant, did you? You simply told him that if he could find out who was taking the jewellery you'd give him a hundred dollars."

"Just a moment, Your Honour," Mason said, "that question is viciously leading and suggestive. Counsel is putting words right in the mouth of the witness."

"Well, this is on redirect examination," Saybrook said, "and I'm simply trying to shorten an examination that has been already too prolonged."

"Come, come," Mason said, "let's not assume that just a few minutes spent inquiring into the issues is going to be——"

"Well, the court's time is valuable and Mr. Bain's time is valuable, even if yours isn't," Saybrook said.

"And think of the defendant," Mason said reproachfully. "If your attempt to save Mr. Bain just two or three minutes of his valuable time is going to obscure the issues, the defendant might be incarcerated in jail for a period of months. She'd have her good name blackened, she——"

"You don't need to go into that," Saybrook said, "that's simply to influence the jury."

"Well," Mason told him, smilingly, "your attempt to justify yourself for putting words into Mr. Bain's mouth was for the purpose of influencing the court."

Judge Peabody smiled. "The vice of a leading question, of course, consists in having asked it. The witness now pretty generally knows what Counsel has in mind. Go ahead, however, Mr. Saybrook, and ask a question so that it is a little less leading."

"Oh, I don't think there's any need of going into all this in any greater detail," Saybrook said.

"You have any further questions?" Judge Peabody inquired.

"That's all."

"Any further evidence?"

"That's the People's case, Your Honour."

Mason smiled at Judge Peabody and said, "We'd like to move at this time that the court instruct the jury to bring in a verdict of not guilty."

"The motion is denied."

"If I may have a ten minute recess, Your Honour," Mason said, "I would like to talk with the one person whom I have subpœnaed as a defence witness. Mrs. Imogene Ricker."

"Very well," Judge Peabody ruled.

In the back of the court-room the housekeeper stood up, gaunt, grim, and defiant. "I refuse to talk to Mr. Mason," she said.

"This woman has been subpœnaed as a defence witness, Your Honour," Mason explained. "She has heretofore refused to make any statement to me."

"I don't have to talk to him," Imogene Ricker said. "I

came to court and that's all I have to do. I obeyed the subpœna. That doesn't mean I have to talk to him."

"Very well, then," Mason said, smiling, "just come forward, hold up your right hand to be sworn, and get on the witness stand."

"Do I have to do that?" she asked Judge Peabody.

"If you have been subpœnaed you have to do that," the Judge said.

She strode past Mason, held up her hand to be sworn, turned and flung herself down in the witness chair. "All right," she said grimly, "go ahead."

"You're a housekeeper in Mr. Bain's employ?" Mason asked.

"I am!" she snapped.

"How long have you been working for him?"

"Six years."

"On the evening of the tenth did you examine your hands by ultra-violet light to see if they were fluorescent?"

"That's none of your business."

Mason smiled. "If your fingers *hadn't* been fluorescent you would have answered the question, wouldn't you?"

"I don't have to tell you that either."

Mason grinned at the sympathetic jury. "Thank you. That's all, Mrs. Ricker. I just wanted the jurors to see how violently partisan you were."

"Oh, Your Honour," Saybrook said, "that——"

"The witness is excused," Judge Peabody ruled wearily. "The jury will pay no attention to comments of Counsel. Who's your next witness, Mr. Mason?"

"I don't have anyone," Mason said. "I think perhaps the jury have a pretty good concept of the case, Your Honour. An attractive jewel case was deliberately put in a position of prominence where anyone would be inclined to pick it up. We insist that——"

"There's been a ruling on the motion for a directed

verdict," Judge Peabody said. "Go ahead and put on your defence."

"I'm certainly not going to put on any defence in the present state of this case," Mason said. "It's not incumbent on the defendant to prove herself innocent. It's up to the prosecution to prove her guilty. All they've proven so far is that this defendant, who was in a room where she was required to be under the terms of her employment, touched the outside of an attractive and unusual piece of bric-à-brac. The defendant will rest right now and we'll submit the case without argument to the jury."

"You have already made an argument," Saybrook said,

"Tut-tut," Mason told him. "I was merely explaining to the court why I intended to rest the defendant's case. Do you wish to submit it without argument?"

"I think I should argue it," Saybrook said.

Mason smiled at him. "Well, as far as I'm concerned I think this jury understands the issue very clearly. I'm satisfied that they're intelligent citizens and I see no reason for wasting their time. You were very concerned about the value of time a few minutes ago. I'll submit the case without argument. Go ahead and argue if you want to."

Saybrook thought the matter over, then said sulkily, "Very well, I'll submit it without argument."

Mason made a little bow to the Judge.

Judge Peabody said, "You ladies and gentlemen of the jury have heard the evidence. It is now the duty of the court to instruct you as to certain matters of law."

Judge Peabody read a stock list of instructions, emphasising the fact that it was incumbent upon the prosecution to prove a defendant guilty beyond all reasonable doubt, and that it was not incumbent upon the defendant to prove himself or herself innocent; that the jurors were the exclusive judges of the fact, although they should take the law as given to them in the instructions of the court.

The jury retired and returned in ten minutes with a verdict of not guilty.

Mason and Nellie Conway walked over to shake hands with the jurors.

The woman juror who had smiled at Mason said, exasperatedly, "That man Bain! You certainly gave him just what he had coming to him. The idea of his keeping a key to his wife's writing desk. Just a snoop, that's what he is! Poor woman, her lying there sick in bed and having a man like that around the place."

"I *thought* you were a pretty good judge of character," Mason said. "I felt as soon as I looked in your eyes that I didn't need to argue the case."

"Well, I certainly told them what I thought of *that* man," she said. "The only trouble was I didn't have a chance to tell them *all* that I thought, because everyone else felt the same way about it I did."

She turned to Nellie Conway. "You poor dear, having to work for a man like that, and now he's gone ahead and had you arrested and sworn to a complaint against you on the ground of theft and blasted your reputation. I certainly think that you should do something about it. I think you should sue him for damages."

"Thank you very much for the suggestion," Mason said. "I was going to advise her something of the sort myself, but I think the fact that the suggestion has come from one of the members of the jury will be something to remember."

"Well, you can certainly quote me. You have my name and address," the woman said, and again gave Mason a cordial smile and another handshake.

6

BACK in Mason's office, as Mason and Della Street were getting ready to close the office, the telephone rang. Della Street, taking the call, cupped her hand over the mouthpiece and said to Mason, "Do you want to talk with Nellie?"

"I definitely want to talk with her," Mason said. "Long enough to explain to her that she's no longer a client."

Mason took the telephone and Nellie Conway said in a calm level voice that was as expressionless as her face, "Mr. Mason, I want to thank you for what you did today."

"That's all right," Mason said.

"I suppose," she ventured somewhat diffidently, "I owe you some more money, Mr. Mason? The one dollar I paid you didn't cover all this extra work, did it?"

Mason said, "Well, of course, if I handled jury cases at a dollar a throw, it would be difficult for me to pay my office rent, my secretarial salaries and my taxicabs back and forth to the Hall of Justice."

"Oh, Mr. Mason, you're being sarcastic now, aren't you?"

"I was just pointing out a few economic facts."

"Can you tell me just how much I owe you? Would another ten or fifteen dollars be all right?"

Mason said, "How much money do you have, Nellie?"

"Does that need to enter into it?"

"It might have something to do with it."

"I'd rather not discuss that, Mr. Mason. I'd rather you'd just tell me how much your charges are."

Mason became serious. "You called me up to ask me that?"

"Yes."

Mason was curious now. "You didn't say anything about any additional compensation after the case was over, Nellie. You just shook hands with me and thanked me. Why have you become so concerned about it now?"

"Well, I . . . I was just thinking that perhaps . . ."

"Look here," Mason asked, "has Bain been in touch with you?"

She hesitated, then said, "Yes."

"And Bain is offering you some sort of a settlement?"

"Well . . . Mr. Bain and I are talking."

"You mean you're talking with Bain at the present moment? You mean he's with you?"

"I'm with him."

"Where?"

"At Mr. Bain's house."

"At the Bain house!" Mason repeated incredulously.

"Yes."

"What in the world are you doing there?"

"Why, getting my things, of course. When the officers took me away they didn't give me any opportunity to pack up my personal things."

"Let's get this straight," Mason said. "Were you *living* there at the Bain house?"

"Why, yes, of course. The day nurse and I shared an apartment over the garage."

"Well, I'll be damned!"

"Why, what's wrong with that, Mr. Mason? Mr. Bain has lots of room here, and——"

"But you didn't tell me that."

"Well, you didn't ask me."

"Who's taking care of the patient now?" Mason asked.

"Why, the same nurse."

"I mean as a night nurse. Who's taking your place?"

"They had a temporary nurse for a few days, but she left very abruptly. The housekeeper has been helping out, and, just as a favour, I'll stay on the rest of the night. Mrs. Ricker will take a spell with me while I'm packing."

"You've seen Mrs. Bain and talked with her?"

"Why, of course. Elizabeth Bain and I are real friendly. She'd like to have me stay right on at my old job. But I don't think I'll stay . . . I had to tell her all about my arrest, of course, and about the way you questioned—well, the witnesses."

"By that I take it you mean the way I tore into her husband on cross-examination?"

"Yes."

"How did she react to that?"

"She thought it was wonderful. She said she wanted to see you. She . . . well, I . . ."

"You mean you can't talk freely?" Mason asked as she hesitated and broke off.

"Oh, yes. That's right. Yes, indeed. Mr. Bain is right here."

"And you're negotiating some sort of a settlement with him?"

"I hope to."

"Then you'll go back to work for him?"

"I think not. Quite a few of Mrs. Bain's relatives are due here some time after midnight. They're flying in from Honolulu. She'll have lots of company. She . . . well, I'll tell you some other time. I wanted to ask you now . . . that is, Mr. Bain wanted to know . . . if you'd set a price on your services so——"

Mason said, "If Nathan Bain is going to pay the fee, you owe me five hundred dollars, and that cleans us up. Do you understand?"

"Well, I should think it would," she said, rather tartly.

"If Bain doesn't pay the fee, we're quits," Mason said. "The one dollar charge is all I'm making."

"Oh."

"You understand that?"

"Yes."

"And," Mason told her, "that winds us up, and let's have one thing understood, Nellie."

"What, Mr. Mason?"

"I'm not representing you in connection with any settlement you make with Bain. If you make a settlement with him that's up to you. I think perhaps you should have some lawyer represent you."

"Then I'd have to pay him, wouldn't I?"

"Most lawyers like to be paid," Mason told her. "They have to support themselves, you know."

"Well," she said indignantly, "I don't see why I should take money and pay it over to a lawyer. Mr. Bain is willing to be reasonable, and as he's pointed out he couldn't be any more reasonable if a lawyer were there to take fifty per cent out of what I am going to collect."

"Did he say that?"

"Yes. He pointed out that it would be coming right out of my pocket."

"All right," Mason said, "use your own judgment."

"I am," she said, "and please, Mr. Mason, so there won't be any misunderstanding, you're not representing me in the settlement. I'm just trying to find out how much I owe you for your lawyer's fees, but I'm not going to pay five hundred dollars."

"You're not," Mason said. "Bain is."

"But I'm not going to let him pay that much. I think it's too much, Mr. Mason."

"How much do you think it should be?"

"Well, I would say not more than fifty dollars. You only did half a day's work."

Mason said, "I told you that if you were paying me you only owed me a dollar. If Bain was paying me, the bill would be five hundred dollars."

"Well, then, I'll get Mr. Bain to pay me and . . . well, I'll think it over, Mr. Mason. I'll . . . I'll do what's right."

"I'm satisfied you will," Mason said. "And now let's get this straight, Nellie. You and I are finished, the slate is wiped clean. I'm not your lawyer any——"

"I'll say you're not. At any such prices as those! Five hundred dollars for just a little over half a day's work . . . Why, I never heard of such a thing!"

And she slammed the receiver in Mason's ear.

The lawyer rubbed his ear, turned to Della Street. "That," he announced, "is gratitude. I have always said, Della, that the time to fix the amount of a fee is when the client is most anxious to secure the services. Miss Nellie Conway now feels ten or fifteen dollars would be ample compensation, and fifty would be munificent.

"Come on, Della, let's close up the joint and go home."

7

WHEN Mason entered his office a few minutes after ten the next morning, Della Street said, "Congratulations, Chief!"

"A birthday or something?" Mason asked.

"You've missed her by five minutes. Therefore congratulations are in order."

"Missed who?"

"Your dollar client."

"Good Lord, don't tell me *she's* been on my trail."

"Called four times after nine-thirty. I told her I expected you'd be in at ten. She said she'd call at exactly ten o'clock and that was the latest call she could possibly make."

"What's it all about, Della?"

"Apparently she feels she may need a lawyer."

"For what?"

"She didn't deem it fit to confide in me."

"What did you tell her, Della?"

"In a nice way I told her she was poison, smallpox, and had B.O., bad breath, and, in short, that she stank. I told her you were far to busy to be able to handle anything else for her. I suggested that she get in touch with some other lawyer who wouldn't be quite so busy and would be more accessible."

"Then what?"

"She said no, she didn't have confidence in anyone else. She had to talk with you."

"Did she call again at ten?"

"Right on the dot. You could have set your watch by it. Just as the second hand on the electric clock got to fifty-nine seconds past nine-fifty-nine the telephone rang and it was Nellie. I told her you weren't here and she said that was a shame because then she couldn't explain things, and she did want to explain things."

"She'll probably call again," Mason said.

"I gathered that she wouldn't."

Mason grinned. "We've probably lost a chance to make another dollar! What else is new? Anything?"

"There's a woman waiting to see you. A Miss Braxton."

"What does she want?"

"Now there," Della Street said, "you have me. She won't tell me what she wants or what it's about."

"Tell her I won't see her then," Mason said. "Hang it, I waste more time talking with people who want some routine legal chore I wouldn't touch with a ten-foot pole—probably wants me to draw a contract or make a deed or——"

"You should see her," Della Street said archly.

"Huh?"

Della Street made motions with her hands as though outlining a feminine figure.

"Like that?" Mason asked.

"Wolf bait," Della Street said. "I mean she's *really* something."

"Now," Mason told her, grinning, "you *do* have me interested. Keep on."

"And," Della Street went on, "I think she's mad about something. She says that what she wants to see you about is a personal matter and too confidential to mention to anyone. She's been waiting ever since nine-fifteen."

Mason said, "I love beautiful women who are mad, Della. How old?"

"Twenty-three, on a guess."

"And neat?"

"Face, figure, clothes, eyes, complexion, even just a trace of the perfume that makes men go nuts. You should see Gertie out at the reception desk. She can't keep her eyes on the switchboard."

"That does it," Mason said. "We're going to see Miss Braxton, but if she doesn't measure up to your build-up I shall resort to stern disciplinary measures."

"Wait until you see her," Della Street said. "You want to take a look at the mail first or——?"

"No, not the mail—the female. Let's go."

"Prepare yourself," Della Street said. "Take a deep breath. Here she comes."

And Della Street went out to the outer office to escort Miss Braxton into Mason's private office.

Mason saw the young woman enter the office with a swinging confident stride, saw her hesitate, bow coolly, then walk over to stand perfectly calm and collected by Mason's desk.

"This is Mr. Mason," Della Street said. "Miss Braxton, Mr. Mason."

"How do you do?" Mason said. "Won't you sit down?"

"Thank you."

She crossed over to the big, overstuffed client's chair, settled herself, crossed her knees, smoothed her dress, and said to Mason, "Will you kindly tell me *just* what is happening to my sister?"

"Now, just a moment," Mason said, noticing the cold steely anger in her eyes. "I'm not certain that I know your sister and I certainly don't——"

"My sister is Elizabeth Bain. Nathan Bain, her husband, is trying to poison her. Just what has been done about it?"

"Wait a minute," Mason said. "You're getting several carts in front of one horse."

Miss Braxton said, "I don't think I was ever so mad in

my life, Mr. Mason. You'll pardon me if I seem to be a little worked up."

"Go right ahead," Mason told her, "only don't take it out on me."

"I didn't come to you for that purpose, Mr. Mason. I'm not mad at you."

"Just why did you come to me?"

"I want to retain you as a lawyer. I think you're the only one who can handle this situation."

"What situation?"

"What situation?" she exclaimed angrily. "Good heavens, Mr. Mason, do you have the temerity to sit there and ask that question in good faith? Good Lord, my sister has been living in a hell on earth and no one seems to have taken sufficient interest to do anything about it?"

"Are you sure you have your facts right?" Mason asked.

"Mr. Mason, let's put it this way. My sister married very much beneath her. The man she married is a cold-blooded, scheming, nasty toad. Do I make myself clear?"

"I gather," Mason said, "that you're endeavouring to convey to my mind that you don't like the man."

"That," she said, "is a close approximation of the truth. I hate the ground he walks on."

"So I gathered."

She went on, angrily, "He married my sister entirely for her money. We warned her about it and—well, that's where we made our mistake."

"Who's 'we'?" Mason asked.

"The family. I'm her half-sister. There's a half-brother and—well, we should have kept our noses out of it. But we didn't, and as a result, there was a certain element of stiffness which crept into the family relations. We'd always been very close prior to that time, just as real brother and sisters, and now—well, thank heaven, now it's different. Now we're all back together again."

"Just what was it you wanted me to do?" Mason asked. "I have already been retained in connection with one matter involving the Bain household."

She threw back her head and laughed.

Mason raised his eyebrows.

"You'll pardon me," she said, "but I heard Nathan's description of what happened to him on the witness stand. I don't think I ever heard anything that amused me quite as much in all my life. The pompous, vain-glorious, self-centred, egotistical toad! And you ripped him up the back and down the front, Mr. Mason. You really did a job on him. Oh, how much I would have given to have been there!"

"You learned about all this from him?"

"From him and from Nellie Conway, the nurse."

"You talked with her?"

"Oh, yes."

Mason said, "I was rather surprised that she went back out to the house."

"I think Nathan was the one who was responsible for that. Nathan was simply frightened stiff, Mr. Mason, and I'll say one thing for Nellie Conway, she certainly knew how to keep pouring it on."

"Just what do you mean?"

"The way she put the hooks into Nathan was really something."

"Let's see if we can get this straight," Mason said. "First, I'd like to find out just what you want me to do and——"

"Why, I thought I'd make myself clear on that. It's not so much what I want you to do as to what my sister wants you to do."

"Elizabeth Bain?"

"Yes."

"What does she want?"

"She wants you to represent her."

"In doing what?"

"In doing lots of things."

"Go ahead."

"Well, in the first place, Elizabeth has now seen Nathan in his true colours. The man tried to kill her. He's been deliberately trying to kill her for some time. Heaven knows what that girl has put up with and heaven knows how many times she's been at the brink of the grave. All of those sicknesses she had, the food poisonings, the things she thought at the time were just stomach upsets, were probably all part of this scheme on Nathan's part to get rid of her."

Mason's eyes narrowed. "This has been going on for some time?"

"She's been living a perfect hell, Mr. Mason, and the poor girl doesn't know even now that her spinal cord is permanently injured. She thinks that after she has gone through a period of recuperation from the accident, someone is going to be able to operate on her, remove the pressure from the spinal cord and she'll walk again."

"And she won't?"

Miss Braxton shook her head. Tears came in her eyes. "She never will."

"What do you know about the accident?" Mason asked.

Her eyes glittered. "I know all about it. Nathan says that the brakes gave way on his automobile. He tried his best to stop it. When he found he couldn't he yelled to Elizabeth to jump. A fat chance she had of jumping! Nathan had very carefully engineered the thing so that he was on the inside of the road and Elizabeth was in the seat that looked right out over a yawning chasm. When Nathan yelled to jump he already had his door open. He just jumped out of the car and turned it loose.

"Elizabeth had sufficient presence of mind to reach over and grab the wheel. Then she tried to keep the thing on the road. When she saw that wasn't going to work, and the car was accelerating into terrific speed, she tried to run the car into the bank."

"The brakes really were out of order?"

"There wasn't a brake on the car," Miss Braxton said. "But that could have been arranged easily enough. All Nathan had to do was to fix it with a string running up through the floorboard so he could cut through one of the hoses on the hydraulic brakes and put the whole system out of order. And he picked a place to do it where the car would have naturally been expected to plunge over a perpendicular precipice. Fortunately Elizabeth's efforts to keep it on the road managed to get her past the most dangerous place so that when it left the road the car only rolled down the steep slope for a couple of hundred feet. Even so, it was a wonder she wasn't killed."

"Did anyone examine the car to see whether it had been tampered with?" Mason asked.

"What do you think?"

"I'm asking you."

She said, "Poor Elizabeth had her spinal cord crushed. She'd received a concussion and was unconscious. They got her to a hospital, and dear old Nathan went right back with a breakdown crew to see what could be done with the car. They managed to get it on a winch and hoist it back up to the highway; then they towed it away—and turned it over to Nathan. And during all the time they were fooling around out there with the winch, Nathan had every opportunity on earth to remove any evidence——"

"In other words, the police weren't called in?"

"The highway patrol made a routine inspection, but that was all. I don't think anyone actually went down to where the car was except Nathan and the garage men who hooked the cable on to the car and winched it back up to the road."

"Go on," Mason said.

She said, "You don't need to be so conservative, Mr. Mason. Nellie Conway told me her whole story this morning. I was never so completely flabbergasted in all my life. To think that such conditions could exist. Well, it certainly is time we got here. That's all I can say!"

"Have you talked with Nathan Bain about it?"

"No, I haven't said a word to him. I heard about you from Nellie Conway and I decided you were the attorney my sister wants. She wants to draw up a will that will completely disinherit him and she wants to file a suit for divorce. She hates the ground he walks on; she wants him out of the house."

"Has Nathan Bain been advised about this?"

"No, Mr. Mason. We want you to tell him."

"Me?"

"That's right. I want you to come out and talk with my sister. She'll tell you what to do, and then I want you to go out and see Mr. Bain, tell him he's done and tell him to pack up his things and get out of the house."

"Who owns the house?" Mason asked.

"My sister. She owns everything."

"Nathan's business is not profitable?"

"I think it's *quite* profitable," she said acidly, "but you'd never find it out from anything he tells you, and you wouldn't find it out from any books he keeps."

"What do you mean by that?"

"He does business on a cash basis wherever possible. He puts the cash in his pocket and no one knows how much it is or how much he makes. He doesn't believe in paying income tax and he doesn't believe in confiding in anyone. He's one of the most secretive men I know."

"Don't you think," Mason asked, "that it would be a better plan for your sister to call him in and tell him that as far as she's concerned she's all finished, that she wants him to leave, that she intends to file a suit for divorce, and——?"

"No, Mr. Mason. I don't think that would be the way to handle it. Elizabeth simply detests the sight of him. She gets almost hysterical every time she thinks of him. Remember that she's not well and she's been taking lots of sedatives which have had an effect on her nervous system. She wants to feel that he is entirely out of her life once and for all, and she doesn't ever want to see him again."

"All right," Mason said, "if that's the way she wants it."

"You'll do it?"

"I see no reason why not."

Miss Braxton opened her purse. "I told Elizabeth I'd come to you and put it right up to you, that if you'd do what she wanted and tell Nathan Bain where he got off, that she could be free of her worries. Elizabeth told me to give you this as a retainer."

She handed Mason a cheque, dated that day, drawn on the Farmer's and Mechanic's National for an amount of five hundred dollars, payable to "Perry Mason, attorney for Elizabeth Bain", and signed in a somewhat wobbly handwriting "*Elizabeth Bain*".

"This is a retainer?" Mason asked.

"That's right."

"And just what is it Mrs. Bain wants me to do?"

"You've started out very nicely showing her husband up. Just keep on doing it. Kick him out of the house and see that things are fixed so he can't ever get a penny of her property."

Mason said, "Your half-sister may make you her agent to deliver the cheque. I'll have to have those instructions from her own lips."

"Of course."

"When I'm alone with her, so I'll know there hasn't been any . . ."

"Undue influence, Mr. Mason?"

"If you want to put it that way, yes."

"Come on out and talk with her."

"I will."

"In the meantime, Mr. Mason," she said, "I want your opinion about this document—that is, Elizabeth does."

Miss Braxton opened her purse and took out a sheet of paper on which the date was written in the same wobbling handwriting that was on the cheque, and then the words:

I, Elizabeth Bain, knowing that my husband has tried to kill me on several occasions, having lost all confidence in him, and all affection for him, make this my last will and testament, leaving everything I own share and share alike to my beloved half-sister, Victoria Braxton, and my beloved half-brother, James Braxton, with the understanding that they will take my property

Mason regarded the piece of paper somewhat quizzically, and said, "Just what is it you want to know about this?"

"Is it good?"

Mason said cautiously, "That depends."

"Well, good heavens, you're a lawyer, aren't you?"

"Yes."

"And you can't say that it's good or that it isn't good?"

Mason smiled and shook his head.

"Why not?"

"Suppose," Mason countered, "you tell me something of the circumstances under which this will was made."

"Well, I don't know as it's so terribly important, Mr. Mason. You'll notice that it's dated today. Elizabeth slept very soundly last night. One of the few good nights she's had. I think it was because she knew we were coming.

"Now, Mr. Mason, when she wakened about five o'clock this morning, she told me to come and see you, and give you that retainer. She instructed me to have you make a will which would fix it so Nathan Bain couldn't profit by her death. And then she . . . well, I don't know, I suppose perhaps . . . well, in a way she's been reading a lot and . . ."

"What are you getting at?" Mason asked.

"Well, of course, in pictures on the screen and in detective stories and all that, a person who is intending to disinherit someone . . . well, the interval that the lawyer is preparing the new will, you know, is always the most dangerous time. So Elizabeth talked that over with me, and decided that if she'd write it out, in her own handwriting, showing just what she wanted done with her property, that it would be good. Now is that right?"

"That's right," Mason said, "up to a certain point."

"What do you mean by that?"

"In this State, and, mind you, I'm talking now only about this State, a will is good if it is made, dated and signed in the handwriting of the testator. It takes those three things, the date, the will and the signature, all in the handwriting of the testator."

Miss Braxton nodded.

"Now," Mason went on, "you'll note that, in the ordinary sense of the word, your sister didn't sign this will."

"But she wrote her name, Elizabeth Bain, in her own handwriting."

"She wrote her name," Mason said, "in describing herself. In other words, there's a question whether the words 'Elizabeth Bain' as they appear in the will were intended as a signature or whether they were intended to be merely descriptive."

"Well, does it make any difference where the name appears on the will?"

"As a matter of law, it does not," Mason said, "provided the courts can establish clearly that the testator intended the writing of the name to be as a signature."

"Well, that's what Elizabeth intended."

Mason smiled and shook his head. "There have been several very interesting cases where the point has been raised. I can't give you the citations offhand, but there are cases where wills such as this have been offered for probate, and the question has always been whether the use of the testator's name was descriptive or whether it was intended as a signature. Now you'll notice one very peculiar thing about this writing."

"What?"

"There is," Mason said, "no final punctuation at the end of it."

"What do you mean by that?"

"After the word 'property'," Mason said, "there is no full stop."

"Well, for heaven's sake! Do you mean to say that a little dot one-tenth the size of a pinhead on a piece of paper would——?"

"I mean to say so very definitely," Mason interrupted. "There's a case somewhere . . . wait a minute, perhaps I can put my hand on it."

He walked over to a shelf filled with books, pulled down a book, ran through the pages, then settled himself for a few minutes' intensive study.

Miss Braxton interrupted him to say, "Well, after all, it isn't that important, Mr. Mason. This is just sort of a . . . well, a stopgap. Elizabeth did it to ease her mind. She thought that if Nathan knew he had already been disinherited it would dissuade him from perhaps trying any last minute final attempt in desperation."

"You mean that he wouldn't try to kill her?"

"That's right."

Mason returned to the book, then said, "From a legal standpoint it's a most interesting question."

"Well, I've heard of a lot of technicalities," Miss Braxton said, "but if you're trying to tell me that a teeny, weeny dot on a piece of paper is going to make any difference as to the validity of a will, I'll say you lawyers are getting altogether too technical."

"The point is," Mason said, "that it goes to the intention of the testator. In other words, when your sister finished with this document, did she consider that it was a complete and final will, or did she start to make a will and was then interrupted by something and never did finish making the will?"

"Oh, I see what you're getting at now."

"For instance," Mason said, "if you're interested in the legal reasoning, here's the Estate of Kinney, reported in 104 Pacific (2d) at page 782, where it was held that the writing of the testator's name only in the beginning of the declaration is a sufficient signing to justify admitting a will to probate, even though there is no affirmative expression adopting the name so placed as the signature of the testator.

"Then in a recent case, Estate of Kaminski, reported in 115 Pacific (2d) at page 21, it was held that the name of the testator at the beginning of an alleged holographic will constitutes a sufficient signature where the instrument appears to be a *complete* testamentary expression of his desires.

"Now, in the Estate of Bauman, 300 Pacific, 62, it was held that in all cases of this sort the entire instrument must be examined to find out whether it was intended to be a complete will. The final expression, the abruptness in closing, and *even the final punctuation* are to be considered for the purpose of determining whether the writer intended to adopt the name as written in the opening clause as a signature or merely as words of description.

"Now you notice that your sister's will has some very peculiar closing words—'*with the understanding that they will take my property*' . . . The testator could very well have been intending to add 'subject to the following trust,' or 'to be used for the purpose of' . . ."

"But she didn't mean that at all," Miss Braxton interrupted. "She simply meant that the understanding was that by this will we were to take all of her property so that Nathan Bain wouldn't have any opportunity——"

"I understand that's your contention," Mason said, "but you hand me a sheet of paper, you ask me a legal question, and I'm giving you the best answer I can."

Miss Braxton smiled. "Well, I guess it won't make two bits' worth of difference, Mr. Mason, because you can draw up a formal will and have it executed with witnesses and everything. How soon can you get out there?"

"When would be convenient?"

"The sooner the better. All you need to do is to prepare a will made in conformity with this will and have it all ready for her to sign and——"

"That might not be advisable," Mason interrupted.

"Why not?"

"I haven't as yet talked with your sister."

"Well, I'm her agent. She sent me up here to tell you what to do, and gave me this cheque for your retainer."

Mason nodded and smiled, "Nathan Bain might contest the will. He might claim there was undue influence on your part."

"But good heavens, Mr. Mason, aren't we crossing a lot of bridges before we come to them? After all, a will wouldn't . . . well, there wouldn't be any occcasion for a will unless Elizabeth should die, and now that Jim and I

are here she's not going to die; and if you can get Nathan
Bain out of the house there won't be one chance in a
million that——"

"A lawyer isn't paid to consider *probabilities*," Mason
told her. "He's paid to consider *possibilities*."

"But that will mean a delay, won't it, Mr. Mason?"

Mason shook his head.

"Why not?"

"I'll take Della Street, my secretary, along with me.
She'll take a portable typewriter, and just as soon as your
sister tells me she wants the will prepared, my secretary
will type it out, call in two witnesses who are completely
disinterested, and——"

"What two witnesses?" Miss Braxton interrupted.

"Miss Street can sign as one witness and I'll sign as
another."

"Oh, that'll be fine," she said, her face beaming. "That's
the way to do it. How soon can you get out there, Mr.
Mason?"

"Under the circumstances, I can get out there at . . .
well, let me see, at two o'clock this afternoon?"

"Could you possibly make it at eleven-thirty this morning, Mr. Mason? That will give me time to get home
and tell Elizabeth that you're coming out, and give her a
chance to get straightened up a bit. After all, a woman
wants to look her best, you know, and her hair's a mess!
. . . They haven't been giving her the affectionate attention that a sister would give . . . you know, those little
personal touches."

"Eleven-thirty will be all right," Mason said. "I'll be
there——"

The telephone rang sharply. Della Street picked it up,
said, "Hello . . . Who is it? . . . Vicki Braxton? . . .
Just a moment, please."

She turned to Miss Braxton and said, "Someone wants

to talk with you on this phone and says it's very important."

"And they asked for 'Vicki'?" Miss Braxton asked.

"Yes."

"Good heavens, I can't understand it. No one in the world knows that I am here, and I'm known as Vicki only to intimates and members of the family. Why, I . . . I can't understand it."

"Well, suppose you take the phone call," Della Street said, "and find out who it is. That is, if you want to."

From the receiver came a rasping chatter and Della Street said, "Just a moment." She placed the receiver to her ear and said, "What was that again? . . . Oh, yes, I'll tell her.

"It's your brother, Jim," she said.

Victoria Braxton walked over to the phone, said, "Hello, Jim. This is Vicki. What is it? . . . What? . . . No! . . . Oh, my God! . . . You're sure? . . . I'll be right over."

She slammed the phone back on the hook, turned around and said to Perry Mason, "My God, it's happened! Elizabeth is dying. They've been looking all over trying to find me. Jim, my brother, happened to remember . . . Let me out of here."

She started towards the door to the outer office, then saw the exit door opening into the corridor, swerved in her course, twisted the knob, jerked the door open, and dashed out.

Mason, looking at Della Street, ran his fingers through thick, wavy hair in a gesture of perplexity.

"This Bain case!" he said.

"I suppose you'd throw me out if I mentioned anything about the bane of your life!"

"I'd draw you and quarter you," he announced, as Della Street ducked defensively. "What happened to that holographic will?"

D

"She grabbed it, put it back in her purse, and took it with her."

Mason said, "There's just a chance, Della, that that document might assume the greatest importance."

"You mean, if Mrs. Bain is really dying?"

He nodded. "The peculiar wording of that last sentence in the holographic will, the absence of any closing punctuation——"

Della Street laughed cynically. "The next time you see that will, Chief, it will have a very complete period at the end of that sentence. Want to bet?"

Mason pursed his lips. "No, I don't think I do, Della. I guess you're right. In that event I'd be in a most peculiar position. I'd be bound to respect my client's confidences on the one hand, but, on the other hand, as an attorney at law, who is an officer of the court. . . . Get Paul Drake on the telephone. Tell him I want information about what's going on out there in the Bain household and I want it fast. Tell him I'm not particularly concerned how he gets it. . . . And Nellie Conway's last call was at ten o'clock?"

"Right on the second," she said.

"And she told you she couldn't call after that?"

"Yes."

"That," Mason said, "makes it exceedingly interesting. Also notice that Miss Braxton said no one knew she was here. That would mean her brother must know nothing about Elizabeth Bain's intentions to retain me, and nothing whatever about that rather mysterious holographic will."

Della nodded. "Shall we say the plot thickens, Chief?"

"Just like that gravy I tried to make on my last hunting trip, Della. It thickened in lumps. 'Thousand Island Gravy', the boys called it."

8

At 11.55 Paul Drake telephoned.

"Hello, Perry. I'm out here at a service station about two blocks from the Bain house. Elizabeth Bain died about ten minutes ago according to information that was relayed to me by back door scuttlebutt."

"The cause?" Mason asked.

"Seems to be no doubt that it's arsenic poisoning. They felt she was too ill to be removed to a hospital. They've had a diagnosis of arsenic ever since nine-thirty this morning and have been treating her for it. Symptoms first appeared a little before nine."

"Any chance that it's suicide?" Mason asked.

Drake said, "The place is crawling with officers from the Homicide Squad. Your friend Sergeant Holcomb is pretty much in evidence."

Mason thought things over, then he said, "Paul, I have a job for you."

"What?"

"I not only want all the dope on everyone out there at Bain's place, but I want you to canvass the airports. I want to find out what planes left at ten-fifteen this morning. I want that done fast."

"Okay. I can check that pretty rapidly," Drake said. "You can check it yourself by calling the airports——"

Mason said, "That's only half of it, Paul. When you find what airplanes left, I want you to check descriptions of every woman on those planes. I'm particularly looking for a mousy, poker-faced woman, who will have signed her name on the passenger list with the initials 'N.C.' That is, her first name will begin with an 'N', her last name will begin with a 'C', and I want information so fast that it isn't even going to be funny. How long will it take?"

"Perhaps an hour."

"Cut that in half," Mason said. "Make it fifteen minutes if you can. I'm going to be sitting right here at the telephone. Get going and call me."

Mason hung up the telephone and began pacing the floor.

"What is it?" Della Street asked.

Mason said, "Probably around nine this morning, perhaps a little before, Elizabeth Bain was taken violently ill. By nine-thirty they had diagnosed it as arsenic poisoning. About fifteen minutes ago she died."

"And?" Della Street asked.

"And," Mason said, "Nellie Conway was frantically trying to get me all morning, but she had a deadline of ten o'clock. She couldn't call me after that. That was the last minute she'd be able to talk with me."

"You mean she's on a plane somewhere?"

"She's on a plane," Mason said, "and let's hope she had sense enough to sign her name as Nellie Conway. In the event she didn't, her baggage is probably stamped 'N.C.' so she'll use a name that will fit with the initials on the baggage."

"And if Elizabeth Bain died from arsenic poisoning?" Della Street asked.

"Then," Mason said, "in view of the fact that I had certain tablets in my possession which Nellie Conway gave me with the story that Nathan had been bribing her to administer them to Elizabeth Bain, and in further view of the fact I gave those tablets back to Nellie——"

"But those were only aspirin tablets," Della Street said.

Mason sighed. "One of them was an aspirin tablet, Della. Whenever a lawyer begins to regard his work as routine and to think in terms of the average and the usual, he's riding for a fall. People don't pay a lawyer to think of what's probably going to happen. They expect him to think of and anticipate everything that could possibly happen.

"Look up Nathan Bain's telephone number. Ring the house. If Sergeant Holcomb's out there I want to talk with him."

Della Street said, "Nellie Conway left us a number, you know. Just a minute, I'll get it. . . ."

She ran through half a dozen cards, said, "Here it is. West 6–9841."

"All right," Mason said, "get Holcomb."

Della Street picked up the telephone, said, "Gertie, ring West 6–9841 and get Sergeant Holcomb on the line. It's important. Rush it."

Della Street held on to the phone for several seconds, then motioned to Mason and said, "He's coming on now, Chief."

Mason took the phone just as he heard a gruff voice saying, "Hello. This is Holcomb. Who is this?"

"Perry Mason."

"Oh, yes, Mason. How did you know I was out here?"

"I've been trying to reach you."

"All right, what is it?"

Mason said, "You will remember, Sergeant, that Nellie Conway, whom I spoke to you about a few days ago, had claimed that Nathan Bain had asked her to administer certain five-grain pills to his wife. I told you about that."

"Yeah, go on," Sergeant Holcomb said.

"And," Mason said, "in order to check her story I had one of those pills analysed. It contained aspirin. I thought you should know."

There was a long period of silence.

"You there?" Mason asked impatiently.

"I'm here," Sergeant Holcomb said.

"Well?" Mason asked.

"I don't remember the conversation that way," Sergeant Holcomb said, and hung up.

Mason jiggled the receiver twice, then dropped the telephone into place.

"Did he hang up?" Della Street asked.

Mason nodded, white-faced with anger.

"Go ahead, Chief," she said. "Let it go. I've heard all of the words before, and this is once I'd like to hear 'em again."

He shook his head.

"Why not?"

"Damn it, Della, I can't afford to get mad. I have to think."

"But, Chief, I was listening to that conversation. I know that you told him that——"

"Your testimony will be somewhat less than conclusive," Mason said dryly. "Moreover, you didn't hear what Holcomb said to me by way of reply."

"What does he *claim* he said?" she asked.

Mason made his lips into a sour grin. "He hasn't had time to think that up yet. What the hell do you think he hung up for?"

She said, "I wish you'd let go and cuss him. It's going to sound unladylike if I voice my thoughts on behalf of the firm."

Mason shook his head. "A good lawyer must always remember one thing. Never get mad unless someone pays him to do it."

"Can you imagine that damn cop deliberately lying?" Della Street asked, indignantly.

"I can imagine him doing anything," Mason said. "Lieutenant Tragg is tough but he's a square shooter. I should have insisted on getting in touch with Tragg; but the thing sounded like such a complete cock-and-bull story . . . I still don't get it. All I know is that I have a distinct feeling I'm in hot water and it's getting hotter."

He began pacing the floor. Della Street started to say something, then, changing her mind, stood watching him with worried eyes as he paced back and forth.

At 12.25 the telephone rang.

Della Street picked up the phone and Paul Drake said, "Hello, Della. I have the information Perry wanted about the airplane passenger."

Mason jerked himself up sharply. "That Drake?" he asked.

Della Street nodded.

"Tell him to give you the dope if he has any," Mason said.

"Shoot," Della said into the phone.

Drake said, "A ten-fifteen plane for New Orleans, Della. A woman who answered the description of the party Mason wanted gave her name as Nora Carson."

Della Street relayed the information to Perry Mason. Mason crossed the office in three swift strides, grabbed the telephone and said, "Paul, get in touch with whatever agency you correspond with in New Orleans. I want four men working in relays. I want Nora Carson picked up as soon as she leaves the plane. I want to have someone on her every minute of the time, and I don't care what it costs. I want to know where she goes, who she sees, what she does and when. Then wire to the Roosevelt Hotel and reserve a suite for two in your name. The registration will be Paul Drake and party.

"Della Street will get us tickets on the first available plane to New Orleans. Tell your men to report to us at the Roosevelt Hotel. Now jump in your car and get up here just as fast as you can because we're leaving on the first available plane and I don't know yet just what the schedules are——"

"There's one at one-fifteen," Paul Drake said, "but we can't make that. We——"

"Who the hell says we can't?" Mason asked. "Drive to the airport. I'll meet you there."

9

WITHIN two hours of the time Mason and Paul Drake had ensconced themselves in the Roosevelt Hotel in New Orleans, a representative of Paul Drake's affiliated detective agency was in the room making a report.

"We have the party located," he said. "She's taken an apartment in the old French Quarter. It was all ready for her. The lease was signed by a man from your city, a fellow by the name of Nathan Bain. Do you know him?"

Mason and Drake exchanged glances.

Mason said, "Go ahead."

"This apartment was leased about thirty days ago and Bain took out a six-months' lease on it."

"What sort of a place?" Mason asked.

"Well, you know how those apartments in the French Quarter are. They're old as the hills, but the place has a certain atmosphere that appeals to tourists and some of the local residents who want high ceilings and low rent. Some of the buildings have been fixed up pretty nice."

"When Bain negotiated for the lease did he say anything about who was going to occupy the apartment?"

"Simply took a lease on the apartment."

"How did he pay for the rent?" Mason asked. "By cheque?"

"No. There's something interesting. He paid by postal money order."

Mason nodded. "The girl is living there?"

"That's right. Living there under the name of Nora Carson, and she's dough-heavy."

"How heavy?" Mason asked.

"I don't know. She has quite a wad of bills in her purse, big bills. Right after she arrived she went to the Bourbon House for dinner and tried to change a hundred-dollar bill. It caused quite a little commotion. She said that was the smallest she had. The manager happened to get a glance at the inside of her purse and saw that it held quite a wad of currency. He thought she was lying and was trying to get rid of a big bill because it might be hot. That made him suspicious. He insisted that she dig up something smaller. She finally left the hundred-dollar bill as security, went out, and was back within twenty minutes with a bunch of small bills."

Mason digested that information. "Anything else?" he said.

"Yes. We've followed instructions and kept her spotted all the time."

"Does she have any idea she's being tailed?"

"Apparently not. She goes about her business just as though it was part of a regular routine. She doesn't seem to pay any attention to people on the sidewalk."

"All right. What's she doing down here?"

"Well, of course, she's only been here three or four hours, but——"

"What's she done to indicate the purpose of her visit in that time?"

"Nothing."

"How big a place is this French Quarter apartment house?" Mason asked.

"Not big. Two apartments to a floor, two floors. It's a narrow, three-storeyed place with a praline store on the ground floor, your party and one other woman have the apartments on the second floor, one bachelor and one vacant apartment on the third floor."

"Who has the other second-floor apartment?" Mason asked.

"A Miss Charlotte Moray. You know how these buildings are in the French Quarter—that is, I'm taking it for granted that you're familiar with it?" The question invited confidences.

"He's familiar with it," Drake said, shortly.

The New Orleans detective regarded Perry Mason thoughtfully. It was quite evident that he was interested in the identity of Drake's mysterious client, but his curiosity stopped short of actual questions.

"How long has this Moray woman been there?" Mason asked.

"About a week."

"Know where she comes from or anything about her?"

"Not a thing. We've only been on the job——"

"Yes, I know. Have you a description?"

The detective took a notebook from his pocket. "Around twenty-four or twenty-five, very dark, good figure, snapping black eyes, dark hair, a lot of personality and pep, wears good clothes and knows how to wear them. We haven't had time to find out much about her. We do know that she gets telegrams every day, sometimes two or three times a day. We don't know where they come from or anything about them, but we do know she gets them."

"Anything else?" Mason asked.

"That covers it to date. That Moray girl is a nice dish. Five feet four, a hundred and twenty pounds, curves in the right places, lots of fire, and evidently she keeps pretty much to herself. No boy friends, no particular interest in the scenery, seems to be fully familiar with New Orleans, knows where to shop, does some cooking in her apartment, eats out some of the time, very unapproachable, but gracious and smiling to the waitresses, just a woman keeping very much to herself."

"One more question," Mason said. "When did Charlotte Moray rent her apartment?"

"She sub-let it before she came here and was all ready to move in when she got off the plane."

"Sub-let it? From whom?"

"Why, this man Bain. I thought you understood. He leased the whole second floor, and——"

"Leased the whole second floor!" Mason exclaimed.

"Why, yes. You see, he——"

"Why the hell didn't you say so?"

"You didn't ask. I mean, you seemed to want information only on this Conway girl. Of course we've been working fast and . . . I'm sorry, sir. I thought you understood."

"The third floor—does Bain lease that too?"

"No, just the second floor, the two apartments there."

Mason turned to Paul Drake. "Pay them off, Paul, and call them off."

Drake raised his eyebrows.

"We're finished," Mason said. "Are these boys pretty good at forgetting things?"

"They should be," Drake said.

"We are," the New Orleans detective assured them, his eyes, however, filled with curiosity as he studied Mason.

"All right," Mason said, "we don't want any more coverage on the case. Lay the men off and be sure everyone is called off the job."

"As soon as we're paid off, we're off the job," the New Orleans detective said. "We're not anxious to work for nothing."

Drake pulled a notecase from his pocket, said, "This is a job where payments are made in cash. Come on in the other room and we'll get straightened up."

Five minutes later when Drake returned he said, "I didn't want to seem rude, Perry, but if I hadn't insisted on a private pay-off it would have been suspicious. He would have thought we were pretty closely associated. I wanted him to think you were just an ordinary client."

Mason nodded. "How soon will he have his men removed from the job, Paul?"

Drake said, "Give him fifteen minutes, Perry. I told him to go out and call the thing off. He said he was starting right away. We'll give him fifteen minutes."

Mason said, "That'll be fine."

"But what gets me," Drake told him, "is why you're so damn crazy to have this gal covered every minute of the day and night, and after the men have been working on her for four hours, you get in such a lather to have them called off the job. I don't get it."

"Because we have the information we want," Mason told him.

"Well, even so, why be in such a rush to get the men off the job?"

Mason lit a cigarette. "Nellie Conway is going to have a visitor, Paul. Later on, the police may be interested in Nellie Conway. They may find out these detectives were on the job and shake them down to find out what they know. If they don't know who this visitor is, they can't tell."

"You seem to be pretty sure of your facts," Drake said.

"I am."

"Then you probably know who this visitor is going to be—the one you don't want the police to find out about."

"I do."

"Who—Nathan Bain?"

"No."

"Who, then?"

"Perry Mason," the lawyer told him.

10

AFTER midnight the French Quarter of New Orleans takes on an individuality all its own.

Escorts who have gone to 'get the car' drive back down the narrow one-way streets, only to find that their party, instead of waiting on the sidewalk, is lingering over a last drink.

The driver sounds an indignant horn.

In the meantime, his car is blocking the choked one-way street. A car pulls up behind him and the driver sounds a couple of blasts just as a courteous reminder. The driver of the stalled car shows his good faith by blasting his horn in protest.

Two or three other cars fall in behind. Each car, from time to time, emits short, courteous reminders of sound, until, patience exhausted, they all start demanding the driver ahead to move on and clear the street.

At such times the exasperated roar of a dozen blasting horns shatters the night silence to ribbons.

Parties emerging from the noisy interiors of the night-clubs say good-bye to new-found acquaintances. There is an exchange of telephone numbers, and because ears and voices are not as yet oriented to the comparative stillness of the outer air, the information is usually given in a voice audible half a block away.

Then there are the exuberant souls who take advantage of the Quarter's custom of putting garbage cans out on the sidewalk for night collection. These revellers release their animal spirits by kicking the covers of garbage cans along the sidewalks.

Shortly before daylight, when other noises have quieted down, the garbage trucks rumble along, banging and clattering the collection of garbage into the big vans.

All in all, the person who craves quiet in the Quarter should not try to sleep before 6 a.m. Most of them don't.

Mason, threading his way through late revellers and denizens of the Quarter, walked twice around the block in order to make certain there were no shadows watching the entrance to the apartment house. Then he entered a narrow passageway which led to a patio, and climbed an ornamental flight of stairs, whose characteristic wrought-iron banisters led in a sweeping curve to the second floor. Here a hundred and fifty years of foundation settling in the damp soil had caused waving inequalities in a typical floor, which, because of habit, the eye interpreted as being level, with disastrous results to the gait of a sober citizen, but seemingly without undue effect on the inebriated.

The door marked '1.A.' was by the head of the stairs. The door was slightly open. Mason could see the illuminated interior of the apartment.

There was a reclining chair by a table on which were newspapers and magazines; a reading lamp shed brilliance over the scene. In the shadowed area behind the reading lamp, heavy curtains had been partially pulled across french doors opening on a narrow balcony, which in turn stretched out over the sidewalk of the one-way street.

A door at the end of the corridor made a noise. Mason heard the sound of a cautious step, then a half-startled scream.

"How did you get here?" Nellie Conway demanded.

Mason said grimly, "Let's get a few things straightened out, Nellie."

They entered the apartment. Mason seated himself and indicated a chair for Nellie Conway.

"This isn't going to take long," he said.

She stood for a moment, dubiously, then fumbled with the catch of the purse which she had been carrying clutched under her arm.

"Honestly, Mr. Mason," she said, "you didn't need to do this. I intended to send you the money."

She sat down, opened the purse and took out two one-hundred-dollar notes, hesitated a moment, added another hundred-dollar note and pushed the three hundred dollars across the table to Mason.

Mason regarded the one-hundred-dollar notes thoughtfully. "Where did you get this?"

"That was part of the settlement."

"What settlement?"

"The one I made with Nathan Bain."

"All right," Mason said, still holding the money in his hand, "tell me about the settlement."

"Well, it was like I told you, Mr. Mason. Mr. Bain was worried and . . .

"Well, of course, when I came to get my things, Mr. Bain was a little embarrassed at first. I asked him about the relief nurse he had taking care of his wife, and it seemed she'd quit the job for some reason or other. The housekeeper was helping out. Mr. Bain said that he expected his wife's relatives to arrive shortly after midnight."

"Then what did you do?"

"I went in and talked with Elizabeth . . . Mrs. Bain, and helped the housekeeper. We managed to get her really quiet. She had the best sleep she'd had since the accident."

"Have any conversations with her?"

"Oh, yes. She asked me a lot of questions."

"What about?"

"About where I'd been and how much she hated to have me leave her, and how she'd missed me while I was gone, and asking me how it had happened that I was leaving."

"Did you tell her the truth—about being arrested and the trial?"

"Of course, why not?"

"I'm just asking," Mason said. "Go on. Did Nathan Bain come in there while you were there? Did he——?"

"Mr. Bain never enters his wife's room. It would have a very adverse effect on Elizabeth. The doctor knows that just as Mr. Bain knows it. It's lamentable, but it's one of the things that——"

"Never mind that," Mason said. "I just wanted to know if he went in."

"No, he didn't."

"And did you tell her about how he had tried to bribe you to give her medicine?"

"Oh, no."

"Why not?"

"That might have been bad for the patient. You shouldn't ever do or say anything to excite your patient."

Mason studied her thoughtfully. "All right. Now tell me about where you got this money."

"That was early in the evening, before I went in to see Mrs. Bain. When I first showed up, Mr. Bain asked me what I intended to do—you know, about the arrest and all that. That's when I telephoned you."

"Go ahead," Mason said.

"Well, I told him that as far as our relations were concerned, that is, Mr. Bain's and mine, they would have to be worked out by attorneys, that I didn't care to discuss that phase of the matter with him. I said I had come to get my things, and not to talk."

"And what did Bain do?"

"Well, then Mr. Bain insisted we make some kind of a settlement. He wanted to have things worked out so we could . . . well, as he said, so we could act civilised about the thing."

"And you made a settlement with him?"

"Well, he explained to me that if an attorney represented me in making a settlement, the lawyer would charge me perhaps fifty per cent of what I received, at least thirty-three and a third per cent. He told me there was no reason why I couldn't have that money just as well as some lawyer. He said that he was willing to acknowledge the fact that he'd made a mistake. He said he'd been betrayed by that private detective who had posed as a smart guy, a sort of know-it-all."

"What kind of a settlement did you finally make?"

"I don't think that needs to enter into our discussions, Mr. Mason."

"What kind of a settlement did you finally make?"

"Well, he said he'd pay me what it would cost him to fight me in court, and in that way the lawyers wouldn't get it all. He said that if I got a lawyer to sue him he'd have to pay a lawyer to fight the case and I'd have to pay a lawyer to bring the case to court, and then they'd suggest a compromise, and he'd pay money to me, half of which would go into the pocket of the lawyer, and his lawyer would then charge——"

"What kind of a settlement did you make?"

"An adequate settlement."

"What kind of a settlement did you make?"

"I felt under the circumstances I had been fairly compensated."

"How much was it?"

She said, "Mr. Bain asked me not to discuss that matter with anyone and I don't feel free to do so, Mr. Mason. I . . . I had enough for your fee. I intended to send you a money order in the morning, the first thing. I really did."

"How much did he pay you?"

"I am sorry, Mr. Mason, I am not at liberty to discuss that. I've paid you your fee and I'd like for you to give me a receipt, please."

Mason said, "This money came from Nathan Bain?"

"Of course, where else would I get it?"

"I mean, did he give you a cheque and did you go to a bank and cash the cheque and then——?"

"No, no. He gave me the cash in currency."

"Did you sign anything?"

"I signed a complete release."

"Had it been drawn up by a lawyer?"

"I don't know."

"Was it typewritten?"

"Yes."

"On legal size stationery, or on letter size stationery?"

"On letter size stationery."

"Do you know whether he'd been to see an attorney?"

"I don't think so. I think he drew it up himself."

"You took the money?"

"Yes."

"How did you happen to come here?"

"I've always wanted to come to New Orleans and just relax and see the city. It has always fascinated me. It's a city with such a romantic background, and they say the restaurants here are——"

"How did you happen to come here?"

"Just an impulse, Mr. Mason."

"Did Mr. Bain suggest that you come here?"

"Mr. Bain? Good heavens, no!"

"How did you happen to get this apartment?"

She lowered her eyes for a moment, then said, "Really, Mr. Mason, I don't think I care to discuss any more of my private affairs. I'm certainly grateful to you but there are some things I can't go into. Please remember that you acted as my lawyer for just one matter. You're not my lawyer now. You defended me, and I've paid you. That winds up all matters between us. I don't want to seem rude, but——"

"Do you know anyone here in New Orleans?"

"Not a soul. No."

"There was no one you came here to see?"

"No."

Mason jerked his head towards the door. "Where were you when I came in?"

"I . . . I'd just dashed downstairs to mail a letter in the mail-box at the next corner."

"Who was the letter to?"

"To you. I wanted you to know where I was and to tell you I'd send you money for your fee."

Mason said, "You had some tablets in a little corked tube."

"You mean the ones we put in the envelope?"

"Yes. What did you do with those?"

She hesitated a moment, then said, "I tossed the whole thing in the trash."

"What do you mean by the whole thing?"

"The envelope, everything."

"You mean the envelope with our names written across the sealed flap?"

"Yes."

"You didn't open the envelope?"

"No."

"Why did you do that?'

"Because, well . . . I don't know. Perhaps I shouldn't have done it, Mr. Mason, but after I had made my settlement with Mr. Bain and he turned out to be . . . well, he was trying to do the square thing and I thought I'd let bygones be bygones."

"Did you tell him you were throwing the tablets away?"

"I'd rather not answer that."

Mason said, "Let's get a few cards face up on the table for a change. Did you tell him what you had done?"

"Yes. He saw me do it."

"Saw you throw the envelope in the trash?"

"Yes."

"What did you tell him?"

"I told him that I wasn't in a position to do what he'd wanted me to, that I'd told you about what had happened when . . . when I talked with you, and that if you'd wanted to, you could have confronted him with that envelope on cross-examination and put him in the position of having tried to see that drugs were given to his wife."

"What did he say?"

"He said that he had been anticipating such a move and that he was prepared for it."

"Did he say how he was prepared?"

"No."

"But he did say he had been anticipating it?"

"He said he thought I might try to pull something like that or that you might."

"And what did you tell him?"

"I told him that you hadn't needed to do anything like that, and that since he was trying to do the right thing by me, I'd try to do the right thing by him, and I took the envelope with that little bottle in it and tossed it into the waste basket back of the cook stove in the kitchen."

"Did you tell him you'd do that before he paid you money, or afterward?"

"I . . . I can't remember."

"Did you tell Nathan Bain you were going to New Orleans?"

"Certainly not. It was none of his business."

"You got off the plane and moved right into this apartment. You didn't go to a hotel first to get oriented, you just moved right in."

"Well, what's wrong with that?"

"Apartments aren't that easy to find in New Orleans."

"Well, what if they aren't? I found this one."

"You had this one before you ever came to New Orleans."

"Well, what if I did? I'm not accountable to you for my conduct."

"How is Mrs. Bain getting along?"

"Splendidly. Of course, she'll never walk again, but she's doing fine. She slept like a log, just the realisation that her relatives were there—and they're very nice people, those relatives of hers."

"You met them?"

"Of course. I was helping with the nursing as much as I could. After Mr. Bain made his settlement with me, I wanted to do what I could, you know."

"You didn't have any idea how long she might live when you last saw her?"

"Oh, she'll live for years."

Mason said, "Now we'll go back to where we started. How much of a settlement did you get out of Mr. Bain?"

"I'm not going to tell you that."

"You collected money from Mr. Bain for my attorney fee?"

"We talked, of course, about the expense I'd been to. That was why he was making a settlement."

"I told you over the telephone that if Mr. Bain was paying my fee, it was going to be five hundred dollars."

"Well, he wasn't paying your fee. I'm the one who's paying your fee."

"Nathan Bain was standing right there by the telephone when you talked with me?"

"Yes."

"And I told you it was going to cost him five hundred dollars for my fee?"

"Something to that effect."

Mason held out his hand.

She hesitated a long moment, then reluctantly opened her purse again, took out two one-hundred-dollar notes and literally threw them across the table.

Mason folded them, put them in his pocket and walked out.

As soon as he had left the apartment, she slammed the door, and Mason heard the sound of a bolt shooting into place.

Mason walked down the corridor, waited for a moment, then tapped gently on the door of Apartment 1.B.

The floor had sagged enough to leave a half-inch crack under the door. Mason could see a ribbon of light through the crack, could see a moving shadow as some person glided gently into position and stood listening intently.

Mason tapped once more with his finger-tips, a barely audible sound on the panels of the door.

The shadow on the other side of the door moved a few inches. The sound of the bolt being drawn back was almost inaudible. The door opened.

The very attractive woman who was standing on the threshold was clothed only in a filmy négligé. Light shining through it outlined her figure in sharp silhouette, the gossamer clothing forming a filmy aura about the well-shaped body.

"Oh!" she said, in an exclamation that was a mingling of surprise and dismay, and started to close the door.

Mason stepped forward.

She struggled with the door for a moment, then fell back.

"I'll scream," she warned.

"It won't get you anything."

"And this won't get you anything!" she retorted angrily.

Mason said, "Let's make this as painless as possible. I want to talk about the woman who was in here a few minutes ago, the one who has apartment 1.A."

"I don't know anything about her, except that I saw a young woman moving in there tonight, carrying a couple of suitcases. I haven't met her yet."

Mason said, "You'll have to do better than that. Let's talk about Nathan Bain. Does that name mean anything to you?"

"Certainly not."

"In case you don't know it already," Mason said, "Nathan Bain is going to be delayed quite a bit in coming to New Orleans. Now if you want to——"

She elevated a scornful chin. "Are you trying to intimate something?"

"Merely that Nathan Bain's plans are going to be changed materially."

"I don't know any Nathan Brame——"

"Bain." Mason corrected.

"All right, Bain or Brame, or whatever you want to call it. I don't know him and——"

"You've never met him?"

"Of course not. Now, if you don't get out I'm going to start screaming for the police."

She waited a few seconds, then started towards the window which opened on the patio.

"No telephone?" Mason asked.

"I don't need one. I'll show you how quickly the police——"

Mason waited until she was within inches of the window, then said, "Elizabeth Bain's death is going to cause Nathan Bain to——"

She whirled. "What are you saying?"

"I was telling you about Elizabeth Bain's death."

She straightened, turned and stood looking at him, as stiffly motionless as a statue. "What are you saying?"

"I'm trying to give you some information that may be of value."

She regained her self-possession. "Who is this Elizabeth Bain?"

"She's the wife of Nathan Bain, or rather she was."

"Would you mind telling me just who you are?"

"The name is Mason."

"And are you connected with the police in some way?"

"No. I'm an attorney."

"And just why do you come here to tell me this, Mr. Mason?"

"Because," he said, "I wanted to find out whether you already knew about Mrs. Bain's death."

"Mr. Mason, you certainly must have me confused with someone else."

She moved over to the big overstuffed chair, standing with one arm on its back, not bothering to hold the négligé. "How did it happen—this death of Mrs. Brame?"

"Calling it Brame the first time was a good act," Mason said. "The second time is corny. She was poisoned."

"Oh, good heavens!" she said, and her knees buckled her into the chair. "Did you say she was . . . was poisoned?"

"Yes."

"Was it . . . sleeping pills . . . suicide?"

"No."

"Oh!"

"However," Mason went on, turning back towards the door, "since you don't know the Bains, the thing can't be of any possible interest to you."

"Wait," she said sharply.

Mason paused.

"Who gave her . . . how did it happen?"

"What do you care? They're strangers to you—remember?"

"I . . . I meant . . . oh, all right, you win. What do you want?"

Mason said, "You look grown-up. I thought you might be able to act grown-up."

"What do you want?"

"Information."

"What information?"

"All you have."

"Suppose I don't give it?"

"That's your privilege."

"And you're a lawyer?"

"Yes."

She said, "Okay, sit down. I'll buy you a drink."

Mason sat down. She went to the sideboard, took out a bottle of Scotch, poured two stiff drinks, splashed in soda and said, "I hope you like Scotch and soda. It's all I have."

"That'll do fine," Mason said.

She brought the drink over to him and sat down in the chair, the *négligé* falling away to show glimpses of a figure that would have won a beauty contest anywhere.

"The sooner you begin," Mason said, "the sooner it will be over with."

"All right," she said. "I have nothing to hide. The big lug!"

Mason sipped his drink.

She said, "I met him at a convention six months ago. A producers' convention. He certainly has a good line and he's a good spender."

"Just what are you looking for?" Mason asked.

She said, "All right, I'll tell you that, too."

She took a couple of swallows from her drink, then met

his eyes and said, "I was a green, trusting kid. I found out that men had a good line. I fell for it. It didn't buy me anything. Now I've started to get wise.

"I've worked, and worked hard, ever since I was seventeen years old. I see other women who don't have anything I haven't got, breezing around in expensvie automobiles with chauffeurs, all dolled up in furs and with some big sap footing the bills and thinking he's sugar when he's only gravy."

Mason grinned and said, "That's better."

"All right," she said, "I met Nathan Bain. I guess at one time he'd been God's gift to women. He can't realise that years and fat do things to a man. He started handing me a line, then when he saw he had to boost the ante he shelled out a little bit here and there."

"Money?" Mason asked.

"Gems, jewels—nice stuff."

Mason was thoughtful. "Did it come by messenger?"

"Don't be silly. He delivered in person," she said. "He'd take a nice little diamond something or other from his pocket, hold it on his hand for a while, then slip it around my neck. I'd go nuts with rapture."

"Nice work if you can get it," Mason said.

"Don't make any mistake about me, brother. I got it."

"Then what?"

"Then Nathan rented these apartments down here in New Orleans. I was to take a vacation down here. He'd have the adjoining apartment just for the sake of appearances. He wasn't supposed even to know me. Ostensibly he was down here on business, and he intended to have a business conference or two in his apartment so he could prove what he was here for if he had to."

"And then what?"

"Then," she said, "the damn fool let his wife get hold of my letters. She got them from his office."

"You wrote him passionate letters?" Mason asked.

"Sure. What did *I* have to lose? I took my pen in hand and drooled all over the paper. After all, I thought the guy had some sense."

"It bothered you when the wife got the letters?"

"Not a damn bit," she admitted. "It bothered him, and then all of a sudden, it bothered me. Up to then I hadn't realised how firmly he was hooked. He was hoping he could find a way to get a divorce with some sort of a property settlement from her, and marry me. Well, I decided to string along on that end of the game for a while."

"And then what?"

"Then," she said, "he got the letters back from his wife. I don't know how he got them but he got them and he sent this girl down to give them to me."

"You mean the one over in apartment 1.A.?"

"Yes. Nora Carson."

"What do you think of her?"

"All right in a negative sort of a way. She's kept herself under wraps until she doesn't know how to let herself go. She hasn't any voltage. She'd like to play the game my way but she doesn't know how it's done and she'll never find out. She doesn't have anything to show, and nothing to deliver. But she'd like to try. Since she delivered the letters, she's made an excuse to run in here three or four times. The way she looks me over you can see she's wondering what I've got she hasn't—and the pathetic part of it is, she'll never find out."

"She was sent here just to deliver those letters?"

"Yes. Nathan sent her down here to bring me my purple letters. Wasn't that nice of him? My 'good name' is safe now. Think of it. I won't have to be a co-respondent after all. I'll be—as though I give a damn—or do I?"

Mason said, "You're giving me a lot of information. Why?"

"Because I like your looks."

Mason smiled and shook his head.

"Yes, I do too. You look like a square shooter. You look like a man who knows his way around. You look like a man who will play square with me if I play square with you."

"And what do you want?"

She said, "I've put my cards face up on the table."

"All right, what do you want in return?"

She said, "If there's a murder, I don't want any part of it. Nathan Bain is a fellow you can have a lot of fun with and he does keep decorating the mahogany, but that isn't going to last. You know that as well as I do. Marriage to him would lead to a career in the kitchen. You have to get what you can out of him and then move on. He likes pastures while they're green and while they're on the other side of the fence. Give him the key to the gate and it would mean nothing."

"Go on," Mason said.

She said, "I have a right guy. He doesn't have quite as much as Nathan Bain, but there's just a chance that I might play it on the up-and-up with him. I've been thinking."

"And what do you want me to do?"

"Tell me what to do, so I can keep from being smeared in a murder case."

Mason said, "Start packing your things. Get out of this apartment within twenty minutes and get out of this city within thirty. You have your letters back. Burn them. The wind is going to blow. Go hunt yourself a cyclone cellar."

"I thought you were a good egg," she said. "Do you know, Mr. Mason, I sort of like this other guy. I might

. . . hell, you don't suppose I'm falling for another line, do you?"

"I wouldn't know," Mason said, "but there's only one way to find out."

"You're right at that," she told him.

Mason finished his drink.

She followed him to the door, put her hand on his arm. "I'll remember you."

Mason said, "I'd get out quietly so that girl in the next apartment doesn't know that you're leaving."

The dark eyes showed sudden bitterness. "You aren't telling *me* anything," she said. "Listen, I've found out that a girl can't trust many men, and she can't trust *any* women."

"Good luck," Mason said, and walked down the narrow, winding stairs to the patio and the night noises of St. Peter Street.

11

BACK in the Roosevelt Hotel, Mason found Paul Drake with his ear glued to a telephone, getting a long report.

When Drake had finished and hung up, Mason said, "Paul, I want to get copies of messages from the local files of the Western Union Telegraph Company."

Drake shook his head. "It's not only darned near impossible, Perry, but it's illegal."

Mason said, "Charlotte Moray, who has the apartment across from the one where Nellie Conway is living, has been receiving telegrams. I think they come from Nathan Bain."

Drake said, "I can help you out on the last one of those telegrams, Perry."

"How come?"

Drake said, "She may not even have received it as yet. Here it is." He picked up a sheet of paper on which he had scrawled pencilled handwriting, and read:

Unexpected and entirely unforeseen developments which may cause complications necessitate immediate conference. I am arriving on plane due nine-fifteen a.m. leaving on plane due to depart New Orleans one-thirty-five p.m. which will get me back here before my absence will have been noticed or commented on.

"And Drake said, "the message is signed 'Your Falstaff'."

"And it was sent by?"

"Nathan Bain."

"How did you get it, Paul?"

Drake said, "Nathan Bain was quote overcome with grief unquote. He enlisted the aid of a friendly physician who quote administered a sedative unquote, put Bain to bed in a private sanatorium and insisted that he remained undisturbed. A rather bad heart condition, you understand."

"Go ahead," Mason said.

"The police apparently fell for it and so did the newspaper reporters, although they grumbled a bit. My man smelled a rat. He found there was an alley exit through a garage. He watched it and sure enough Nathan Bain, showing no evidence whatever of having been given a hypodermic, came boiling out of the back, jumped into a closed car and was whisked away.

"My man followed as best he could, but I think he'd have lost the guy if Bain hadn't been so damn anxious to send this telegram. There was a branch of Western Union office about ten blocks down the street and Bain's car stopped there. Bain ran in and scribbled his message."

"How did your man get the copy?" Mason asked.

"That's a trick of the trade, Perry."

"Go on, come through," Mason told him. "If there's any way of getting Western Union messages that easy I want to know about it."

"It was dead easy, Perry."

"How much did it cost?"

"A dollar and ten cents."

"How come?"

"Bain grabbed a pencil and wrote this message down on a pad of telegraph blanks that was lying on the counter. My man boldly stepped up as soon as Bain had sent the message, took the same pad of telegraph blanks, tore off a couple of sheets and sent a telegram to his mother telling her he was too busy to write but that he wanted her to know he was thinking of her. The message cost him a dollar and ten cents. Naturally he didn't write it on the sheet of paper that had been immediately under the one on which Bain wrote his message. So it was only necessary for my man to take that sheet of paper, illuminate it with transverse lighting, photograph it and decipher the message which had been indented in the paper underneath by Bain's pencil. Bain writes with a heavy fist."

Mason grinned. "Good work, Paul."

Drake said, "Here's some stuff you won't like so well. The police searched the trash can back of Bain's kitchen stove. In there they found an envelope that had been sealed, and your name and the name of Nellie Conway had been written across the flap. Then the envelope had been torn open and——"

"Was a phial in there?" Mason asked.

"Apparently not, but an outline on the envelope showed it had contained a little phial or bottle."

Mason thought that over. "Can the police tell just when the poison was administered, Paul? She must have taken some food——"

"It wasn't taken in food," Drake interposed.

"How was it taken?"

"It was taken in the form of three five-grain tablets washed down with a glass of water followed by coffee, and given by Mrs. Bain's sister, Victoria Braxton."

"Are you sure?"

"The police are," Drake said.

"How do they know?"

"Elizabeth Bain told them. Her half-sister gave her the tablets."

"What does Victoria Braxton have to say to that?" Mason asked.

"Apparently nothing," Drake said, "because the police can't find her."

"Oh-oh!"

"Your friend Sergeant Holcomb, seems to have taken charge of the affair. For some reason he had a sudden desire to search the Bain house from cellar to garret. He ordered everybody out just as soon as Elizabeth Bain died. He told them to go to hotels and report to the police where they were."

"So what happened?"

"So they did," Drake said, grinning. "Nathan Bain went to his club. He reported to the police that he was there. James Braxton and his wife, Georgiana, went to a down-town hotel, registered and stayed there. Victoria Braxton went to another hotel, registered and notified the police she was there, and the police seem to be having some difficulty finding out exactly where she is. They want to question her. All they can learn so far is that she's completely broken up over her sister's death, is staying with friends somewhere and isn't in her room."

"What else do you know, Paul?"

Drake said, "Bain got a new night nurse after Nellie Conway was arrested. Evidently he made passes at her and she walked out in a huff.

"Mrs. Ricker, the housekeeper, had been on duty all day, but she said she'd try to see that the patient was comfortable. Then Nellie Conway walked in. Nathan Bain made a settlement of some sort with her, patched up his differences with her and put her to work.

"Mrs. Bain had a fine night. She went to sleep early and slept like a log, which was something she hadn't been doing. Sometime after midnight the plane bringing her half-brother, James Braxton, and her half-sister, Victoria Braxton, and Jim Braxton's wife, Georgiana, landed, and all three of them went directly to the house.

"Since Elizabeth Bain was sleeping, they decided they wouldn't disturb her at the moment, but would wait until she wakened.

"She wakened about three a.m. and asked if the folks had come. On being assured they had, she said she wanted to see them. She seemed a little sleepy and groggy, and a lot less nervous and hysterical than she had been. She greeted them warmly and went back to sleep.

"Now get this, Perry. Nellie Conway wasn't really working. She'd gone back to get her things. She made some sort of a settlement with Nathan Bain and she was just helping out because the housekeeper had been up all day. Nellie had said she'd help out until the folks came and then they could take over with the nursing."

Mason nodded.

"But," Drake went on, "the travellers had been flying from Honolulu and felt a little worn. They decided they'd get a little sleep, and Nellie Conway volunteered to stay on for a while longer.

"After about an hour's sleep, Victoria Braxton came in and told Nellie Conway she was completely rested now and Nellie could leave. The housekeeper had already gone to bed. I'm giving you all of this because I think it's important, Perry."

"Go ahead."

"Now, as nearly as we can tell, the doctor, a fellow by the name of Keener, had left three five-grain tablets to be given Mrs. Bain when she wakened at any time after six o'clock in the morning, but they weren't to be given to her before six. Those tablets had been left with Nellie Conway who was the nurse in charge."

"So what happened when Nellie Conway went off duty?"

"She put the tablets on a little saucer, put them on the table and told Victoria Braxton that she was to give them to Elizabeth Bain at any time after six o'clock, but not to wake her up to give them to her, to wait until she wakened naturally."

"Go on," Mason said.

"Mrs. Bain woke up around five o'clock, I believe, and was awake for a while, talking with her half-sister. Then she went back to sleep, wakened at right around seven o'clock.

"She still felt drowsy and completely relaxed. She didn't want any breakfast, but said she'd like coffee. She had a cup of coffee and took the three pills. Anyway, that's what she told the doctor. And get this, Perry, that coffee and the three pills are all that she took into her stomach from somewhere around eight-thirty the night before. So the arsenic *had* to be in the pills."

"Or in the coffee," Mason said.

"You can discount the coffee, because the coffee came out of an urn and several people drank it."

"Perhaps in the sugar?"

"She didn't take sugar or cream. She took the coffee black."

"Then what, Paul?"

"The day nurse came on duty at eight o'clock. She found Victoria Braxton on duty. Victoria said she wanted to take a bath, clean up and then she was going up-town for a while. The day nurse took over. Understand, this was a case where they only had two nurses. The night nurse worked from six to eight because she didn't have it quite so hard, and the day nurse worked from eight to six."

"Go on, Paul."

"The day nurse found Mrs. Bain sleeping, but she was twitching and moaning as though she might be in pain of some sort, but since she was sleeping soundly the nurse didn't disturb her.

"Mrs. Bain had been very restless, you know, and it

was considered important for her to get sleep whenever possible, so, as it happened, the day nurse didn't do a darned thing about straightening up the room or anything. She just sat down and left everything the way it was so Mrs. Bain wouln't be disturbed. That's important because it means that the evidence was left undisturbed."

"Go ahead, Paul. Then what?"

"Well, sometime shortly before nine, Mrs. Bain wakened and was immediately and violently ill, and she had such typical symptoms of arsenic poisoning that the day nurse, who seems to have been a really competent girl, and who had had training as a nurse, notified the doctor that she suspected arsenic poisoning. The doctor got on the job in a hurry, and by nine-thirty they had a definite diagnosis of arsenic—but in view of Mrs. Bain's weakened condition and the fact that she'd been sleeping so heavily and had absorbed so much of the arsenic before her stomach began to reject it, she couldn't pull through. She died sometime shortly after eleven-thirty.

"Victoria Braxton got home about a quarter to eleven. I think at that time Elizabeth Bain knew she was dying. Anyway, Miss Braxton told everyone to get out of the room, said she wanted to be alone for just two minutes with her sister, and since they were a little alarmed about Mrs. Bain's nervous condition, the doctor said that Victoria Braxton could see her for just five minutes. No one knows what they talked about."

"No question that it was arsenic poisoning?"

"Absolutely no question. They are making an autopsy and making an analysis of the vital organs, but the doctor saved some of the stomach contents."

"How about the time element?" Mason asked. "Is that all right?"

"That checks, Perry."

"Do the doctors say so?"

"The doctors aren't saying a damned thing, except to the District Attorney, but I've had my researchers making an investigation."

"What do you find?"

Once more Drake consulted his notes and said, "Well, take Professor Glaister's Medical Jurisprudence and Toxicology. He says that the symptoms usually appear within an hour. In one case, where the stomach was empty, the symptoms did not appear until after two hours. Then, of course, there have been cases where the symptoms didn't develop for seven to ten hours."

"And fifteen grains is a fatal dose?" Mason asked.

"Oh, sure. There has been a fatal case recorded where the amount of arsenic was only two grains, according to Professor Glaister.

"Gonzales, Vance and Helpern, in their book entitled Legal Medicine and Toxicology, state that three grains of arsenic absorbed into the system will kill a man of average weight. Of course, there have been cases where large doses have been taken without fatal results, but usually the poison was rejected by the stomach before it could get into the system."

The telephone rang sharply.

Drake answered, said, "Yes, hello . . . Yes, sure he is . . . Okay, I'll put him on."

He said, "Della Street calling you, Perry."

Mason glanced at his watch. "Gosh, there must be some major emergency to cause Della to call me at this hour."

He picked up the telephone, said, "Hello," and heard Della Street's voice, sharp with excitement, saying, "Chief, I don't want to mention names over the telephone, but do you remember the client who consulted you about the will?"

"The one that didn't have the dot at the end?"

"That's right."

"Yes, I remember her. What about her?"

"She's with me. People are looking for her, lots of people, and she doesn't want to see anyone until she's talked with you. Can she get in touch with you down there if she——?"

"Not very well," Mason said. "I'm coming back. Is there something she's trying to conceal?"

"She thinks someone is trying to frame something on her and——"

"All right," Mason said, "tell her not to say anything to anyone. Can you keep her out of circulation, Della?"

"I think so."

"All right. There's a plane leaving here at one-thirty-five in the afternoon. I'll be on it."

Drake's face showed surprise. "That's the plane that Bain——"

Mason nodded at Paul Drake, and said into the telephone. "I'll try and get that plane leaving here at one-thirty-five, Della."

"Okay."

"Don't let anything happen until I get there—you know what I mean."

"I'll try."

Mason said, "Okay, Della. I'll be seeing you."

Mason hung up the telephone, and as soon as he did so the bell started ringing rapidly and insistently.

Drake picked it up, said, "Hello," and then waited while the receiver rattled with a voice that was pouring words into it with a rapid insistence.

After a full two minutes, Drake said, "Thanks. I owe you one for that. We'll remember it."

He hung up.

"What gives?" Mason asked.

"That was the detective agency we hired to tail Nellie Conway," Drake said. "They were just giving me a tip. They have connections down here, you know."

"Go ahead."

"Seems the California police became interested in Nellie Conway. They found she'd taken the plane as Nora Carson. They phoned police here. They questioned the taxi drivers who cover the airport. The result is they spotted Nellie Conway in that apartment, and they got on the job just as you were leaving the joint.

"On general principles they tailed you here. Then they picked up Nellie. Where does that leave you?"

Mason looked at his watch. "Okay, Paul, I want that one-thirty-five plane. I don't want anyone to know that I'm taking it. Get a ticket in your name. Pay for the ticket, then go out to the airport, rent one of the parcel lockers, put the ticket in that locker, deposit twenty-five cents which will pay for twenty-four hours, close the locker, take the key out, and leave it with the girl at the news-stand. Tell her that when I show up and ask for the key to the locker, she's to give it to me without any question. Describe me if you have to."

"Will you know which locker?" Drake asked.

"Sure," Mason said, "the locker number is stamped on the key."

Drake asked, "Why don't you get a ticket in your own name? They may have tailed you here, Perry, but you're clean. You can tell——"

Mason shook his head. "I have five one-hundred-dollar bills in my pocket that may be hot as a stove lid. Here, Paul, put them in an envelope. Address and stamp the envelope and drop it down the mail chute.

"And I don't want to have any ticket for that plane in my pocket because I don't want anyone to know I'm on that plane when it gets in.

"I haven't time to explain, but this is one time I'm skating on thin ice——"

He broke off as knuckles sounded on the door. With a significant glance at Paul Drake, he tossed the folded five one-hundred-dollar notes far back under one of the twin beds, and opened the door.

Two men stood on the threshold.

"Either one of these the guy?" one of the men asked a plain-clothes man who was standing back in the corridor.

"This is the guy right here at the door."

The detective threw back his coat, showed a badge. "Come on, you're going places, mister," he said. "Somebody important wants to talk with you."

12

THE taxicab drove up to police headquarters. Mason was escorted into an office where the stale, close air gave forth that peculiar smell which clings to a room which is customarily occupied for twenty-four hours a day.

A desk sergeant said, "We don't like out-of-town guys who bust in here with a muscle racket. What's your name?"

"Suppose I should tell you it's John Doe?"

"Lots of 'em do. We'll book you that way if you want. Then when we throw you in the tank, we'll take all the stuff out of your pockets and maybe find a driving licence or something that will tell us who you are. But you'll still be booked as John Doe."

"What's the charge?"

"We haven't thought one up yet, but I think it's going to be vagrancy. You've been paying unchaperoned calls on single girls at two o'clock in the morning, and——"

"Is that a crime in this city?" Mason asked.

The desk sergeant grinned. "Could be, particularly if the California officers are interested. It'd be vagrancy. After we saw your driving licence, Mr. Doe, we'd know a lot more. Perhaps you'd like to co-operate a little better."

Mason took his wallet from his pocket, handed a card to the sergeant and said, "The name's Perry Mason. I'm a lawyer. I came here to interview a witness."

The desk sergeant whistled in surprise, took Mason's card, stepped out of the office, walked down the corridor and was back within two minutes.

"The Captain wants to see you," he said.

Officers escorted Mason down the corridor to a door that said 'Captain', opened the door and pushed Mason in.

A big, middle-aged man with sagging pouches under his eyes, a close-clipped greying moustache, sat behind a desk. At a table beside the desk a shorthand stenographer was taking notes. At the other side of the room Nellie Conway sat on the edge of a plain wooden chair, her gloved hands folded in her lap, her face without expression, her eyes staring straight ahead.

She showed no sign of recognition as Mason was pushed into the room.

The police captain looked across at her. "Is this the man?" he said.

"Yes."

"This is Perry Mason, the lawyer, you're talking about?"

"Yes."

The police captain nodded to Mason. "Sit down."

Mason remained standing.

The captain said, coldly, "You're playing hard to get along with. That isn't going to get you anywhere, not in this town. You aren't in California now. Don't try throwing your weight around because in this place you haven't any weight to throw around. Do you want to sit down or do you want to stand up?"

"Thank you," Mason said, coldly. "I'll stand up."

"Want to make any statement?" the captain asked.

"No."

The captain turned to Nellie Conway. "All right," he said, "you said you did every single thing you did under the advice of counsel. You said the name of the lawyer was Perry Mason. Now this is Perry Mason. Go ahead and keep talking."

Mason said, "I'll advise you not to say a word, Nellie. You——"

"Shut up," the captain said.

"Are you going to keep right on being my lawyer?" Nellie Conway asked, eagerly.

"No."

"Then I'd better listen to these people," she said.

The captain grinned.

Mason took a cigarette case from his pocket, lit a cigarette.

"Keep talking," the captain said to Nellie Conway.

She said, "Nathan Bain gave me those pills. He offered to pay me five hundred dollars in cash if I would give the pills to his wife. I thought they were poison. I went to see a lawyer."

"What lawyer?" the captain asked.

"Perry Mason."

"That's the gentleman here?"

"Yes."

"What did he say?"

"There were four tablets," she said. "He took one of them out of the bottle and put it in an envelope and wrote his name on it. He put the other three tablets back in the bottle, corked the bottle, put it in an envelope, sealed the envelope and had me write my name across the flap of the envelope, and he wrote his name across the flap of the envelope, and he told me to save the envelope because he was going to find out what was in the tablets and was going to communicate with the police."

"Then what?" the captain asked.

"Then Nathan Bain had me arrested."

"Then what?"

"Then Mr. Mason got me acquitted and told me there

wasn't anything in the tablets except aspirin. He intimated that I had been telling him a lie and trying to take him for a ride."

"Then what?"

"Then I went back to the Bain residence to get my things and Nathan Bain talked with me. He was very much concerned because he was afraid I was going to bring a suit against him for false arrest. He said there was no reason why we couldn't get along. He said we could act civilised about the thing. He said he wanted to make a settlement."

"What happened?"

"We talked for a while, and then he told me that he'd give me two thousand dollars and an airplane ticket to New Orleans and a key to an apartment where I could stay for two weeks and have a vacation. He told me all I had to do was to sign a release and give the three tablets to his wife.

"I thought those three tablets contained nothing but aspirin because that's what Mr. Mason had told me was in them, and I didn't see any reason why I shouldn't. I'd tried to do the best I could for myself under the circumstances. If a girl doesn't look out for herself, it's a cinch no one else is going to."

"So what did you do?"

"I signed a release Mr. Bain had drawn up. I got twenty one-hundred-dollar bills. I was helping that night with nursing his wife. I gave her the three pills about eight-thirty or nine o'clock."

"Did you tell Mr. Bain you had done so?"

"Yes."

"Did you have any trouble giving them to her?"

"Of course not. I was the nurse. I told her it was the medicine the doctor had left for her."

"What did she say?"

"She said she'd already had the medicine the doctor had left for her. I told her this was some other medicine, some special medicine that the doctor wanted her to have in addition to the regular medicine."

"Then what happened?"

"The medicine didn't hurt Mrs. Bain a bit. She took it and went right to sleep. I think it really must have been aspirin. It quieted her and she had a nice night. I left about seven o'clock in the morning, about an hour before the day nurse took over. I tried to see Mr. Mason to tell him what had happened, but I couldn't get him. He didn't come into his office before ten o'clock. That was the last minute I had to call him. My plane left at ten-fifteen and they called for passengers to get aboard at ten o'clock. I called him right on the dot of ten o'clock. His secretary said he hadn't come in."

"Did you leave word for him to call you?"

She hesitated. "No."

"Did you tell him where you were going?"

Again she hesitated.

"Come on," the captain said, "let's get this straight."

"No," she said, "I didn't tell him where I was going."

"When did you see him again?"

"About half-past two o'clock this morning."

"What did he do?"

"He came to my apartment."

"What did he want?"

"He wanted five hundred dollars."

"Did you pay him that?"

"Yes."

"Out of the money you received from Nathan Bain?"

"Yes."

"Did you tell him that's where you got the money?"

"Yes."

"And he took the five hundred dollars?"

"Yes."

"Did he give you a receipt for it?"

"No."

The captain turned to Perry Mason. "You've heard the statement that has been made in your presence, Mr. Mason. Do you wish to deny it?"

Mason said, "I don't like the way you run things down here. I don't intend to say a damn word."

The captain said, "Stick around and try to cut corners down here and you'll like the way we run things a hell of a lot less. The accusation has been made that you told this woman it was all right to give those three pills to Mrs. Nathan Bain. Do you deny that?"

Mason said, "I'm not making any statement. I will say, however, that she is entirely incorrect in that statement."

"I'm not either, Mr. Mason," Nellie Conway said with some spirit. "You told me that those tablets contained nothing but aspirin."

"The tablet that I took out of the bottle contained nothing but aspirin," Mason said.

"How do you know?" the captain asked.

"That's something I'll discuss at the proper time and in the proper place."

"All right, these statements have been made in your presence. You have an opportunity to deny them and make an explanation here and now if you want to."

"I have nothing to say."

The captain said to Mason, "That's all. You can go now. Don't try to cut corners here because we don't like smart guys. California may want you. Go back to your hotel and don't try to leave town until we tell you you can. You may be wanted as an accessory on a murder charge—five hundred dollars to give his wife three aspirin pills! You're a hell of a lawyer!"

Mason turned to Nellie Conway. "Nellie, what time did you give——?"

"I said you could go," the captain said.

He nodded to the two officers.

They each took one of Mason's arms, spun him around and propelled him out of the door.

The door slammed shut with an ominous bang.

13

THE taxi that had taken Mason and the detectives from the hotel was parked in front of police headquarters.

Mason said in a weary voice, "Take me back to the Roosevelt Hotel."

"Yes, sir. Have a little trouble, sir?"

"Just lost a little sleep, that's all."

"Oh, well, you can always make that up."

"I suppose so," Mason told him, and settled back on the cushions.

At the Roosevelt Hotel, Mason paid the cab driver off, entered the hotel, walked to the desk, asked for the key to the suite, and, swinging the key carelessly, Mason entered the elevator and said, "Fifth floor."

Mason got off at the fifth floor and promptly walked back down the stairs as far as the mezzanine.

From the mezzanine he could look down and see the house detective who waited until the elevator had returned to the ground floor, then went over to the desk and put through a phone call. Mason, watching his opportunity, slipped down the stairs, went to the door at the other end of the block, and found a taxicab waiting.

"Drive straight down the street," he said. "I'll have to get the address I want."

"Going to be a nice day," the cab driver said. "You're up early."

"Uh-huh. What time do you quit work?"

"Me? I just went on about twenty minutes ago. I quit at four o'clock this afternoon."

Mason said, "That sounds like a nice shift."

"It is while I have it. I have to switch around."

"That doesn't sound so good."

"It isn't."

"Know the town pretty well?" Mason asked.

"Sure."

Mason said, "I've got a day in which I just don't have to do a damn thing. How much would it cost to get this cab by the hour?"

"Well, that depends on whether you want it for shopping and right around town, or——"

Mason took out a fifty-dollar note from his wallet, said, "I'll tell you what I'll do, driver. I'll just give you fifty dollars for the day. Is it a go?"

"What do you mean by all day?"

"Until you quit at four o'clock this afternoon."

"It's a go!"

Mason said, "Okay, shut off your radio because the damn thing makes me nervous. Tell your headquarters that you're going to be out of service all day."

"I'd have to telephone in and get permission, but I'm satisfied it can be done all right."

Mason said, "Okay. Tell them that you're going to go to Biloxi."

"I thought you said you wanted to look around the town."

"Hell, I don't know what I want to do," Mason said. "I used to know a girl in Biloxi."

"That's a long way to go for a girl," the cab driver said. "There are lots of good-looking women nearer than Biloxi."

"Are there?"

"So they tell me."

"Well," Mason said, "tell them you have a passenger to Biloxi. Ask them if fifty dollars is all right for a round trip."

"Okay. Wait and I'll telephone."

The cab driver went into an all-night restaurant, tele-phoned, came back and said, "I'm sorry. They say I'd have to get seventy-five for all day under circumstances like that. I think it's a stick-up but——"

"What do we care?" Mason said. "Just so we have fun. Here's a hundred dollars. Now you're paid off for all day and we can go to Biloxi or not, just as we damn please. The extra twenty-five is for you."

"Say," the cab driver said, "you're a real sport."

"No, I'm not," Mason said. "I'm tired of a lot of routine and I want to settle down and enjoy life for a day without having a lot of telephones and a lot of radio. A little later on you can take me to a good place where we can get a nice breakfast and just sit around and enjoy life without being hurried."

The cab driver said, "I can find you a place all right. I hate to take all this money on a mileage basis to Biloxi and then let the company get rich just driving around town. If you're going to start to Biloxi we should get go——"

"I've changed my mind," Mason said. "I'll——"

"I can phone in and get a better rate for just being around the city."

"No, let the cab company get rich," Mason said. "I'll tell you what you do. Start your meter going and we'll run on the meter. Mileage and waiting time won't amount to as much as the price they gave you, and you can tell them afterwards that your passenger changed his mind."

"Okay, boss. Anything you say. I can sure use the money but I want to be on the up-and-up. You'd be surprised how strict they get with us and how closely they watch us. Lots of times they plant somebody to see if we'll cut a corner or——"

"There isn't any rule against cruising around with your meter running, is there?" Mason asked.

"Not a bit."

"Okay, let's go cruise."

They drove slowly around the city, the driver pointing out places of interest, then, after a while, as Mason started to doze, the driver asked, "How about that breakfast place now?"

"A good idea," Mason told him.

"Okay. I know a place that's run by a woman who's a friend of mine. She doesn't run a regular restaurant but she'd be glad to fix up any friend of mine. You'd get a lot better food than you'd get in any of the restaurants."

"That's what I want," Mason told him. "A chance to relax and feel that I don't have a darn thing to do."

"That's swell. This woman has a couple of daughters that are knockouts."

"I don't want to be knocked out this early in the morning."

The cab driver laughed. "Anyway, you'll like the food, and I mean there's some of the most marvellous Louisiana coffee you ever tasted, made with hot milk. Mister, you're going to have some cooking today that you'll remember as long as you live."

The cab driver drove toward the outskirts of town, stopped once to telephone ahead, then took Mason to a neat house where a negro admitted them to a spacious dining-room, with the morning sun just beginning to stream in through windows covered with lace curtains which, according to the cab driver, were "genuine heirlooms".

An hour and a half later, Mason, once more in the cab, suggested that they drive out to the airport. He said that he liked to watch planes come and go and it would be a good chance to see the town.

The driver felt that Mason might spend his time more profitably, but drove the lawyer out to the airport.

Mason sat in the cab.

The nine-fifteen plane was twenty minutes late.

Nathan Bain hurried from the plane towards a taxi. Two broad-shouldered men fell into step on each side. Bain's face showed startled surprise. The men piloted him across the street to a black sedan. They entered and drove away.

"Don't you want to get out and look around any?" the driver asked.

Mason stretched, yawned, said, "No, I'd like to find some place where we could walk and stroll around . . . Say, haven't you got a park here?"

"A park!" the cab driver exclaimed. "We've got several of the best parks in the world! Why, say, we've got parks here with live oaks that are bigger than any tree you ever saw in your life. We've got lawns and walks, and a zoo with all kinds of animals, lakes, canals——"

"That's for me," Mason said with enthusiasm. "Let's go down to a park some place where we can get out and lie on the grass and just bask in the sun, and then we can go out and look around the zoo and get some peanuts to feed to the animals, and after that . . . well, after that we'll do just as we damn please."

The cab driver said, "If I could only get a fare like you just about once every ten years, it would make up for all the grouchy old crabs that yell because I have to go around a block in order to get headed right on a one-way street. Come on, mister, you've called the turn. Say, do you like to fish? I know where we can get some fishing rods and get some of the best fishing . . ."

"Sounds good," Mason said. "Let's go."

Around eleven o'clock, Mason decided he was hungry. The cab driver found a quaint, isolated place, where Mason had an oyster cocktail, bouillabaisse, oysters Rockefeller, and a firm, white-meated fish that seemed to dissolve on the tongue. An olive-skinned girl with limpid, dark eyes, and exceedingly long lashes, served the meal, and from time to time glanced sidelong under her long lashes at Perry Mason, who was drowsily oblivious of everything except the food.

Shortly before one o'clock, Mason decided he would once more like to go down to the airport and see the planes come in.

This time he got out of the cab and said, "I'll walk around for a while."

"About how long?" the cab driver asked.

"Oh, I don't know," Mason said. "I just do things on impulse. Come on along, if you want."

Escorted by the cab driver, Mason moved slowly around the air terminal, then said, "I think I'll buy a newspaper."

He walked over to the news-stand while the cab driver was standing out of earshot, bought a newspaper and said, "I believe there's a key left here for me."

The girl looked at him curiously and said, "Yes, your friend said your bags would be in the locker."

She handed him a key.

Mason thanked her, gave her a two-dollar tip, walked back to the cab driver and said, "Go out and wait in the cab, will you? In case I don't show up within half an hour, shut your meter off, pocket the rest of the money and report back to duty."

Mason went to the locker and found that Paul Drake had packed his overnight travelling bag and left it in the locker, together with a letter in a plain envelope.

Mason opened the envelope and found the aeroplane ticket, together with a note which read:

Della knows you'll be on this plane. Things are moving too fast for me. I'm crawling into a hole and pulling the hole in after me. This is where I check out. I've had police in my hair at intervals all morning and have

"She did give the poison after all. Nathan bribed her to do it."

Mason raised his eyebrows in silent interrogation, then smoked in silence.

The woman looked at him and said, "You're not saying a word, Mr. Mason."

"Your husband isn't saying a word," Mason said.

She laughed nervously. "He's a great listener. I'm the talkative one of the family. I go rambling on and on and on."

Mason nodded.

"We'd like to know what you think of it and what your ideas are concerning the case."

Mason said, "Lots of people would like to know that."

"I'm afraid I don't understand."

Mason said, "You tell me that you're Mr. and Mrs. Jim Braxton. I've never seen you before in my life. For all I know you could be newspaper reporters trying to get an exclusive interview."

"But, good heavens, Mr. Mason, your own secretary told us where we'd find you. We took a plane into El Paso and got in there just half an hour before this plane of yours pulled in. We've certainly been stewing and worrying and we wanted to see you at the earliest possible moment and warn you of what you're up against."

"Thanks."

"Mr. Mason, you must believe we're who we are. We . . . Jim, don't you have something, some means of identification?"

"Sure," Jim said, promptly rising to the occasion. "I have a driving licence."

"Let's take a look at it," Mason said.

He studied the licence which the man handed him, then said, "Perhaps I can clear the matter up by asking a few questions. Where were you up until a few days ago?"

"Honolulu."

"Who was with you?"

"Just the three of us together. It was a family party. My sister, Vicki, and I have always been very close, and she gets along fine with Georgiana."

"Got any more means of identification on you?" Mason asked.

"Certainly. I have lodge cards, business cards, club memberships . . ."

"Let's see them," Mason said.

Mason went through the collection of cards which the man presented, said finally, "Okay. I guess that does it. Now suppose you tell me the thing Miss Street wanted you to tell me. She didn't have you fly down here just to ask me questions."

"Well," the woman said, laughing nervously, "I was just trying to get acquainted."

"We're acquainted now. What was it you told Miss Street that caused her to send you down here?"

"It sounds such a horrible thing to say," she said after a few moments, "when you blurt it right out this way."

"But, my dear," Jim Braxton interposed, "Mr. Mason is our lawyer. You have a right to tell him anything. You're supposed to tell him. Isn't that right, Mr. Mason?"

Mason said, "If you have any information which throws any light on the death of your sister-in-law, I suggest by all means that you tell me what it is."

She turned to her husband. "Jim, for the life of me I can't understand you. For the past year whenever I've mentioned that, you've told me I should keep my mouth shut, that I could get in serious trouble, and now you want me to tell the story to a man I've only known for a few minutes."

"But, dear, the situation is entirely different now. This would be . . . well, the law would protect you in this."

Mason glanced at his wrist watch. "We don't have too long to stall around, you know. There may be reporters coming aboard the plane at Tucson."

"Well," she said, "I may as well blurt it right out, Mr. Mason. Nathan Bain poisoned his first wife."

"She was supposed to have eaten something which disagreed with her," James Braxton said mildly.

"The symptoms were those of arsenic poisoning," Mrs. Braxton asserted.

"How do you know?" Mason asked.

"Because," she said, "I was suspicious of Nathan Bain from the moment he set foot in the house and started making eyes at Elizabeth."

"Go on," Mason said.

"Well, that's it, Mr. Mason. He's always said he didn't want to talk about it, but one time he told us all about it. It seems she had eaten something which disagreed with her, and the way he described the symptoms . . . well, I just started thinking, that's all."

"What about the symptoms?"

"All of the typical symptoms of arsensic poisoning. They are not very nice to describe, Mr. Mason, but I can assure you she had *all* of the typical symptoms."

"How do you know what the symptoms are?"

"I made it a point to read up about it."

"Why?"

"Because I was suspicious of Nathan Bain from the minute I clapped my eyes on him. I felt certain that he'd . . . I think he's a toad."

Mason said, "Let's get back to the death of his first wife. That *could* be one of the most important things in the case."

Jim Braxton said, "Your secretary thought so too. She wanted us to get in touch with you and tell you about it."

"Then tell me about it," Mason said. "And tell me how

it happened that Nathan Bain got your sister to marry him. I gather that she was rather an attractive young woman."

"She was."

"Two and a half years ago Nathan Bain was a lot better looking than he is now." Jim Braxton interposed. "And he sure has a smooth line."

"But he was fat even then," his wife countered. "Don't you remember how he was complaining about his clothes being tight? He was always saying he was going to take off weight. First he'd say he was going to take off five pounds in the next six weeks. Then he said ten pounds in the next three months, then twenty pounds in the next six months.

"And all the time he kept putting it on. His clothes were always six months behind his figure. I always felt he was going to burst every time he leaned over. He just wouldn't watch his appetite. He ate everything. All the rich foods—used to boast about his stomach. He'd eat——"

"That isn't telling me about his first wife," Mason said impatiently, "and we haven't got all night."

"Well," she said, "his first wife died about three years before he married Elizabeth."

"Did he profit by her death?" Mason asked.

"I'll say he profited by her death! He picked up about fifty thousand dollars. He used that to gamble in the stock market and get himself established in the produce business. And then when he made some poor investments and found out that the financial shoe was pinching, he deliberately went out and set his cap for someone who had money.

"I tell you, Mr. Mason, that was all that he wanted of Elizabeth. He just wanted her money, that was all. I knew that the minute I clapped my eyes on that man. I could just look at him and tell.

"I've always been good at judging character that way. I can take a look at a person and tell what he's thinking about within the first ten minutes. And what's more, I never have to change my opinion of people. I come to a decision and I don't have to change it."

"She's good," Jim Braxton said.

Mrs. Braxton tried to look modest and failed.

"Go on," Mason said.

"Well, that's all there is to it, Mr. Mason. There's one thing I'll say about Nathan Bain. He's a marvellous talker. Give him a chance to get started and he can talk the birds right down out of the trees.

"And when he set his cap for Elizabeth he really made a good job of it. He was just the nicest, most considerate man you have ever seen. But as far as I was concerned, I could see the hypocrisy oozing out all over him. It was just like something filled with slime. He didn't fool me for a minute, and he knew it."

"You told Elizabeth how you felt?"

"I certainly did. I told her exactly how I felt about that man. I warned her against him and . . . well, she wouldn't listen to me."

"Then what?"

"Well, of course, that made the relationship a little strained because she was completely hypnotised. Nothing would do but she must run right to Nathan and tell him how I felt."

"Now, wait a minute, dear," Jim interposed. "You don't know that she went to Nathan and——"

"You mind your own business," Georgiana interrupted tartly. "I guess I know what she did and what she didn't do. I could tell the minute she spoke to Nathan. I could just see the change come over him. Before that time he'd been trying to hypnotise me as one of the members of the family, but the minute he knew I was on to him he drew into his shell and got on the defensive."

"Go ahead," Mason said. "Let's get down to something that we can use as evidence if we have to."

"Well, I'm just telling you, Mr. Mason, that after he married Elizabeth for a while he was the most attentive husband. Butter wouldn't melt in his mouth. He was always dancing attendance on her hand and foot. He did let himself go terribly when it came to putting on weight. He started to get real fat. He just ate and ate and ate——"

"Never mind that," Mason said. "Let's get back to first principles."

"Well, as I say, he was very nice for a while, always, however, trying to get Elizabeth to finance this and finance that, and then trying to get her to let him manage her property. But Elizabeth was too smart for that. She was a pretty shrewd business woman and she kept her own property so that she had it entirely in her own hands, and she intended to keep it that way.

"Well, you could just see Nathan change the minute he realised that he had tied himself up for life to a woman who wasn't going to let loose of her property, but was going to keep on handling it herself and regarding it as her own.

"I just knew something was going to happen. I told Jim a dozen times if I told him once. I said to him time after time, 'Jim', I said, 'you watch that man, he's going to——'"

"We were talking about his first wife," Mason interrupted.

"Well, one day when he had been drinking and was unusually talkative, he was telling us about his early life, and then he mentioned his first wife, which was something he very seldom did."

"What was her name?"

"Marta."

"And what happened?"

"Well, they had been married about two years or a little better, and they went down into Mexico and she was supposed to have eaten some sea-food, and she became terribly, terribly ill. He described what a nightmare it was, driving her back across the border and getting to a point where they could get competent medical attention. By the time he got her home to her family doctor she was in very bad shape. The doctor said it was undoubtedly a case of food poisoning from eating tainted sea-food. Well, she died, and that's all there was to it."

"How do you know the symptoms were those of arsenic poisoning?"

"I'm telling you the man went into details, Mr. Mason. It was positively indecent, but he'd been drinking at the time and he told about all of the trouble he'd had driving this very sick woman through miles and miles of wild country. And it was then he mentioned the candy.

"With all Nathan Bain's craving for rich foods, there's one thing he can't touch, chocolate.

"Well, he told me about Marta having taken this box of chocolate creams along in the car, and the minute he said that, the very minute, mind you, I knew what had happened.

"I looked up the symptoms and, sure enough, there they all were. Marta was poisoned by arsenic in that box of candy which she opened and ate right after the sea-food luncheon."

"Where did she get the candy?" Mason asked.

"Heavens, how should I know? But you can bet one thing, he's the one who put the arsenic in it."

"He didn't go to a Mexican doctor?"

"No. Marta didn't want one and he didn't think it would be advisable. According to the way Nathan tells the story now, they both felt that she was suffering from food poisoning and that as soon as her system was cleaned out, she'd be all right. So they made a dash to get home.

"If you ask me, the reason he wanted to get her home

was because he had a friendly doctor that he used to play golf with, and he knew the doctor would sign a death certificate without asking any embarrassing questions. The doctor accepted their diagnosis of sea-food poisoning, and when she died two days later, he very obligingly filled out the death certificate."

"Where were they living at the time?" Mason asked.

"San Diego."

"And what happened to Marta's body? Was she cremated or——"

"That's one thing," she said. "*He* wanted to have the body cremated, but her mother and father insisted that the girl be buried, so they had their way. She didn't leave any will or anything directing what should be done with her body, so she was buried."

"Where?"

"In San Diego, in the cemetery there."

"All right," Mason said, "that's fine. I'm glad you've told me that. Now we have something to work on."

"You see," Jim Braxton said to his wife, "I told you that was important."

Mason said, "Now I want you to get this and get it straight. I don't want either one of you to say a word about this to anyone until I tell you. Do you understand?"

They nodded.

Mason said, "This thing is terribly important. The facts in this case are all scrambled. Nellie Conway says that Nathan Bain wanted to pay her to give his wife medicine that would make her rest better and get her over being so nervous. She brought that medicine to me. I took one of the tablets and had it analysed It was aspirin. . . . The thing simply doesn't make sense.

"Now then, Elizabeth Bain is dead. Nathan Bain is going to try to worm out from under. In order to do that he's going to try to involve everyone else. At the proper time I want to hit him with this thing so it will be a bomb-shell. . . . And I don't want any word of this to leak out in advance. Do you understand?"

"Anything you say," Braxton said.

"Well, that's it," Mason said, "and I want you to follow instructions on that to the letter. It may be a lot more important than you realise at the present time."

"Well, I guess *I* know when to keep my mouth shut," Mrs. Braxton said, "and as for Jim, he never talks, do you, Jim?"

"No, dear."

"And you'll follow Mr. Mason's instructions, won't you, Jim?"

"Yes, dear."

"You don't have anything to worry about," she said to Perry Mason."

Mason gave a wry grin. "That," he announced, "shows all you know about it."

14

It was a calm, clear night. Stars were blazing down steadily, but paled into insignificance in the floodlights at the airport.

Mason joined the stream of passengers walking briskly to the exit.

Pursuant to his instructions, Jim and Georgiana Braxton had been among the first to leave the plane. Mason was at the tail end of the procession.

As the lawyer climbed up the ramp to the main floor level of the air terminal, he gave a swift searching glance, looking for Della Street.

She was not there.

Worried, Mason started crossing the big air terminal and suddenly caught sight of Lieutenant Tragg carrying a brief-case and pacing restlessly back and forth, his eye on the big clock.

Mason hurriedly walked towards the exit, carefully keeping his back turned to Lieutenant Tragg. He was just about to push his way through the heavy glass door when Tragg called his name, sharply, peremptorily.

Mason turned with every evidence of surprise.

Tragg was hurrying towards him.

"Hello, Tragg," Mason said, and waited, obviously impatient to be on his way.

Tragg, tall, intelligent, alert and a dangerous antagonist, gripped Mason's hand. "How are you, Counsellor?"

"Pretty good. How's everything?"

"I understand you were in New Orleans?"

Mason nodded.

Tragg laughed. "Police there reported that they told you not to leave New Orleans without permission."

"The New Orleans police," Mason said, "are abrupt, arbitrary, short-tempered and disrespectful."

Tragg laughed, then asked more seriously, "*Did* you have their permission to leave?"

"I'm not accustomed to asking *any* permission from any police officer before I do *anything*," Mason said.

Tragg grinned good-naturedly. "Well, let's hope nothing happens to change your habits."

"I don't think anything will."

"You always were an optimist."

"Are you here to meet me?" Mason asked.

Tragg said, "I have no official interest in you at the moment, Mason. My interest is in an airplane which is scheduled to leave for New Orleans sometime within the next twenty minutes. I'm one of those nervous travellers. I can't sit down and wait until someone calls the plane, but I have to pace the floor and look at the clock as though my eyes would push the minute hand around faster."

"Going to New Orleans to talk with Nellie Conway?" Mason asked.

"Officially," Tragg said, "I'm not supposed to make any statements, but off the record, Mason, there are some rather interesting developments in New Orleans."

"Of what sort?"

Tragg shook his head.

Mason said, "You don't need to be so damn secretive. I guess everyone knows Nathan Bain flew to New Orleans and was picked up by police as soon as he got off the plane."

Tragg tried to keep from showing surprise. "Is that so?"

Mason raised his eyebrows. "You didn't know I knew about that, eh?"

"You know lots of things, Mason. Sometimes you amaze me when I find out what you do know, and then again there are times when I'm afraid I never do find out what you know. So I have to try to keep you from finding out what I know."

"So," Mason said, "the fact that Nathan Bain was picked up by the police, that Nellie Conway was picked up by the police and was talking, and that you are impatiently pacing the terminal, waiting for a plane to take off for New Orleans is a pretty good indication that Nathan Bain has made some sort of a statement that is of the greatest importance, or that you expect him to by the time you get there."

Tragg said, "You really should get a turban and a crystal ball, Mason. Then you could go into the business of fortune-telling, mind-reading and predicting the future. It's a shame to have these talents wasted on an amateur."

"Has Bain confessed to the murder?" Mason asked.

"Why don't you look in your crystal ball?" Tragg asked.

"Not giving out any information, Lieutenant?"

Tragg shook his head.

Mason said, "I'm going to have trouble with your man, Holcomb, Tragg."

"You've had trouble with him before. It won't be anything new."

"I mean I'm going to have some real trouble with him. I'm going to put him on a spot."

"Are you?"

"You're damn right I am."

"What's he done now?"

"It's what he hasn't done. He's having a very convenient memory in connection with a conversation I had with him, in which I told him all about Nellie Conway."

Tragg was serious and thoughtful. "Sergeant Holcomb

knows Nathan Bain. They've had quite a few talks together."

"So?"

"Just a matter of friendship, of course. Holcomb signed up for a class in public speaking that was open to police officers and deputy sheriffs—given under the auspices of one of the service clubs. Nathan Bain was one of the instructors at that class. He made quite an impression on Holcomb.

"Bain is a smooth, convincing talker. He has a good deal of personality when he's on his feet. Holcomb was very much impressed. He made it a point to compliment Bain, and they had quite a talk.

"A couple of months later Bain rang up Holcomb and told him that he was suspicious that a nurse named Nellie Conway, who was taking care of his wife, was stealing jewellery, and asked Holcomb what to do. Holcomb said it was out of his line and offered to refer it to the larceny detail, but after they'd talked for a while Holcomb suggested Bain get a private detective, and recommended James Hallock.

"Now does that answer your question?"

"It explains a lot of facts," Mason said. "It doesn't answer my question because I wasn't asking any question. I was making a statement."

"Well," Tragg said, "I thought you'd like to know the low-down on that. Naturally, when you approached Holcomb with a story about the medicine, Holcomb thought you were rigging up an elaborate defence for Nellie Conway, so you could use it later to trap Nathan Bain on cross-examination and get your client released."

A feminine voice on the public address system announced that passengers for Tragg's plane were being loaded at Gate 15, and Tragg, welcoming the interruption, grinned and said, "Good luck to you, Counsellor."

"Thanks, the same to you. Hope you bring back a confession from Nathan Bain and drop it on Holcomb's desk."

"Any message for the New Orleans police?" Tragg asked.

"Give them my love," Masons told him.

"They may want you back there."

Mason said, "If the New Orleans police want me back there, they can telegraph a fugitive warrant for my arrest, then they can try and find some law I've violated in the State of Louisiana so they can get me extradited. You might explain to them some of the legal facts of life, Lieutenant."

Tragg grinned, waved his hand and started walking briskly towards the gate.

Mason watched him out of sight, and was just turning, when he heard the patter of quick steps behind him, and Della Street came running up to him.

"Hello, Chief."

"Hello. Where have you been?"

She laughed. "You can imagine where I've been. When I saw Lieutenant Tragg waiting around here, I didn't know whether he was looking for you or for me, or just taking a plane. So I retired to the one place where Lieutenant Tragg and his minions would be unable to follow."

"And then?" Mason asked.

"Then," she said, "I kept watch on the situation, decided Tragg was taking a plane to New Orleans, and kept where I could watch him, hoping I would find an opportunity to tip you off, but he would have to be one of those big, restless he-men, and pace back and forth with one eye on the clock as befits a nervous traveller."

"Where's Victoria Braxton?"

"We're staying at an auto court."

"Registered all right?"

"Under our own names. That's the way you wanted it, isn't it?"

"That's fine. I'd hate to have it appear she was a fugitive from justice."

"She isn't."

"Anyone looking for her?"

"Newspaper people, but as nearly as I can find out, that's all. She's wanted for questioning at the district attorney's office at ten o'clock tomorrow morning."

"Have they notified her?" Mason asked.

"No, but it's in the press. They did notify her brother, Jim, and Georgiana. I see that they made connections with the plane all right. What did you think of them, Chief?"

"Okay," Mason said, "except that once that woman gets started she certainly talks a blue streak."

"She told you about . . . ?"

Mason nodded.

"What are you going to do with it? Do you want it released to the press so we can . . . ?"

"No," Mason said. "I want that information put in cold storage, to be used at the proper time, in the proper manner, and at the proper place. If Nathan Bain confesses to the murder of his wife, we'll pass the information on to Lieutenant Tragg—although Tragg will probably know all about it before we have a chance to tell him.

"On the other hand, if the police try to give Nathan Bain a coat of whitewash, we'll slap them in the face with it."

"Why should they try to give Nathan Bain a coat of whitewash?"

"Because," Mason said, "our dear friend, Sergeant Holcomb, has been taking lessons in public speaking from Nathan Bain. Isn't that just too ducky?"

"Quite a coincidence, isn't it?"

"It's a coincidence, if you want to look at it in one way."

"And if you want to look at it in another way, what is it?"

Mason said, "Suppose you were planning to commit a murder. Suppose you were a member of a service club that was asking for volunteers to coach a class in public speaking that was to be composed of top-flight detectives and peace officers. Suppose you were a smooth, forceful speaker and felt you could make a good impresson on people. Wouldn't that be a nice way to make yourself a whole handful of friends who'd be in a position to do you some good, or, to look at it in another way, who'd be in a position to keep anyone from doing you harm?"

Della Street nodded.

"Well," Mason said, "apparently Sergeant Holcomb and Nathan Bain are just like that," and Mason held up two crossed fingers.

"And that may complicate the situation?" Della Street asked.

"That may raise hell with it. Where's the car, Della?"

"In the parking lot."

"Okay, I'll get my bag, you get the car, and I'll meet you in front. No newspaper reporters are expecting me back?"

She laughed. "Apparently not. They've been trying to get in touch with you, but they called the New Orleans police and were assured you wouldn't be leaving Louisiana until the police there had completed their investigations."

"Well, isn't that something!" Mason said.

"What did you do? Put up bail and then jump it?"

Mason said, "I walked out. Where did they get that idea that they could tell me not to leave town? The situation would have been different if a crime had been committed in Louisiana. They're trying to investigate a crime that was committed in California. To hell with them!"

"To hell with them is right," Della Street said, laughing. "Don't get so worked up about it, Chief. You're fifteen hundred miles from New Orleans now. You get your bag and I'll get the car."

She flashed him a quick smile and ran towards the parking place. Mason secured his bag from a porter and was standing by the kerb as she drove up. He tossed the bag in the back of the car, slid in the seat beside her and said, "Let's make sure we aren't wearing a tail, Della."

"Okay, you keep watch behind and I'll cut around some of the side streets."

Mason turned so he could watch the road behind him. "How's Vicki, Della?"

"She bothers me, Chief?"

"Why?"

"I don't know. There's something I can't put my finger on."

"Anything more about the will?"

Della Street said, "That will isn't the same now as when you saw it."

"No?"

"No."

"What's different about it?"

"At the end of the sentence," Della Street said, "there is now a very perfect piece of punctuation, a nice round dot made with ink."

"How nice."

"Chief, what could they do in a situation like that?"

"What could who do?"

"Would that be forgery?"

"Any mark that would be put on a document for the purpose of deceiving others and made after the document had been signed, would be an alteration of the document."

"Even a teeny-weeny dot no bigger than a fly speck?"

"Even a dot half that big, provided it was a significant part of the document and was intended to be such."

"Well, it's there now."

"Have you asked her about it?"

"She *said* her sister put it there."

There was an interval of silence.

Della Street said, "How are we coming, Chief?"

"No one seems to be taking any undue interest in our driving, Della."

"How about it? Do we hit the main boulevard?"

"Take one more swing, and then start travelling. I want to hear Vicki Braxton's story about the full stop at the end of the will."

15

VICTORIA BRAXTON, attired in a neatly tailored suit, looking very efficient and business-like, was waiting up for Perry Mason and Della Street in the well-furnished living-room of the de luxe auto court where Della Street had registered.

Mason lost no time with preliminaries.

"I don't know how much time we have," he said, "but it may be a lot shorter than we hope for, so let's hit the high spots."

"Can you tell me what happened in New Orleans?" she asked.

Mason shook his head. "It's too long to go into now."

She said, "I'd like to know. I'm very much interested in anything Nathan does."

"So are the police. We'll talk about that after a while if we have time. Right now I want to know certain things."

"What?"

"Exactly what happened in connection with Mrs. Bain's death."

"Mr. Mason, *I* gave her the poison."

"You're certain?"

"Yes."

"How did it happen?"

"Nellie Conway put those tablets on the saucer. She said to me, 'The first time Elizabeth wakes up after six o'clock in the morning she's to have this medicine. Don't give it to her before six but give it to her just as soon after six as she wakes up.'"

"There were three tablets?"

"Yes."

"Placed on a saucer by the side of the bed?"

"Yes."

"And then what happened?"

"Well, that's it, Mr. Mason. She wakened and I gave her the medicine. It must have been those tablets."

"To whom have you told this?"

"To Miss Street and to you."

"Did you tell it to the officers?"

"No, Mr. Mason, I didn't, because at the time—well, when the officers were out there making an investigation, we were all excited, and at the time it never occurred to me that by any extreme possibility could *I* have been the one who administered the poison."

"That's fine."

"What is?"

"That you didn't tell anyone. Don't tell anyone, don't mention it, don't say anything to the police, don't say anything to anyone."

"But, Mr. Mason, don't you understand, it's only through my testimony that they can really connect Nellie Conway with my sister's death, and Nellie Conway, of course, is the connecting link that leads to Nathan Bain."

"For the moment," Mason said, "we'll let the police worry about their connecting links."

"Mr. Mason, I don't think that's right. I think I should tell them. Those tablets Nellie left in that saucer were poison."

"Don't tell them."

"Will you please tell me why?"

"No," Mason said, "there isn't time. Now tell me about that will."

"What about it?"

"All about it. I don't think your brother or your sister-in-law know about it."

"Does that make any difference?"

"It might."

"Elizabeth didn't want Georgiana—that's Jim's wife—to know anything about it."

"Why not?"

"Because it would have made her even more extravagant, just the idea that she'd maybe some day come into some of Elizabeth's money."

"Is Georgiana that way?"

"Terribly—and she's always jumping at the wildest conclusions from the most trivial data. As it is now, she keeps poor Jim in debt all the time. Heaven knows how much they owe. If she knew about this will—I mean, if she had known about it—the way Elizabeth was injured and all—well, she'd have gone on another spending spree."

Mason digested that information thoughtfully. "Did you and Elizabeth discuss that?"

"Yes."

Mason said, "That may or may not explain something."

"What do you mean by that?"

Mason said, "There are some things about your story I don't like."

"What?"

"To begin with, when you came to my office you told me that your sister had sent you there, that you were to retain me and I was to draw a will."

"Well, what's wrong with that?"

"Then, when somebody telephoned and asked for 'Vicki', you were surprised. You said only your intimates called you Vicki and no one knew you were there."

"Oh, you mean my brother and sister?"

"Yes."

"Well, they didn't know I was there. Only Elizabeth

knew where I was, and I knew that Elizabeth wouldn't telephone me. But Jim knew I'd asked Nellie Conway where your office was—and he thought I might have gone up there to ask you something about her case or the settlement.

"They were, of course, trying frantically to get me. He tried half a dozen places and then he tried your office, just on a blind chance."

"All right, let's put cards on the table. Why didn't your brother and sister know you were there?"

"For the very reason I've been telling you, Mr. Mason. They weren't to know anything about the will. Elizabeth discussed it with me."

"When?"

"When she woke up about . . . oh, I guess it was about five o'clock in the morning."

"All right. Tell me what happened."

"Well, you understand, she woke up first sometime about three o'clock. We all went in there then and talked with her. It wasn't much of a talk. Just greetings and generalities. She kissed us and told us how glad she was to see us."

"Then what?"

"Then she went right back to sleep. We left Nellie Conway in charge and we all went into the other room to lie down for a while. I slept an hour or an hour and a half, and then I came back and told Nellie I was wide awake and could take over."

"Then what?"

"That was when she put the tablets on the saucer and told me to give them to Elizabeth whenever she woke up at any time after six a.m."

"Where had the tablets been before then?"

"In a little box in the pocket of her uniform—anyway, that's where she got them when I first saw them."

"Why didn't Nellie Conway leave them in the box and simply tell you that——?"

"Apparently she was afraid I'd forget them. She took the saucer out from under the glass that had the water in it, and put the tablets right there in plain sight by the side of the bed."

"How far from Elizabeth?"

"Why, right by the side of the bed. Not over . . . oh, a couple of feet perhaps."

"How far from you?"

"I was sitting right near there. They couldn't have been over three or four feet from me."

"How far from the door of the room?"

"The door of the room was right by the stand. It wasn't over . . . oh, eighteen inches or two feet from the door of the room."

"I just wanted to get it straight," Mason said. "Now, what happened after that?"

"Well, Elizabeth was sleeping. She wakened about five o'clock and that was when she started to talk with me. Then was when she made out the will."

"Then what?"

"I was thinking I'd give her the medicine—I guess it was about twenty minutes to six—but she went back to sleep again. She didn't wake up until around a quarter to seven, and then I gave her the medicine with some coffee."

"Tell me a little more about what happened when you were talking."

"She talked to me I guess for half an hour, Mr. Mason, telling me about what she'd been going through, about the fact that Nathan had been trying to kill her, that she had been talking with Nellie Conway about you, and that she wanted you to be her lawyer, that she wanted you to go out and tell Nathan Bain that he was all finished, that she intended to file a suit for divorce, and that she wanted to make a will disinheriting Nathan."

"Did she say anything about her grounds for divorce, about what proof she had?"

"She didn't go into details, but she told me she had documentary proof."

"*Documentary* proof?" Mason asked sharply.

"That's right."

"She was intending to get a divorce because he'd been trying to kill her, wasn't she?"

"I don't know—I presume so."

"And she had *documentary* proof?"

"That's what she said. I think it related to infidelity."

"Where did she keep it?"

"She didn't say."

"All right," Mason said, "go on. What happened?"

"Well, she told me that she wanted to have you come out and prepare a will for her to sign, and she asked me to go and see you. She asked for her cheque-book and told me it was in her purse in a bureau drawer. I brought it to her and she wrote out that cheque for you."

"Then what?"

"Then we had some discussion about the fact that she was really afraid of Nathan and she felt that before you could draw up a will and have her sign it, something might happen to her."

"That was rather melodramatic, wasn't it?" Mason asked.

"Not in the light of subsequent events," Miss Braxton said sharply.

"All right. Go ahead."

"Well, I told her I didn't think it was necessary. I told her I could go to see you and tell you what she wanted, and that you could probably be out there before noon with a will ready for her to sign. She said that she thought it would be better to execute a will first and have Nathan know that no matter what happened she wasn't going to let him have a cent of her money. She said she'd been thinking it over and had come to that conclusion, and that that was the thing to do."

"So what did she do?"

"She took a piece of paper and wrote out that will."

"Let me take another look at that will."

"But you've seen it, Mr. Mason."

"You have it with you?"

"Yes, of course."

With obvious reluctance she opened her purse and handed the will to the lawyer.

Mason looked at it carefully, then moved over to study it under the light.

"There's a full stop after the last word now," he said.

Victoria said nothing.

"When you came to my office," Mason said, "there was no stop at the end of the will. I pointed that out to you."

"I know you did."

"So then you took a fountain pen and added a stop," Mason said. "In order to try and gild the lily you've probably put your neck in a noose. They'll have a spectroscopic analysis made of the ink on that stop. If they have any idea that——"

"You're thinking that they'll show it was made with a different ink and a different fountain pen?" she asked. "Well, you don't need to worry about that, Mr. Mason. That stop was made with Elizabeth's fountain pen and it's the same pen that wrote the will."

"When did you do it?" Mason asked.

"I didn't do it."

"Who did?"

"Elizabeth."

"Do you," Mason asked, "know any more funny stories?"

She said, "I'm going to tell you the truth, Mr. Mason. I was very much disturbed about that stop not being at the end of the sentence. After you pointed it out to me, I realised that if anything happened—and then, of course, something did happen; I received word that Elizabeth had been poisoned. I dashed out there in a taxicab just as fast as I could get there, and I went right into the room. Elizabeth was very, very ill. She was suffering excruciating agony, but she was conscious. I told everyone to get out and leave me alone for a few minutes, and then I said, 'Elizabeth, Mr. Mason says you neglected to put a stop at the end of that will,' and I took the fountain pen and handed it to her."

"Did she reach for it?"

"Well, I . . . she was very sick at the time."

"Did she reach to take the fountain pen when you handed it to her?"

"I put it into her hand."

"And then what did you do?"

"I held the will close to her so she could make a dot at the proper place."

"Did she raise her head from the pillow?"

"No."

"How did she see where to make the dot then?"

"I guided her hand."

"I see," Mason said dryly.

"But she knew what was being done."

"I like the way you say that," Mason said. "In place of saying she knew what she *was doing*, you say that she knew what was *being done*."

"Well, she knew what she was doing, then."

Mason said, "You still aren't telling me the truth about that will."

"What do you mean?"

"I mean that the story you told isn't the right story."

"Why, Mr. Mason, how can you say that?"

"You're talking to a lawyer. Let's cut out the kid stuff and try the truth for a change."

"I don't know what you mean."

"That will wasn't finished when you brought it to my office, and you know it."

"Well, it certainly . . . it certainly is finished now."

"Why did Elizabeth Bain break off in the middle of making that will?"

Victoria Braxton hesitated. Her eyes moved around the room as though seeking some means of escape.

"Go ahead," Mason said remorselessly.

"If you *must* know," she blurted, "Elizabeth was writing the will when Georgiana opened the door and looked in the room to see what she could do—that is, too see if there was any way that she could help."

"That's better," Mason said. "What happened?"

"Elizabeth didn't want Georgiana to know she was making a will, so she whipped the piece of paper down under the bedclothes. Georgiana asked how everything was coming and if we were getting along all right, and I told her yes, to go back and go to sleep."

"Then what?"

"Then she went back into her room. Elizabeth waited a few moments, lying there with her eyes closed, and then suddenly I realised she'd gone to sleep. So I took the fountain pen from her fingers, but the will was under the bedclothes and I couldn't find it without waking her up. I decided I'd wait until I gave her the medicine and then get the will. I thought she'd entirely finished with it, because of something she said . . . she'd quit writing for a good minute or two before Georgiana opened the door."

"And when did you get the will?"

"Well, when I gave her the medicine, she took it with

water but she wanted some coffee right after that, so I rang the bell and asked the housekeeper for some coffee. At about that time the day nurse came on and she said she'd give her the coffee. I only had time to fish the will out from under the bedclothes. Elizabeth saw what I was doing and smiled and nodded and said, 'It's all right, Vicki.' So I knew that she felt she'd finished it. Now that's the real honest-to-God truth, Mr. Mason."

"Why didn't you tell me that before?"

"Because I was afraid you might think that . . . well, that you might think the will really hadn't been finished."

"And no one else was in the room from the time Nellie Conway put those tablets on the saucer?"

"No."

Mason said, "We're going to drive you to the airport. I want you to take the first available plane for Honolulu. I want you to send a wire from the plane to the District Attorney that certain business matters in connection with your sister's affairs have made it necessary for you to rush to Honolulu, that you will keep in touch with him, and that he can count on your co-operation, but that there are business affairs of such a serious nature that your attorney advised you to make a personal trip to Honolulu at once."

"But what affairs?"

"Your sister owned property in Honolulu, didn't she?"

"Yes. Lots of it. We were staying at one of her cottages there. She has a whole string of them."

Mason said, "You don't need to tell anyone what the business affairs are."

"But, good heavens, what will I do when I get there?"

"You won't get there."

"What do you mean?"

"I mean you'll be called back."

"Then why go?"

Mason said, "Because it's a nice way to get you out of

circulation. You're not running away, because you've sent the District Attorney a telegram under your own name. You're taking your travel transportation under your own name, and I'm taking the responsibility as your attorney for sending you there."

"That sounds like such a crazy thing to do," she said.

"That," Mason said, "far from being crazy, is the only sensible thing to do. Now, I'm warning you—do not discuss this case with anyone. Under no circumstances ever tell anyone you gave Elizabeth those tablets. Under no circumstances discuss the case with the police or the District Attorney unless I am there. Do you understand?"

"I still don't see——"

"Will you follow my instructions?"

"Yes."

"To the letter?"

"Yes."

Mason turned to Della Street and said, "Okay, Della. Take her to the airport."

16

Early the next afternoon, Paul Drake stopped in to see Perry Mason.

Mason made no attempt to disguise his anxiety. "Paul, what's happening in New Orleans? Has Bain made a statement?"

"The police aren't releasing one single bit of information, Perry. . . . Well, I'll amend that statement. They have released one."

"What's that?"

"They have a warrant for you."

"What's the charge?"

"Vagrancy."

"Anything else?"

"You mean as a charge?"

"Yes."

"No. Isn't that enough?"

Mason grinned and said, "They can't extradite me on vagrancy. They know it. They made the charge just as a gesture."

"They're mad."

"Let them be mad. But you didn't come here just to tell me that."

"Lieutenant Tragg has uncovered something."

"What?"

"Something big."

"Evidence that Nathan Bain murdered his wife?"

"Apparently," Drake said, "evidence that he did not."

"I'd like to see *that* evidence."

Drake said, "I can tell you one thing, Perry. They have some secret evidence in this case, some evidence that they're keeping so closely guarded that no one knows what it is."

"What sort of evidence?"

"I can't find out."

"Does it point to Nathan Bain, does it point to the fact she committed suicide, or . . . ?"

"All I know is that it's some super secret evidence."

"Any chance you can find out?"

Drake said, "The grand jury is in session today. They're doing something in connection with this case. I have a man up there who has a pipeline into the grand jury. He may be able to give us the low-down.

"I also know that the District Attorney's office is furious because Victoria Braxton didn't show up for questioning."

"She's on a trip," Mason said. "She has business interests in Honolulu that she absolutely has to look after."

"So you told me," Drake said dryly.

"She is," Mason said, "as far as the business angle is concerned, acting on the advice of her counsel."

"Well, that makes it fine. Only the D.A. doesn't think so."

"He wouldn't. Anything else, Paul?"

"The police have been in consultation with Lieutenant Tragg in New Orleans. Something broke there this morning that they consider highly impor——"

The phone rang sharply. Della Street answered, then said, "It's for you, Paul."

Drake picked up the phone and said, "Hello . . . Yes . . . Okay, give it to me. . . . Who else knows about this? . . . Okay, thanks. Good-bye."

He hung up the telephone, turned to Mason and said, "There's your answer. The grand jury has just returned a secret indictment against Victoria Braxton, charging her with first-degree murder."

Mason whistled. "What's the evidence, Paul?"

"The evidence is secret."

"It won't be if they've put it before the grand jury."

"Don't worry, Perry, they didn't put anything before the grand jury that they aren't willing to shout from the housetops—that is, officially. They probably whispered something in the ear of the grand jury."

Mason said, "I had a hunch something like that might be in the wind."

He turned to Della Street. "Della, we'll send a wire to Victoria Braxton, on the plane en route to Honolulu, telling her to come home. I thought we'd have to do that, but I felt it would be a summons from the grand jury rather than an indictment."

"Telling her what's in the wind?" Della Street asked.

"No. We have to protect Paul Drake's pipeline. We don't dare to let it out that we know what the grand jury did—not yet."

"What do you want to tell her?" Della Street asked, holding her pencil over the notebook.

Mason thought a moment, then grinned wryly. "Take this wire," he said, "COME HOME AT ONCE ALL IS UN-FORGIVEN."

17

THE trial of the People of the State of California versus Victoria Braxton opened with all of that electric tension which underlies a championship prize fight between two men who have heretofore been undefeated.

Hamilton Burger, the big grizzly bear of a District Attorney, savagely triumphant in the assurance that at last he had a perfect case which contained no flaw, was making his preliminary moves with that quiet confidence which comes to a man who knows that he holds the winning cards.

Perry Mason, veteran court-room strategist, worked with cautious skill, taking advantage of each technicality which he felt could be of any possible benefit, feeling his way with caution, realising only too well that the prosecution had prepared a trap for him, and that at any moment the legal ground might fly out from under him.

Inside information was to the effect that the prosecution had carefully saved, as a surprise, evidence that would be completely devastating once it was introduced, and that Perry Mason, despite using every legal trick in the quiver to try and make the prosecution disclose its hand, had finally been forced to enter the court-room without any knowledge of his opponent's case other than the bare outline which had been utilised to support the indictment of the grand jury.

Betting among insiders was five to one against Mason's client.

Little time was wasted in selecting a jury. Mason had

indicated that he wanted only a fair and impartial trial for his client, and Hamilton Burger had quite evidently been willing to accept any twelve individuals who would be guided by the evidence in the case.

Newspaper reporters waited eagerly for Hamilton Burger's opening statement to the jury outlining the case he expected to prove, but veteran lawyers knew that Burger would not even give a hint of the nature of his trump cards this early in the game.

After outlining the fact that he expected to prove Victoria Braxton had poisoned her sister by administering three five-grain tablets of arsenic, knowing that her sister had made a will leaving a full one-half of her property, valued at some half-million dollars, to the defendant, Burger went on to announce:

"I will further state to you, ladies and gentlemen of the jury, that in this case the prosecution has no desire to take any technical advantage of the defendant. The prosecution will produce evidence from various witnesses which will make you familiar with the chain of events which led up to the death of Elizabeth Bain.

"This evidence will not follow the usual legal pattern, but will be in the nature of unfolding a story. We will paint for you, ladies and gentlemen, a broad picture with swift, sure strokes of factual evidence. We want you to see the entire background. You will, perhaps, find the evidence in this case somewhat unusual as far as the ordinary cut-and-dried procedure is concerned, but if you will follow it closely you will be led to the inescapable conclusion that the defendant is guilty of first-degree murder, carefully and deliberately planned, executed in a most heartless manner, under such circumstances that it will be necessary for you to return a verdict of guilty of first-degree murder without recommendation, making mandatory the death penalty."

Hamilton Burger, with vast dignity, walked back to the counsel table, seated himself, and glanced significantly at the judge.

"Does the defence wish to make any opening statement at this time?" Judge Howison asked.

"Not at this time, Your Honour. We prefer to make our opening statement when we present our case," Mason said.

"Very well. Call your first witness, Mr. District Attorney."

Hamilton Burger settled back in the big counsel chair and turned the preliminary proceedings over to his two deputies, David Gresham, the assistant prosecutor, and Harry Saybrook, the deputy, who, having been ignominiously beaten by Mason in the trial of Nellie Conway, was thirsting for revenge, and so had managed to get himself assigned as an assistant in the present case.

In rapid order, witnesses were called to the stand, proving that Elizabeth Bain had died, that prior to her death she exhibited evidences of arsenic poisoning, that after her death an autopsy had shown sufficient quantities of arsenic in her vital organs to have made it certain that her death was produced solely by arsenic poison.

A certified copy of the probate record showed that a holographic will had been made in the handwriting of Elizabeth Bain, dated the day of her death, and leaving all of her property share and share alike to her half-brother, James Braxton, and her half-sister, Victoria Braxton, the defendant in the present case.

After these preliminaries were over, Hamilton Burger moved in to take personal charge of the case.

"Call Dr. Harvey Keener," he said.

Dr. Keener was a slim, professional-looking man with the air of a doctor, even to the well-trimmed Vandyke beard, the cold, analytical eyes, and the dark, plastic-rimmed spectacles.

Taking the witness stand, he speedily qualified himself as a practising physician and surgeon, who had been such on the seventeenth of September last.

"Now, early on the morning of September seventeenth," Hamilton Burger asked, "you were called on to treat one of your patients on an emergency call?"

"Yes, sir."

"At what time were you called, Doctor?"

"At approximately eight-forty-five. I can't give you the exact time, but it was somewhere between eight-forty-five and nine o'clock."

"And you immediately went to see that patient?"

"I did. Yes, sir."

"Who was that patient?"

"Elizabeth Bain."

"Now, Doctor, directing your attention specifically to the symptoms which you yourself found at the time you arrived and not those which may have been told to you by the nurse, will you tell us just what you found?"

"I found the typical symptoms of arsenic poisoning, manifested in a gastro-enteric disturbance, an intense thirst, painful cramps, typical vomitus, tenesmus, feeble irregular pulse, a face that was anxious and pinched, the skin cold and clammy. I may say that these are progressive symptoms, and I am referring to them as over a period of time, from approximately the time of my arrival until the time of death, which occurred around eleven-forty that morning."

"Was the patient conscious?"

"The patient was conscious until approximately eleven o'clock."

"Did you make any chemical tests to check your diagnosis?"

"I saved substances which were eliminated for more careful analysis, but a quick chemical check indicated the presence of arsenic in the vomitus, and the symptoms were so typical that I was virtually certain of my diagnosis within a few minutes of the time of my arrival."

"Now then, did you have any conversation with the patient in regard to the manner in which this poison might have been administered?"

"I did."

"Did she make any statement to you at that time as to who had administered the poison?"

"She did."

"Will you please state what she said as to the manner of administration of the poison, and by whom?"

"Just a moment, Your Honour," Mason said, "I object to this as incompetent, irrelevant and immaterial, and quite plainly hearsay."

"That is not hearsay," Hamilton Burger said. "The patient was even then dying of arsenic poisoning."

"The point is, Your Honour," Mason said, "did she *know* she was dying?"

"Yes," Judge Howison ruled. "I think that is a very essential prerequisite to a so-called death-bed declaration, Mr. District Attorney."

"Very well, if Counsel wishes to be technical, I will dispose of that feature of the case."

"Did the patient know she was dying, Doctor?"

"Objected to as leading and suggestive."

"The question is leading, Mr. Burger."

"Well, Your Honour," Burger said, with exasperation, "Dr. Keener is a trained professional man. He has heard the discussion and certainly understands the purpose of the question. However, if Counsel wishes to consume time with technicalities, I will go about it the long way. What was Mrs. Bain's mental condition at the time with reference to hope of ultimate recovery, Doctor?"

"Objected to on the ground that no proper foundation has been laid," Mason said.

"Surely," Judge Howison said, "you are not questioning Dr. Keener's qualifications now, Mr. Mason?"

"Not as a doctor, Your Honour, only as a mind reader," Mason said. "The test of a dying declaration, or a deathbed declaration as it is sometimes known, is whether the patient states as part of that declaration that the patient is dying and knows that death is impending, and with the solemnity of the seal of death placed upon the patient's lips, then proceeds to make a statement which can be used as evidence."

"Your Honour," Hamilton Burger said irritably, "I propose to show as part of my case that the defendant was left alone in this room with Elizabeth Bain, that medicine was placed on a saucer to be given to Elizabeth Bain, that the defendant surreptitiously substituted for this medicine three five-grain tablets of arsenic, that when the decedent wakened at approximately six-forty-five, the defendant said to the decedent, 'Here is your medicine,' and gave her the three tablets or pills which had been substituted for the medicine which had previously been left by Dr. Keener."

"Go ahead and prove it then," Mason said, "but prove it by pertinent and relevant evidence."

"I think in order to show a death-bed declaration, you are going to have to show that the patient knew death was impending," Judge Howison said.

"That is exactly what I intend to do," Hamilton Burger said. "I have asked the doctor the question as to the patient's frame of mind."

"And that question," Mason said, "is to be answered not by the doctor's attempting to read the mind of the patient, but only by what the patient herself may have said."

"Very well," Hamilton Burger conceded. "Limit it to that point, Doctor, to what the patient said."

"She said she was dying."

Hamilton Burger smiled triumphantly at Mason.

"Can you give me her exact words?"

"I can," Dr. Keener said. "I made note of them at the time, thinking that they might be important. If I may be permitted to consult a memorandum which I made at the time, I will refresh my recollection."

The doctor's glib patter and his bearing on the witness stand indicated that he was no stranger to the court-room, and knew quite well how to take care of himself.

He produced a leather-backed notebook from his pocket.

"Just a moment," Mason said, "I'd like to consult the memorandum, that is, I'd like to look at it before the witness uses it to refresh his recollection."

"Help yourself," Hamilton Burger said sarcastically.

Mason walked up to the witness stand and examined the notebook.

"Before the doctor uses this to refresh his recollection," Mason said, "I would like to ask a few questions for the purpose of having it properly identified."

"Very well," Judge Howison ruled. "You may ask the questions."

"Doctor, this entry which appears here is in your own handwriting?"

"Yes, sir."

"It was made when, Doctor?"

"It was made at approximately the time the statement was made to me by the patient."

"And by the patient you mean Elizabeth Bain?"

"Yes, sir."

"It is written in pen and ink?"

"Yes, sir."

"What pen, what ink?"

"My own fountain pen filled with ink from a bottle which I keep in my office. I can assure you there is nothing sinister about the ink, Mr. Mason."

There was a ripple of merriment which Judge Howison frowned into silence.

"Quite so, Doctor," Mason said. "Now, at what time was this statement made?"

"It was made shortly before the patient lost consciousness."

"Shortly is a relative term, Doctor. Can you define it any better than that?"

"Well, I would say perhaps half an hour."

"The patient lost consciousness within an hour after this statement was made?"

"Yes, sir. There was a condition of coma."

Mason said, "Let me look at this notebook if you will, please, Doctor," and, without waiting for permission, he turned some of the pages.

"Just a moment," Hamilton Burger interposed. "I object to Counsel pawing through Dr. Keener's private documents."

"It's not a private document," Mason said. "It's a notebook which he is attempting to identify for the purpose of refreshing his recollection. I have the right to look at the adjoining pages of the notebook and to cross-examine the doctor on it."

Before Burger could make any answer, Mason, holding the notebook, turned to Dr. Keener and said, "Is it your custom, Doctor, to make entries in this notebook methodically and in consecutive order, or do you simply open the book at random until you come to a vacant page and then make a note?"

"Certainly not. I keep the book in an orderly manner. I fill one page and then turn to the next page."

"I see," Mason said. "Now this entry which you have made here, and which you wish to use at the moment to refresh your recollection as to the words that Elizabeth Bain used in stating that she was dying, are the last words which appear in this notebook?"

"Yes, sir."

"That has been some little time ago, and I take it that you have treated quite a few patients since then?"

"I have. Yes, sir."

"Why then did you not make any further entries in this notebook after Elizabeth Bain made this statement to you?"

"Because I read the statement to the police when they appeared at the scene, and the police promptly took that book as evidence, and it has been in their possession ever since."

"Until when, Doctor?"

"Until this morning, when it was returned to me."

"By whom?"

"By the District Attorney."

"I see," Mason said smiling. "The idea was that the District Attorney was to ask you if you had jotted down the exact words of the decedent, and you would whip the notebook from your pocket——"

"I object," Hamilton Burger shouted. "That's not proper cross-examination."

"I think it goes to show the bias of the witness, Your Honour."

"I think it goes more to show the skill of the prosecutor," Judge Howison said, smiling. "I think you have made your point, Mr. Mason. I see no reason for permitting the question to be answered in its present form. The witness has already stated that the notebook was taken by the police and that it was returned to him this morning."

"And that is the reason there are no entries in the notebook subsequent to the entry by you of the statement made by Elizabeth Bain that she was dying and that she had been poisoned?"

"Yes, sir."

"Now, perhaps you will permit the witness to go ahead with his testimony," Hamilton Burger said sarcastically.

"Not now," Mason said, smiling. "I have a few more questions to ask concerning the identification of this written memorandum. This is in your own handwriting, Doctor?"

"Yes, sir."

"And was made within a few minutes of the time the statement was made?"

"Yes, sir."

"What do you mean by a few minutes?"

"I would say within four or five minutes at the most."

"You made notes of that statement because you considered it important?"

"I did."

"You knew that it would be important to get her exact words?"

"I did."

"In other words, you have been a witness in court before this, you knew the legal requirement of a death-bed statement, and you knew that in order to get a death-bed statement admitted, it would be necessary to show that the patient knew she was dying?"

"Yes, sir."

"And you made these notes because you were afraid to trust to your own memory?"

"I wouldn't say that. No, sir."

"Why *did* you make them then?"

"Because I knew some smart lawyer was going to ask

me what her exact words were, and I decided I'd be able to tell him."

Again there was a ripple of merriment.

"I see," Mason said. "You knew that you were going to be questioned on this and you wanted to be in a position to cope with counsel on cross-examination?"

"If you want to put it that way, yes, sir."

"Now, then," Mason said, "without saying what her exact words were, did the patient make a statement to you as to who had administered the poison?"

"She did. Yes, sir."

"And yet you didn't consider that statement particularly important, Doctor?"

"Certainly I did. That was the most important part of the whole thing."

"Then why didn't you make a note of that in your notebook so that if some smart lawyer started to ask you for the exact words of the dying patient, you would be able to give them?"

"I did make such a notation," Dr. Keener said angrily. "If you will look back a page you will find the notation giving the exact words of the patient."

"And when was that notation made?"

"Within a few minutes of the time the patient made the statement."

"Within five minutes?"

"Within five minutes, yes. Probably less than that."

"Within four minutes?"

"I would say it was within one minute."

"And what about this statement that the patient made that she was dying? What's your best recollection as to when that was written in your notebook?"

"I would say that also was written within one minute."

"But," Mason said, smiling, "the statement from the patient as to who had administered the medicine to her is made on the page preceding her statement that she was dying."

"Naturally," Dr. Keener said sarcastically. "You have already questioned me about that. I told you I made my entries in this notebook in chronological order."

"Oh, then the statement as to who had administered the medicine was made *before* the patient said she knew she was dying?"

"I didn't say that."

"Well, I'm asking it."

"Frankly," Dr. Keener said, suddenly aware of the trap into which he had been led, "I can't remember the exact sequence of these statements."

"But you do know, do you not, Doctor, that you make your entries in this book in chronological order? You have said so very emphatically on at least two occasions."

"Well, yes."

"So that at the time the patient made the statement to you in regard to the administration of medicine, she had not made any statement to you to indicate that she knew she was dying?"

"I can't say that."

"You don't have to," Mason said. "Your notebook says it for you."

"Well, that's not exactly my recollection."

"But your recollection is hazy, isn't it, Doctor?"

"No, sir."

"You had reason to doubt it?"

"What do you mean by that?"

"You were afraid that you couldn't remember exactly what had happened and the exact sequence in which it happened, so you didn't trust your memory but made entries in this notebook so that no smart lawyer could trap you in cross-examination?"

Dr. Keener shifted his position uneasily.

"Oh, Your Honour," Hamilton Burger said, "I think this cross-examination is being unduly prolonged and I am sure——"

"I don't," Judge Howison ruled. "As the court understands the law it is plainly a prerequisite to a death-bed declaration that the person making it knows of impending death and makes a statement to that effect, so that the knowledge which is within the mind of the patient can be communicated to others."

"Well," Dr. Keener said, "I can't answer that question any better than I already have."

"Thank you," Mason said. "That's all."

"All right," Hamilton Burger said, "Counsel apparently is finished. Go ahead and state what Elizabeth Bain said, refreshing your recollection from the entry in your notebook, Doctor."

"I now object to the question," Mason said, "on the ground that it is incompetent, irrelevant and immaterial. It appears that the doctor is now testifying to a statement made by the patient at some considerable time interval after the statement made by the patient concerning the administration of the medicine, which the District Attorney is trying to get into evidence."

"The objection is sustained," Judge Howison said promptly.

Burger's face purpled. "Your Honour, I——"

"I think the situation is obvious as far as the testimony is concerned at the present time. If you wish to make a further examination of Dr. Keener for the purpose of showing the relative times at which these entries were made, those questions will be permitted, but in the present state of the evidence the objection must be sustained."

"Well, I will withdraw Dr. Keener from the stand

temporarily and call another witness," Hamilton Burger said with poor grace. "I'll get at it in another way."

"Very well," Judge Howison said. "Call your next witness. That's all, Doctor. You may stand aside for the time being."

"Call Nellie Conway to the stand," Hamilton Burger said, with the manner of a man getting ready to play his high trumps.

Nellie Conway came forward to the witness stand, was sworn, and, after the usual preliminaries as to her name, address and occupation, was asked by Hamilton Burger, "You are acquainted with Nathan Bain, the surviving husband of Elizabeth Bain?"

"Yes, sir."

"And were employed by him as a nurse to nurse Elizabeth Bain?"

"Yes, sir."

"And on the evening of the sixteenth and the morning of the seventeenth of last September, you were so employed there as nurse?"

"Yes, sir."

"Now, did you at any time on the evening of the sixteenth or the morning of the seventeenth, give instructions to the defendant in this case as to medicine that was to be given to Elizabeth Bain?"

"I did. Yes, sir."

"And those instructions were communicated to the defendant?"

"Yes, sir."

"And the medicine was left where?"

"The medicine was left in a saucer on a bedside table within some two feet of Elizabeth Bain."

"What did the medicine consist of?"

"Three five-grain tablets."

"Who had given you that medicine?"

"Dr. Keener had left it with me to be given to Mrs. Bain."

"Where had this medicine been left?"

"It had been given me personally by Dr. Keener."

"When?"

"About seven o'clock on the evening of the sixteenth when Dr. Keener made his evening call."

"Who was present in the room when you had this conversation with the defendant?"

"Just Elizabeth Bain, who was sleeping, and Victoria Braxton."

"And what did you tell her?"

"I told her that if Mrs. Bain awakened after six o'clock in the morning she was to have this medicine, that it was not to be given to her before six."

"And that was medicine which you received directly from Dr. Keener?"

"Yes, sir."

"Cross-examine!" Hamilton Burger snapped.

Perry Mason's tone was casual and conversational. "You don't know what was in the medicine?"

"I know it was three tablets, that's all."

"It was part of your duties to give Mrs. Bain medicine which had been left by the physician?"

"Yes, sir."

"And you did do that?"

"Yes, sir."

"You were paid to do that?"

"Yes, sir. Although I wasn't paid for my services the night of the sixteenth and the seventeenth, that is, not specifically."

"Do you mean you weren't paid by anybody to give any medicine to Mrs. Bain on the night of the sixteenth and seventeenth?"

"I know what you're trying to get at," Hamilton Burger

said, "and you don't need to go at it by indirection, Mr. Mason. The prosecution has no objection. The door is open, walk right in."

And Hamilton Burger smiled smugly.

Nellie Conway said, "I was paid some money by Nathan Bain on the night of the sixteenth. It was not a payment for services I was to render, it was payment for a settlement that had been made, but I did give Mrs. Bain some medicine that Mr. Bain wanted me to give her."

"Medicine?" Mason asked.

"Well, some pills or tablets."

"How many?"

"Three."

"What size?"

"Five-grain."

"And they had been given you by Mr. Bain to give to his wife?"

"Yes, sir. There had been four originally but I had given one of them to you, and the other three remained in my possession, and when Mr. Bain asked me to give them to his wife, I did."

"At what time?"

"Shortly after Dr. Keener had left, I gave Mrs. Bain those three pills or tablets."

"The ones that had been given you by Nathan Bain, her husband?"

"Yes, sir."

Hamilton Burger sat grinning delightedly.

"Where did you get these tablets that you gave Mrs. Bain?"

"From her husband."

"I mean immediately prior to administering them. Where were they?"

She said, as though she had carefully memorised the words, "I had taken those tablets to your office. I had told you about the conversation, and you had told me that the medicine was harmless, that it was nothing but aspirin. And you charged me a dollar for advice. You had returned three of those tablets to a small tube-like bottle which was just big enough to hold five-grain pills. That bottle had been sealed in an envelope with your name and my name written on it.

"So when Mr. Bain asked me once more to give those pills to his wife, I decided to do so since you had told me they contained only aspirin."

"Did I tell you that?" Mason asked.

"Yes, and you charged a fee for telling me so. I have the receipt."

"I told you that the pills you had contained only aspirin?"

"Well, you took one of the pills to be analysed and told me that it contained aspirin."

"One of the four," Mason said. "You don't know what was in the other three."

"No, only I supposed that if they had been anything harmful you wouldn't have given them back to me so I could give them to Mrs. Bain. I went to you for advice and paid you your fee."

Hamilton Burger chuckled audibly.

Mason said, "Then am I to understand that on the evening of the sixteenth you opened this envelope and took the three remaining tablets from the small bottle or phial, and gave them to Mrs. Bain?"

"I did. Yes, sir."

"With what effect?"

"No effect, except that she had a better and quieter night than she had had at any time."

"As far as you know," Mason said, "those pills might have contained arsenic or any other poison?"

"All I know is what Mr. Bain told me, that the pills

were to give his wife a good sleep, and what you told me, that they were aspirin," she said, with the quick, pert manner of one who is giving a well-rehearsed answer to an anticipated question.

Hamilton Burger was grinning broadly.

"So," Mason said, "as far as you know of your own knowledge, you yourself may have given Elizabeth Bain three five-grain pills of arsenic on the evening of the sixteenth at some time shortly after seven o'clock in the evening?"

"I gave her the pills a little after eight o'clock."

"That's all," Mason said.

"No further questions," Hamilton Burger said. "Now we'll recall Dr. Keener to the stand if the Court please."

"Very well. Return to the stand, Doctor."

Dr. Keener returned to the witness stand.

"Doctor," Hamilton Burger said, "I want to ask you, in your opinion as a physician, if three five-grain arsenic tablets had been given to Elizabeth Bain at approximately eight o'clock on the evening of the sixteenth of September, when would the first symptoms of poison have manifested themselves?"

"In my opinion, and because of my knowledge of the patient's condition," Dr. Keener said, "I would have expected symptoms to have manifested themselves within a period of one to two hours after ingestion, a maximum period of two hours, certainly not later than that."

"Now then," Hamilton Burger went on, "you have heard the testimony of the last witness that you gave her three five-grain tablets to be administered to Elizabeth Bain in the morning."

"That's right. At any time when she wakened after six in the morning."

"What were the contents of those pills or tablets, Doctor?"

"They contained soda, acetylsalicylic acid and phenobarbital."

"There was no arsenic in them?"

"None whatever."

"Those pills or tablets had been compounded under your direction, Doctor?"

"In accordance with a prescription which I had given. There were certain very definite proportions. I may state that the problem at the time was that of administering proper sedatives which would, over a course of time, not upset the stomach, but would control a condition of extreme nervousness which had characterised the patient's reactions to her injuries and to surrounding circumstances."

"Now then," Hamilton Burger said triumphantly, "did you at any time after you gave those three tablets to the nurse, Nellie Conway, on the evening of the sixteenth, see those same three pills again?"

"I did. Yes, sir."

"When?"

"At about three p.m. on the afternoon of the seventeenth."

"Those same tablets?"

"Those same tablets. Yes, sir."

"Now then," Hamilton Burger said, smiling, "you may cross-examine, Mr. Mason."

"How do you know they were the same tablets?" Mason asked.

"Because I analysed them."

"You analysed them personally?"

"It was done under my supervision and in my presence."

"And what did you find?"

"I found they were the tablets I had prescribed. They contained identical proportions of soda, phenobarbital and acetylsalicylic acid."

"Where did you find those pills?" Mason asked.

"I found them in a waste-basket that was in the room for the purpose of collecting bandages which had been used, bits of waste cotton and other matter, which had been thrown away while the patient was being treated, things that were used in the treatment, in other words."

"What time were those pills or tablets found?"

"They were found——"

"Just a minute," Mason interrupted. "Before you answer that question, let me ask you one more. Did you find them yourself personally?"

"Yes, sir. That's right, I did. I suggested that a search be made of everything in the room. Frankly, I was looking for——"

"Never mind what you were looking for," Mason said. "Just answer the question, Doctor. You know better than to volunteer information. You've been a witness before. I am simply asking whether you personally found them."

"Yes, sir. I personally went through the contents of this waste-basket and I found one tablet, then I found two more."

"Then what did you do?"

"They were placed in a receptacle, called to the attention of the police, and certain tests were made."

"Can you describe the nature of those tests?"

"Just a moment, Your Honour, just a moment," Hamilton Burger objected. "That is not proper cross-examination. I have asked the witness on direct examination as to whether he ever saw those same pills or tablets again. Now I have no objection as to this witness testifying on cross-examination as to any tests that were made to determine the *identity* of the tablets, but as to any other matters, I object."

"But wouldn't the test be for the purpose of

determining the identity of the pills?" Judge Howison asked.

"Not necessarily, Your Honour."

"Well, I feel that the objection is well-taken if the question is deemed to call for tests which were made for any other purpose and with which the witness is familiar. However, I don't see——"

"It will be explained in due time," Hamilton Burger said, "but I wish the privilege of putting on my own case in my own way, Your Honour."

"Very well, the witness will understand that the question is limited as to tests which were made for the purpose of identifying the tablets."

"Those tests were made by me, by a chemist of the police force, and a consulting chemist from one of the pharmaceutical houses, in the presence of two police officers. The tests disclosed unquestionably that these were the tablets I had prescribed. Those were the same three tablets that I had left to be given to Mrs. Bain after she wakened at six o'clock in the morning. There is no question but what a substitution had been made——"

"Just a moment, Doctor," Mason rebuked sharply. "You keep trying to go ahead and interject your surmises and arguments into the case. Please confine yourself to answering questions and stopping."

"Very well," Dr. Keener snapped. "There is no question but what they were the same tablets."

"In other words, they had an identical formula as the ones you had prescribed?"

"That's right."

"And, by the way, Doctor, do you use the term pills and tablets interchangeably?"

"Loosely speaking, the way we have been talking in lay terms, yes. I usually prefer to refer to a pill as something that is a ball of medication with a coating on the outside, whereas a tablet is more of a lozenge, a compressed, flat substance. However, in lay language I use the terms interchangeably."

"But technically what were these?"

"Technically these were tablets. It was a mixture that had been compounded and then compressed into small, lozenge-like tablets."

"How long had you been having trouble with a nervous condition on the part of the patient?"

"Ever since the accident—the injury."

"And you had used varying methods of sedation?"

"I used hypodermics for a while until the pain had subsided, and then, as I was dealing with a condition of nervousness that threatened to become chronic, I tried to get a treatment that would be a palliative yet without containing sufficient medication to be perhaps habit-forming."

"So this medication of soda, acetylsalicylic acid and phenobarbital was a part of a continuing treatment?"

"Yes, I had continued it for some time."

"How long?"

"About one week on this particular formula."

"And the patient responded?"

"As well as could be expected. I was, of course, finding it necessary to diminish dosage. After all, a patient cannot expect to depend indefinitely upon medication to control nervousness. The patient must co-operate, and there must be an adjustment to circumstances. Therefore, I was continually decreasing the dosage and, of course, the patient was, at the same time, developing a certain tolerance to the medication; therefore results were not entirely satisfactory from a layman's point of view, although as her physician I was keeping a careful watch on the situation and felt that progress was as good as could be expected."

"The point I am making," Mason said, "is that you didn't mix up these pills three at a time. The pills were mixed in quantities."

"Oh, I see what you're driving at," Dr. Keener said, with a somewhat nasty smile. "However, I will state that I was very careful never to leave more than three of these pills at any one time, so that these three must necessarily have been the ones that I left that evening on my departure. I had previously given the patient three similar pills or tablets, which I administered personally."

"Thank you for the benefit of your conclusions, Doctor," Mason said, "but all you know is that these three tablets had identical drug content with the ones you had prescribed. You don't know whether they were the three tablets you had left for her that night, or day before yesterday, or a week ago, do you?"

"I certainly do."

"How?"

"I know, because they were found in the trash basket, and the trash basket was emptied——"

"How do you know it was emptied?"

"The nurse reported it was emptied. Those were the orders that I had left."

"You didn't empty it yourself?"

"No."

"Then you're trying to testify from hearsay evidence, Doctor. You know better than that. I'm asking you of your own knowledge. As far as you're concerned, they might have been tablets that you had left for the patient to take the morning before or the morning before that, or the morning before that."

"Well, the patient would have told me if she hadn't been given the medicine, and the nurse would have reported——"

"I'm talking of your own knowledge, Doctor. Let's

not engage in statements as to the probabilities of a given situation, but as to your own knowledge, is there any way you have of *knowing* that those tablets were the same tablets that you had left that morning, purely from the chemical content?"

"Not from the chemical content, no. However, there were other matters that——"

"I think I've pointed out, Doctor, that we're not going into those other matters at this time," Hamilton Burger interrupted sharply. "The questions that you are being asked concern entirely the chemical compounds of the pills or tablets, and the place and time at which they were found."

"Very well," Dr. Keener said.

"The point I am making," Mason said, "is that for perhaps the last four days you had been giving the patient identical medication?"

"For the last five days prior to her death, I had been giving her the same medication. Prior to that time the dosage had been somewhat stronger. I will further state that because I was afraid the patient might develop suicidal tendencies, I was very careful not to leave any surplus of pills or tablets so that the patient could accumulate a lethal dosage. Now does that answer your question, Mr. Mason?"

"That answers it very nicely," Mason said. "Thank you very much, Doctor."

Judge Howison glanced at Hamilton Burger. "It's four-thirty, Mr. Burger. Do you have some witness that you can put on who——?"

"I'm afraid not, Your Honour. The next witness is going to take some time, but I think we may as well get at it, because I expect his cross-examination will consume a very considerable period."

"Very well, go ahead."

"Call Nathan Bain."

Nathan Bain came forward and was sworn.

It was quite evident from the moment he took the witness stand that this was an entirely different Nathan Bain from the man whom Mason had made to appear at such disadvantage during the trial of Nellie Conway.

Nathan Bain had obviously been carefully prepared, thoroughly coached, and was enough of a public speaker to take full advantage of the situation.

Hamilton Burger stood up and faced the man with a manner which created the impression of a simple dignity and straightforward sincerity.

"Mr. Bain," he said, "you are the surviving husband of Elizabeth Bain, the decedent?"

"Yes, sir."

"And under the terms of the will, which has been filed for probate, you are not to inherit any part of her estate?"

"No, sir. Not one penny."

"You have heard the testimony of Nellie Conway that you gave her certain medication to be administered to your wife?"

"Yes, sir."

"Will you please tell me, and tell the jury, very frankly what the circumstances are in connection with that affair, Mr. Bain?"

Nathan Bain took a deep breath, turned and faced the jury.

"I had," he said, "placed myself in a most unfortunate and lamentable predicament, entirely through my own ill-advised stupidity. I regret that very greatly, but I wish to state the facts——"

"Go ahead and state them," Mason interrupted. "I object, Your Honour, to this man making an argument to the jury. Let him answer the question by stating the facts."

"Go right ahead and *state* the facts," Hamilton Burger said, with something of a smirk.

Nathan Bain's manner was that of a man who is baring his chest to his accusers. He said, in a voice that dripped with sorrow and humility, "For the past few months my relations with my wife had been anything but happy. I gave Nellie Conway four tablets and asked her to administer those tablets to my wife without the knowledge of her doctor or anyone else."

"What was the nature of those tablets?" Hamilton Burger asked.

"Those tablets," Nathan Bain said, "were four in number. Two of them were five-grain aspirin tablets, two of them were barbiturates."

Hamilton Burger, veteran jury lawyer and court-room strategist, managed to put into his tone just the right amount of feeling and sympathy, indicating that he disliked to subject Nathan Bain to this ordeal but that the interests of justice made it necessary.

"Please tell the jury the cause of the difference between you and your wife at the time of her death."

Once more Nathan Bain turned to look the jurors straight in the eyes, then lowered his own eyes, and in a voice of shamefaced humility said, "I had been untrue to my wife, unfaithful to my marriage vows, and she had learned of my infidelity."

"Was that the only cause?" Hamilton Burger asked.

"We had been drifting apart," Nathan Bain admitted, and then, raising his eyes to the jury in a burst of candour, he said, as though baring his very soul, "If it hadn't been for that I wouldn't have sought affection elsewhere, but . . ."

He broke off, made a little gesture of futility and once more lowered his eyes.

"You will understand that I dislike to go into this as

much as you dislike to have me," Hamilton Burger said, "but I feel that it is necessary in order to give the jury a complete picture of the situation. Why did you want your wife to have this one dose, this heavy dose, of bar-biturates?"

Nathan Bain kept his eyes on the floor. "My wife had intercepted certain letters, certain documentary proof of my infidelity. She was planning to bring a suit for divorce. I didn't want this to happen. I loved her. My other affair was simply one of those flings that a man will take heed-lessly, thoughtlessly, when temptation offers, and with-out proper consideration of the horrible consequences which must inevitably develop. I didn't want my wife to get a divorce."

"Why did you arrange to give her the pills?"

"She wouldn't let me come in the room, yet the door was always unlocked. The nurses were not in there all the time. They came and went. When she was asleep the nurse would step out down to the kitchen to get some hot milk or coffee, or something of that sort. I wanted an opportunity to go into the room and search and find those letters."

"Couldn't you have done it without drugging her?"

"She was very nervous and very restless after the accident. The poor girl's spine was crushed and I suppose that that injury had a deep-seated effect upon her entire nervous system, but in addition to that there was, of course, the knowledge of her injuries, and I think towards the last she had the feeling that she might never be able to walk again. She slept very fitfully, wakening at the slightest noise. I knew that if she detected me in the room, trying to get those documents, it would be disastrous. Even my presence in the room irritated her, and Dr. Keener had warned me not to excite her. He had told me definitely to stay out of the room."

"How long had that situation been in existence?"

"From the day she returned home from the hospital."

"So what happened on the evening of the sixteenth?"

"On the evening of the sixteenth, this dosage of barbiturates, added to the phenobarbital that Dr. Keener had prescribed, put my wife in a deep, restful sleep. She was drugged to a point of insensibility. I waited until both the housekeeper, Imogene Ricker, and the nurse, Nellie Conway, were out of the room. They were down in the kitchen drinking coffee and talking. I felt certain they would be there for some minutes, because my wife was sleeping very soundly that night, and they knew that for some reason she was having a very deep, restful sleep. So I entered the room and after some five minutes' search found the documents and took them back into my possession."

Nathan Bain looked down at his shoes, took a deep breath and let it out in a sigh. His attitude was that of one who condemns himself most strongly, yet who, after all, recognises that he has been actuated only by human frailties which are a part of every man's make-up. It was a consummate job of acting.

It would have been possible to have heard a pin drop in the court-room.

Hamilton Burger managed to give the impression of one who is respecting another's great sorrow. "What did you do with these documents after you recovered them, Mr. Bain?"

Bain said, "I arranged to return the letters to the woman who had written them so she could destroy them."

"And I believe you went to New Orleans immediately after your wife's death?"

Judge Howison looked down at Mason and said, "Of course, an objection is usually up to opposing counsel, but it seems to me that some of this matter is entirely collateral."

"I think not," Hamilton Burger said, with slow, ponderous dignity. "I want the jury to get the entire picture here. We want to put all our cards face up and on the table, those that are good and those that are bad. We want the jurors to see the interior of this man's house. We want them to see into his mind, into his soul——"

Mason interrupted dryly, "One of the reasons I hadn't been objecting, Your Honour, was that I knew Hamilton Burger had this touching speech all prepared and I didn't want to give him his cue."

There was a slight ripple of merriment. Judge Howison, himself, couldn't help but smile, and Burger frowned as he realised that this emotional release was undermining the effect he was trying to create.

He drew himself up and said with simple, austere dignity, "If Court and Counsel will bear with me, I think I can convince them of this man's sincerity, of his repentance and of his grief."

And without waiting, Burger turned to Nathan Bain and said, "Why did you go to New Orleans, Mr. Bain?"

"I went there," Bain said, 'because the woman who had entered into my life was there, and I wanted to tell her personally that I never wanted to see her again, that the affair had been the result of an unthinking venture and had left me emotionally bankrupt."

Nathan Bain's words and manner carried conviction. A veteran speaker would have noticed that much of this was due to tricks of delivery, carefully studied, synthetic oratorical accessories, but the average listener heard only a bereaved husband being forced by the exigencies of the situation to make public confession of his wrongdoing, and trying his best to conceal a broken heart beneath a rigid exterior of Spartan self-control.

"Now then," Hamilton Burger went on, "you spoke of a settlement that had been made with Nellie Conway, and there has been some talk here of a settlement. Will you describe that and tell us what that actually was?"

"That," Nathan Bain said, "was an attempt on my part to adjust what had been a wrong."

"Tell us about it, please."

"I was instrumental in having Nellie Conway arrested for theft. I realise now that not only was my action impulsive, but that it was ill-advised. She was represented by Mr. Perry Mason, the attorney who is now representing Victoria Braxton, and Mr. Mason, I am afraid, caused me to cut rather a sorry spectacle in the court-room. That was because I hadn't fully thought over the various ramifications of the situation. I am afraid I was tempted to act hastily—much too hastily."

"Just what did you do, specifically?"

"I appealed to the police, and, on their advice, hired a private detective. Things had been missing from the house and I had reason, or thought I did, to suspect Nellie Conway. I took my wife's jewel casket from the desk where it was kept under lock and key, and left it out in plain sight. I filled it with synthetic costume jewellery and made an inventory of the articles. I dusted the outside of the casket with a fluorescent powder."

"Just describe that to us, if you will, Mr. Bain."

"Well, it was a powder which was furnished me by the private detective whom I employed. I understand it is quite generally used by private detectives for the purpose of catching sneak thieves, particularly in the case of locker burglaries and schoolroom sneak thieves."

"Can you describe this powder?"

"It is virtually . . . well, it's rather neutral in shade, and when you put it on an object such as this leather-covered jewel case which belonged to my wife, it is practically invisible. It has a quality which makes it adhere to the fingers. It is remarkable in its clinging qualities, yet there is no feeling of stickiness in connection with it."

"Now you have described that as a fluorescent powder?"

"Yes, sir. When ultra-violet light shines upon that powder it gives forth a very vivid light, that is, it fluoresces."

"I would, if possible, like to have you tell the jury something more about the case against Nellie Conway. In other words, I want to have it appear why you paid her such a sum of money."

"Because of the false arrest."

"You're now satisfied it was a false arrest?"

"After Mr. Mason got done with me," Nathan Bain said, with a wry smile, "I don't think there was anyone who had any doubt about it, myself included."

Some of the jurors smiled sympathetically.

"How much did you pay her, by the way?"

"Two thousand dollars for herself, and five hundred dollars for an attorney fee."

"Now just go ahead and describe the arrest a little more, if you will, please."

"Well, we dusted the fluorescent powder on this jewel case."

"And I take it the powder wasn't placed anywhere else?"

"No, sir. Only on the jewel case."

"And what happened?"

"Well, from time to time, the detective and I would look at the contents of the jewel case to keep an inventory. Nothing was missing until shortly after Nellie Conway came to work, then a diamond pendant was missing. By that I mean a synthetic diamond pendant, a bit of

costume jewellery. We made an excuse to switch off the
lights and switch on the ultra-violet light, and Nellie
Conway's finger-tips blazed into brilliance. That was
circumstantial evidence and we jumped at conclusions
from it, and naturally jumped at the wrong conclusion,
as Mr. Mason so ably pointed out."

"What happened in that case?"

"Nellie Conway was found not guilty in, I believe,
record time."

"By a jury?"

"Yes, sir."

"Now then," Hamilton Burger said, "with reference to
those three tablets which were found in the waste-basket,
according to Dr. Keener's testimony, were you there when
the basket was searched?"

"I was. Yes, sir."

"And what was done with those three tablets?"

"Well, they were examined and placed in a small box
and . . . well, when it began to appear that in all human
probability the substitution must have been made by the
defendant in this case, I suggested to the police officers
that when I had told the defendant something about the
case against Nellie Conway and how it had been handled,
the defendant had wanted to see the jewel case. So I
opened the desk, got out the jewel case and let the
defendant look at it."

"Did she handle it?"

"Yes. She took it in her hands."

"Did anyone else handle it?"

"No, sir. At about that time the defendant's brother,
who was upstairs, called to her, and she returned the
jewel case to me. I hurriedly placed it on top of the desk
and followed her upstairs."

"Later on, you told the police about this?"

"Yes, sir. I told them that perhaps some of the

fluorescent powder which still adhered to the jewel case might . . . well, I suggested to the police officers it might be well to look at those three tablets or pills under ultra-violet light."

"Did they do so in your presence?"

"Yes, sir."

"And what happened?"

"There was a very faint, but unmistakable fluorescence."

There was a startled gasp from the spectators in the court-room, then the buzz of whispering.

It was at that moment that Hamilton Burger, apparently suddenly aware of the time, of which he had previously been unconscious, glanced apprehensively at the clock on the court-room wall, and said, "Your Honour, I find that I have exceeded the time of adjournment by some ten minutes."

"So you have," Judge Howison said, his voice plainly indicating that he himself had been so interested in this dramatic phase of the testimony that he had not noticed the passing of time.

"I'm sorry," Hamilton Burger said simply.

Judge Howison said, "It appearing that the examination and cross-examination of this witness will occupy a very considerable period of time, and it now having passed the usual hour for the evening adjournment, the Court will take a recess until tomorrow morning at ten o'clock. During that time the members of the jury are admonished not to discuss the case among themselves or with others, nor permit it to be discussed in their presence. You jurors are not to form or express any opinion as to the guilt or innocence of the defendant until the case is finally sub-mitted to you. The defendant is remanded to custody. The Court will adjourn until tomorrow morning at ten o'clock."

Judge Howison left the bench and there was instantly

a great commotion of voices throughout the court-room.

Mason turned to Victoria Braxton. "Did you handle that jewel chest?" he asked.

"Yes. I was curious. I asked him about it. He took me downstairs and opened the desk. When we went back upstairs he left it on the top of the desk. But while I am the only one who handled it at the time, the others did later."

"What others?"

"Why, Jim and Georgiana."

"Did you see them handle it?"

"No, but they went downstairs, and Georgiana asked me when she came back up why Elizabeth's jewel case was out in plain sight—so if they saw it they must have handled it. Georgiana has an insatiable curiosity."

"And Nathan Bain handled it when he gave it to you, didn't he?"

"Why, yes. I hadn't thought of that."

"And who put it back in the desk? Did he?"

"The housekeeper, I think."

"It's the same old story," Mason said. "Everyone handled it, yet by building up to this climax just at adjournment, the District Attorney conveys the impression he's proven your guilt.

"That's always the way with these fluorescent powder cases. The thing is so dramatic, the fluorescent finger-tips seem so damning, that everyone loses his mental perspective.

"Now, couldn't Nathan Bain have opened the door of his wife's bedroom, picked up the tablets from the saucer and switched the poison tablets?"

"No . . . I don't think so, not while I was there."

"They were close to the door?"

"Yes. If he'd opened the door to look in he could have done it, but he didn't. But couldn't he have substituted them while Nellie Conway had them, carrying them around in that box?"

"Don't worry," Mason interrupted. "I'm going to cover that phase of the case on cross-examination. What I'm asking now is whether he could have made the substitution *after* Nellie Conway had put the tablets on the saucer and left them with you."

"No. That would have been impossible."

"And what time was it that you were handling the jewel case and got that powder on your fingers?"

"Shortly before three in the morning. We got to the airport at one-forty-five, and by the time we arrived at the house it must have been two-thirty."

"And at about three o'clock you went in to see Elizabeth?"

"Yes."

"The three of you?"

"Yes."

"Keep a stiff upper lip," Mason said, as the deputy sheriff touched her arm.

"Don't worry," she told him, and followed the officer to the prisoner's exit.

Jim Braxton and his wife, waiting for Mason immediately outside the bar which segregated the space reserved for attorneys and officers of the court from the rest of the court-room, grabbed the lawyer, one by each arm.

It was Georgiana who did the talking.

"That dirty hypocrite," she said. "He's sitting there so butter wouldn't melt in his mouth, and the worst of it is, he's getting away with it. That's what I told you about him, Mr. Mason, the . . . the toad, the big, fat toad! That's all he is, a toad!"

"Take it easy," Mason said. "It's not going to do any good running up a blood pressure over it."

"He's sitting there just trying to lie his way out of it. He's fixed it up with this Nellie Conway, and between them they're telling a great story for the jury, trying to make it appear that Vicki must have been the one who gave her that poisoned medicine. Mr. Mason, you've simply got to do something, you can't let him get away with this."

"I'm going to do the best I can," Mason said.

"We all know who murdered Elizabeth. It was Nathan Bain, and he and that Conway woman have cooked up a story that will look good in print and will lull the suspicions of the jurors. We know the real Nathan Bain, Mr. Mason, and he's not like this at all. He's just a shrewd, selfish, cunning individual—unbelievably cunning —but he does have the knack of standing up and talking to people in a way that makes it seem he's baring his very soul, that he's giving them an insight into his innermost thoughts. Actually the man's innermost thoughts are just as black and impenetrable as . . . as . . . as an inkwell full of ink."

Mason said, "I've torn him wide open once. I may be able to do it again, but this time he's been very carefully coached."

"Hmph!" she said. "The probabilities are he's the one who coached that District Attorney. Between them they're putting on a great show."

"Aren't they?" Mason said.

"Couldn't you have objected to a lot of that stuff?" Jim interposed timidly.

"Sure," Mason said, "but I want it in. The more of this stuff he's putting in, the more latitude it gives me in cross-examination. The more I try to keep out, the more the jurors suspect we're afraid to have them learn all the facts."

Georgiana said, "Don't depend too much on cross-examination. He's been prepared for that. Between him and that District Attorney they've rehearsed that act until they're black in the face. They're both birds of a stripe— I mean a feather. Just a couple of actors putting on a big razzle-dazzle. If you could only know Nathan the way he *really* is, and then see him the way he is on the witness stand, you'd appreciate some of the things I've been telling you."

"Well," Mason said, reassuringly, "perhaps we can find some way of letting the jury see him the way he really is."

18

Mason, in midnight conference with Paul Drake and Della Street, paced the floor of his office.

"Damn Burger," Mason said. "He has some devastating bomb he's going to drop."

"That fluorescent powder? Could that have been it?" Paul Drake asked.

"No. That doesn't really prove as much as they're trying to make it appear. Anyone in the house could have touched the casket. Nathan Bain saw the defendant touching it, but . . . that damn housekeeper, Paul, what have you been able to find out about her?"

"Just what our reports have shown, Perry. She keeps pretty much to herself, and has no close friends. She apparently was devoted to Bain's first wife and she was devoted to Elizabeth. How she feels toward Nathan is a question."

"If she felt that Nathan Bain poisoned Elizabeth . . ."

"But she doesn't, Perry. She's positive Vicki Braxton did it. She says Vicki is a pretty smooth article, and she knows about other evidence in the case. She's positive Vicki wheedled Elizabeth into making a will, and then when Elizabeth became suspicious and refused to complete the will, Vicki poisoned her."

Mason thought that over, then said, "If she could be made to believe that Nathan poisoned Elizabeth, and then that he might have poisoned his first wife, Marta, don't you think she then might tell us something that could help?"

Drake said, "I don't know. I've had one of my cleverest woman operatives make her casual acquaintance, and get her talking as well as anyone can. Of course, we've asked no questions about Marta's death. The housekeeper says the doctor gave Nellie those three pills. Nellie had them in a little box. She saw them on the kitchen table when she and Nellie had coffee together just before midnight, and knows they were the same pills. She says Hamilton Burger can prove they were, that it had to be Nellie or Vicki who made the switch. The police have positive proof. And, of course, she says Nellie had no motive."

Mason, pacing the floor, said, "How do we know she had no motive? That's only what the housekeeper says."

"We can't find any motive, Perry. Vicki, of course, had the big motive."

"Nellie had enough motive to give those three sleeping tablets, Paul."

"Sure—money."

"Well, why couldn't more money have been the motive for the poison tablets? Those extra three tablets after the confession stuff on the first three would be a masterly touch. Good Lord, Paul, we have every element of proof. Bain gave Nellie money to administer sleeping tablets. They both admit it. Then he gave her more money, and someone changed the doctor's three tablets to poison tablets. Nellie and Nathan Bain knew that if he gave her a lot of money it would be traced, so instead of being surreptitious about it, he did it right under our noses.

"He arrested Nellie on a charge where he had no real proof. Nellie had previously contacted me, so he knew I'd rush to her rescue. Then I get her acquitted, and Nathan pays her a lot of dough and puts her back in the room where she has the last three tablets Elizabeth ever took."

Drake said, "Gosh, Perry, when you look at it that way it sure seems dead open-and-shut."

"Sure it does, Paul. It's all this razzle-dazzle stuff that confuses the issues."

Drake said, "Just strip the issues down to bare fact like that, Perry, and you may be able to sell the jury on the idea—unless Burger comes up with something new. Even I never realised how damning the bare facts are. It's only when they're all dressed up in this hocus-pocus that they seem to become innocuous. Nellie and Bain could have staged that whole act, the fluorescent powder and everything.

"When you come right down to it, that fluorescent powder on the tablets and on Vicki Braxton's fingers is a terribly damning bit of circumstantial evidence—and yet it was deliberately planted by Bain. By using the case against Nellie as a red herring . . . dammit, Perry, I believe you're right!"

Mason, continuing to pace the floor, said, "The only thing that I have to be sure of is that Hamilton Burger gets the door wide open."

"What do you mean?"

"Opens the door so I can start cross-examining Nathan Bain about the death of his first wife, without having Burger be in a position to yell that it's incompetent, irrelevant and immaterial; and that because he didn't touch on anything dealing with her in his direct examination, I can't cross-examine on it."

"Of course," Drake said, "you haven't made a move toward getting the body exhumed."

"Why should I? I'm going to put that up to the prosecution. I'll dare them to do it."

"They'd never try to exhume that body in a thousand years. If it *should* turn out she'd died of arsenic poisoning, it would knock the case against Victoria Braxton sky-high. They know that."

"That's fine," Mason told him. "We'll leave the body

in the grave but we'll certainly drag her ghost in front of that jury—if I can only find some way to make it relevant and material. Tell me all you've found out about her, Paul."

Drake said, "She came from a rather wealthy family. Her parents were opposed to the marriage. They're Eastern people. This girl, Marta, evidently had a lot of spirit. She fell for Nathan Bain like a ton of bricks. Between you and me, Perry, Nathan Bain, with that ability to impress people and that gift of gab, must have been quite some ladies' man before he started putting on all that weight."

"Appparently so. Go on, Paul. Tell me more about Marta."

"Well, Marta was independent and high-strung. She had some money of her own, quite a little money. It had come to her from an uncle and was in trust, to be delivered to her when she was twenty-five. Prior to that time she had the income from it."

"How much money?"

"Something over fifty thousand."

"Go ahead. What happened?"

"Well, either Nathan Bain convinced her that her parents were persecuting him, or she got the idea in some way. Anyhow, after the marriage there was a very distinct coolness—she tried to be the dutiful daughter all right, but she had thrown in her lot with Nathan Bain and she wanted her parents to understand it. The old folks thought it was simply the fling of a high-strung, impetuous girl, and that she'd get over it and would probably come back home."

"Tell me some more about the fifty thousand bucks."

"She was twenty-five on the seventeenth of June. She got the money in her own name. On the first of August of the same year she was dead. Nathan Bain got the money. He was a big shot for a while, and then horse racing and poor investments got him down, and he picked out another girl with money. This time a good wad of money. Elizabeth Bain had at least half a million, and it may run more than that. He thought he was going to get his hands on her money, and she had other ideas, so then Elizabeth Bain died. The trouble is that he made a couple of false passes first and she became suspicious, so she disinherited him with that will. Good Lord, when you summarise the naked facts they make Bain look like a fiend, but when you see him on that witness stand, clothed in grief, humility and repentance, and being so damned human about it all. . . . Hell, Perry, I'll bet there isn't a man on that jury but what's found himself in Bain's shoes at one time or another. I tell you Bain has won them over.

"Perry, I don't want to inquire into your business when it's none of my business, but does it seem to you that there's anything phony about that will?"

"What about it?"

"Well, it was made in the handwriting of the decedent on the morning of the date she died, but the wording sounds a little funny, as though she had been interrupted in the middle of the thing in some way. The housekeeper tells my operative she thinks Vicki was trying to high-pressure Elizabeth into making the will and that Elizabeth balked and refused to complete it and sign it."

Mason said, "That's something Nathan Bain's lawyers will have to prove in the Probate Court."

"I was wondering if you'd noticed the way the will seems to break off in the middle."

Mason's reply to that was complete silence.

"Well," Drake said, "that's the story, Perry. I *could* have people whisper a word or two into the ears of Marta's parents. . . ."

Mason shook his head. "Then it wouldn't come as any surprise to Hamilton Burger, and he'll keep the door closed so I can't use it on Bain's cross-examination. No, Paul, I'm going to go into court tomorrow and when Hamilton Burger gets the door opened so I can cross-examine Nathan Bain, I'm going to spring the point. Just as soon as I've done that, I want you to get Marta's parents on the phone, tell them what's happened, and get them to raise hell yelling for an exhumation and autopsy. Remember, Paul, do that the minute I spring the point. Have it so you can get to a phone at once."

"Leave it to me," Drake said. "If you play it right you may blast Bain out of that humble, repentant sinner act. And if you can't do it, Perry, that jury's going against you."

"I know it," Mason said, grimly. "You're not telling me anything, Paul."

19

As court convened the next day, Hamilton Burger's manner gave no doubt but what he was now moving in for the kill.

Once or twice he glanced sidelong at Perry Mason, a glance of sneering triumph.

"Your Honour," he said, "Nathan Bain was on the stand, and I'll ask him to resume his place on the witness stand if he will."

Nathan Bain, moving like an elephant walking on eggs, marched up to the witness stand, composed himself in the chair, and looked at Hamilton Burger with the expression of a repentant but loyal dog, quite evidently a man who had stripped himself to the bone in the interests of justice, and was willing, if necessary, to make even further sacrifices.

"Mr. Bain, directing your attention to events which took place immediately after your wife's death."

"Yes, sir."

"Did you assist the officers in making any search of the premises?"

"I did. Yes, sir."

"Now will you describe the premises, please, generally?"

"Well, the house is a two-and-a-half-storey house. There is a garage at the back, and a patio."

"Is there shrubbery in the patio?"

"Surrounding the patio, yes. Shrubbery and a hedge."

"Now in searching this patio did you find anything, or

were you present when the officers found anything?"

"Yes, sir."

"What?"

"A bottle wrapped in paper."

"Were you present when the officers unwrapped that paper?"

"I was. Yes, sir."

"And what was in the paper?"

"A bottle containing a label from a Honolulu drugstore, with the word 'arsenic' printed on it."

Perry Mason heard a commotion back of him.

Victoria Braxton got to her feet, choked, started to say something.

The deputy sheriff, who had her in custody, rushed to her side, and then suddenly wild screams of hysterical laughter penetrated the court-room as Victoria Braxton, laughing, screaming and crying, had hysterics.

"Pardon me," Hamilton Burger said, with a bow at Perry Mason. "Your client seems to be emotionally upset. I think, Your Honour, we should have a recess until the defendant is able to proceed with the trial."

"Recess until eleven o'clock," Judge Howison said, banging his gavel on the desk. "Is there a physician in the court-room?"

"Dr. Keener is here."

"He'd better have a look at this defendant," Judge Howison said, and promptly retired to chambers.

Complete pandemonium broke loose in the court-room, spectators surging forward, deputy sheriffs in attendance grappling with Victoria Braxton, newspaper photographers battling for places to secure photographs from a point of vantage, the jurors, heedless of the admonition of the court, craning their necks to get a glimpse of what was going on.

It was almost forty-five minutes before a white,

emotionally-shaken, trembling Victoria Braxton could even talk with Perry Mason in a witness room adjoining the judge's chambers.

"Well?" Mason asked, coldly.

She said, "Don't start blaming me or I'll blow my top again. I took a chance on disposing of that arsenic, and lost, that's all."

"Would you mind telling me what it's all about?"

She said, "It's simple. I bought that arsenic in Honolulu for a cat that had been making life hideous there in the bungalows. The bottle was in my baggage. When I got back to the house and learned that Elizabeth had died from arsenic poisoning, I suddenly remembered having it and thought perhaps the possession of it might be misconstrued. I'd signed the poison register in Honolulu and . . . well, I knew that the police were snooping around and I felt quite certain they'd manage to inspect my baggage, so I stepped to my upstairs bedroom window and threw it out into the shrubbery. Someone must have seen me, otherwise I can't imagine why they'd have searched the premises. Now that's the whole story."

Mason was silent.

"How bad is it?" she asked.

Mason said, "Short of some sort of a legal miracle, it's bad enough to get you a verdict of first-degree murder at the hands of the jury, probably with the death penalty."

"That's what I thought," she said.

Mason got up and started pacing the floor.

"What do we do?" she asked. "Or is there anything we can do?"

Mason said, "I could probably get a continuance for a couple of days on the ground that you're emotionally upset. If I did that, it would ruin whatever last faint, glimmering chance we have. If you're telling the truth and can get on the stand and tell it so you convince at least one of the jurors, we can get a hung jury. Our only hope now is to hurry this trial to a conclusion so fast that public opinion doesn't have a chance to crystallise into a feeling of complete hostility. Do you feel that you can go back to the court-room and go through with the thing?"

"I can go through with anything now, I guess. I'm shaking like an autumn leaf, but I'll take it on my chin now."

Mason said, "You *might* have told me this before, you know."

"If I had, you wouldn't have handled my case. I'm grown-up, Mr. Mason. I'm a big girl now. I took a gamble and I lost. Don't rub it in. I'm the one who will be executed, not you."

"Let's go back to court," Mason said, tersely.

"Will you," she asked, "make any explanation of my hysterics to the jury?"

"Sure."

"When?"

"When I can think up an explanation that won't raise more hell with your case," Mason said.

There was sudden hope in her eyes. "Do you think you can do that now—before the bad impression I made has had a chance to sink in?"

"No," Mason said, "we can't make any explanation until we can win at least one friend on that jury. Come on, we're going to have to face it." Turning, he walked back to a court-room which now regarded him with a concentrated stare of sullen hostility.

Judge Howison took the bench and called the court to order. Hamilton Burger, unduly solicitous, inquired of Mason. "Is your client able to proceed?"

"Quite!" Mason snapped at him.

"Very well," Hamilton Burger said. "But I can appreciate the shock she has sustained. The prosecution wishes to be just, but it wants to be humane. If this upset, white-faced, trembling defendant is in as bad shape as she seems, we——"

"She isn't," Mason interrupted. "Go on with the case and save your sympathies for your star witness."

"I can understand and so forgive your short temper," Burger said with a smirk. "Mr. Nathan Bain, will you resume your position on the stand? Now, Mr. Bain, I am going to ask you if you would know that bottle when you saw it again."

"Yes, sir. My initials are marked on the label as well as those of the officers who were participating in the search."

"Is this the bottle?"

Hamilton Burger handed him a box with a glass top, containing a small bottle.

"That is it."

"We ask that this be received in evidence, Your Honour," Hamilton Burger said.

Mason said shortly, "Objected to as incompetent, irrelevant and immaterial. No connection whatever has been shown between the bottle and the defendant, and the Court will notice that this bottle contains a white powder. The unmistakable evidence is that if Elizabeth Bain was poisoned she was poisoned with three five-grain tablets."

"Just a moment," Hamilton Burger said. "We can connect this up if the Court please, but it will be necessary to call two witnesses in order to do so. In view of Mr. Mason's objection, I will ask that Mr. Bain now step aside for just a moment and make way for two witnesses who will be able to dispose of the points raised in the objection."

"In that case," Judge Howison said, "I would suggest that you simply mark the exhibit for identification and then, after you are finished with this witness, you can put the others on."

That did not suit Burger's strategy and his face showed it. "Your Honour," he said, "one of these witnesses is from Honolulu. It is very important that he get back. If I could call him just briefly."

"What's he going to testify to?" Mason asked.

Hamilton Burger welcomed the opportunity to turn to Mason. "That witness," he said, "is a clerk in a drug-store on Hotel Street in Honolulu. He is going to identify the defendant as being the woman who entered his drug-store and asked for arsenic in order to poison a cat that had been terrorising the neighbourhood, killing kittens, carrying off birds, and making a general nuisance of himself. He is going to produce a poison register on which will appear the date and the signature of the defendant."

Mason said casually, "Why, there's no need to call *him!* We'll stipulate to all that."

"You'll stipulate to it?"

"Good heavens, yes," Mason said. "Of course we'll stipulate to it. It's the truth."

"Oh, I see," Burger said slyly. "In view of the defendant's hysterics——"

"That will do," Judge Howison said tartly. "Confine your remarks to the Court, Mr. District Attorney. In view of the stipulation of Counsel, the statement of proof just made by the District Attorney will be considered as part of the evidence in this case."

"And," Hamilton Burger went on, obviously taken aback, "he will identify the bottle and the label as being the bottle that was given to the defendant, and will produce samples of typewriting made on the typewriter of the drugstore, which we expect to prove by a handwriting expert will show that this label——"

"No question about it," Mason said. "We'll stipulate it. We admit it."

"And by that stipulation, that, too, will be considered in evidence," Judge Howison said. "In view of Mr. Mason's stipulation, that disposes of the defendant's objection that the bottle has not been connected with the defendant?"

"Quite right, Your Honour," Mason said, smiling urbanely. "I just wanted to make sure the proof was in. That was the sole object of my objection. Now then, I would like to ask at this time if there is any *other* proof connecting this bottle with the defendant? If there is, let's have it all at this time and then we'll stipulate the bottle can be received in evidence."

Hamilton Burger said, "There is other evidence."

"Let's have it."

"I would prefer to introduce it later."

"Then," Mason said, "I'll renew the objection to the fact that the bottle is incompetent, irrelevant and immaterial. There is no evidence connecting this particular bottle with the defendant."

"Oh, all right," Hamilton Burger said. "The wrapping paper contains a finger-print of the defendant in the same fluorescent powder that was dusted on that jewel box. It fluoresces under ultra-violet light and it can be seen and identified as a finger-print of the defendant."

"You are certain of that?" Mason asked.

"I'm certain of it, and I have a finger-print expert sitting right here in court who can swear to it."

"Then I'll stipulate it," Mason said, cheerfully.

Judge Howison frowned. "I am not certain that in a case of this gravity I want Counsel to make stipulations as to such an important piece of evidence. I think, Mr.

District Attorney, I'm going to ask you to put that witness on the stand."

"Very well," the District Attorney said. "If the Court will permit Nathan Bain to step to one side, I'll call Sergeant Holcomb."

"Very well," the Court said, "for this limited purpose of identifying the bottle, we will call Sergeant Holcomb."

Nathan Bain left the stand. Sergeant Holcomb held up his right hand, was sworn, and took the witness stand.

Nor could he resist a glance of triumph at Perry Mason.

Hamilton Burger said, "I show you this bottle and ask if you have ever seen it before?"

"Yes, sir."

"Where?"

"It was found on the seventeenth day of September on the premises of Nathan Bain, in a hedge in the patio."

"I now hand you a piece of paper and ask you what that paper is?"

"That is the paper that surrounded the bottle, in which the bottle was wrapped."

"Did you make any test of that paper?"

"I did. Yes, sir."

"What did you find on it?"

"I found the finger-print of the middle finger of the right hand of the defendant. That finger-print, incidentally, bore faint traces of fluorescence. In other words, in ultra-violet light it showed the same unmistakable characteristics as the powder which had been placed on the jewel case in the living-room of Nathan Bain."

"Cross-examine," Hamilton Burger said.

"That paper was on the *outside* of the bottle?" Mason asked.

"Yes, sir."

"And the finger-print was on it?"

"Yes, sir."

"Any other prints?"

"No prints that were such as could be identified, but there were numerous smudges which were faintly fluorescent. In other words, they had been made with the fingers of a hand that had touched fluorescent powder, but they were mere smudges."

"And the fluorescence was quite faint?"

"Yes, sir."

"Now how did that compare with the fluorescence on the tablets which were found in the waste-basket?"

"That on the tablets was much stronger."

"There were no fluorescent prints, smudges or traces on the bottle, on the label on the bottle, or the inside of the paper in which the bottle had been wrapped, or in fact, on any single thing inside that paper?"

"Well, no."

"And if the defendant, with enough of that fluorescent powder on her fingers to have left smudges or prints on the paper covering the bottle, had opened the paper to get at the bottle, or had opened the bottle to get at the contents, there would have been such traces of fluorescence, would there not?"

"I am not prepared to say."

"Why? You're testifying as an expert."

"Well . . . I don't know when she got the arsenic out of the bottle. That may have been before . . . I don't know, Mr. Mason. I can't answer your question. There are too many uncertain factors involved."

"I thought you couldn't answer it," Mason said with exaggerated courtesy. "Thank you very much, Sergeant. That is all."

"Nathan Bain, will you return to the stand, please," Hamilton Burger said. "Now, Your Honour, I renew my offer that this bottle and the wrapping paper be received as People's exhibits."

"They will be so received. Now let's see, the three tablets have been identified as People's Exhibit A, the bottle will be People's Exhibit B, and the wrapping paper will be People's Exhibit C."

"Cross-examine the witness, Bain," Hamilton Burger said sharply.

Mason glanced anxiously at the clock. He had time for only a few questions before the noon adjournment. Any impression he was to make on the jury before adjournment must be done quickly.

"You were estranged from your wife, Mr. Bain?"

"Yes. Yes, sir. Unfortunately . . . and as I have been forced to admit, due entirely to my fault."

It was apparent that any further attempt on the part of Mason to persecute this repentant sinner could only result in further alienating the jury.

Mason said, "Did you see your wife in her last illness?"

"At the very end, yes, when she was hardly conscious."

"You have been married once before?"

"Yes."

"Your first wife died?"

"Yes, sir."

"You did not see your wife, Elizabeth Bain, during the first part of her illness?"

"No. Due to the matters I have mentioned, she did not wish me to be in the rooom with her."

"Were you interested in learning about her symptoms?"

"Certainly I was interested. I paced the floor of my bedroom in an agony of self-torture, Mr. Mason. I asked for bulletins from my wife's bedside. I asked the doctor to describe her symptoms. I wanted to make certain that everything that could possibly be done by medical science was being done."

"You knew that those symptoms as described to you were said to be those of arsenic poisoning?"

"Yes."

"You were familiar with those symptoms?"

"No."

"You were not?"

"No."

"You had never seen them before?"

"Why, certainly not, Mr. Mason."

Mason got to his feet. "I will ask you, Mr. Bain, if at the time of her final and fatal illness your first wife, Marta, didn't exhibit each and every symptom that was exhibited by your wife, Elizabeth Bain?"

"Oh, Your Honour," Hamilton Burger shouted, "this is certainly going too far. This is an attempt by innuendo. Why, this is an inhuman, illegal——"

"I don't think so," Judge Howison said, watching Nathan Bain's face shrewdly. "The prosecution threw all doors wide open with this witness. I think under the circumstances I am going to give the defence every latitude for cross-examination. The objection is overruled."

"Answer the question," Mason said.

"That was different," Nathan Bain told him, his manner suddenly stripped of all its poise. In his own way he was as badly shocked as Victoria Braxton had been, and he showed it.

"What was different about it?"

"It was a different cause. She died from food poisoning. The doctors said so. The death certificate shows——"

"Was there any autopsy?"

"No. I tell you there was a certificate of death."

"An autopsy *was* performed on your wife, Elizabeth, was it not?"

"Yes, sir."

"For the purpose of *proving* that she died of arsenic poisoning?"

"I believe the District Attorney ordered the autopsy."

"But no autopsy was performed on your wife, Marta?"

"No." Nathan Bain seemed to have sagged within his clothes.

"You stood to inherit some half a million dollars from your wife, Elizabeth?"

"Apparently not. She seems to have left a will that——"

"You are going to contest that will, are you not?"

"Now, Your Honour," Hamilton Burger interposed, "I wish to object to this on the ground that it is calling for something that is far afield——"

"It goes to show the state of mind of this witness," Mason said. "He has testified at great length in mealy-mouthed repentance. Let's find out how deep that repentance goes."

"I think your language is unduly vigorous, Mr. Mason," Judge Howison said, "but I'm going to permit the witness to answer the question."

"Answer the question," Mason said. "Are you going to contest the will?"

"'Yes," Nathan Bain snapped. "That will is a complete phony. It is——"

"You expect to keep it from being probated, do you not?"

"I do."

"And thereby you will inherit some half-million dollars?"

"Possibly," Bain said, savagely angry.

"Now then," Mason said, "tell the jury how much you inherited after your first wife so unfortunately passed away with symptoms so similar to those exhibited by Elizabeth Bain during *her* last illness."

"Your Honour!" Hamilton Burger shouted. "This is an insinuation that is not warranted by the evidence. This is not proper cross-examination——"

"I think I will sustain that objection in the form in which the question is asked," Judge Howison ruled.

"Can you," Mason said, "point out to the jury any symptom that your wife, Marta, had that was not a symptom of your wife, Elizabeth Bain, in her last illness?"

Nathan Bain was uncomfortably silent.

"Can you?" Mason asked.

"I wasn't there to see the symptoms of Elizabeth's illness," Nathan Bain said at length.

"How much money did you inherit from your first wife, roughly speaking?"

"Objected to," Hamilton Burger said. "That is——"

"Overruled," Judge Howison snapped.

"Fifty thousand dollars."

"How long were you married to her before her death?"

"About two years."

"How long were you married to Elizabeth Bain before her death?"

"Two years, approximately."

Judge Howison glanced at the clock. "I dislike to interrupt Counsel's cross-examination," he said, "but this examination has already continued some few minutes past the usual hour for the Court's recess."

"I understand, Your Honour," Mason said.

"Court will adjourn until two o'clock this afternoon," Judge Howison said. "The defendant is remanded to custody and the jurors will remember the admonition of the Court."

Nathan Bain took advantage of that moment to dash down from the witness stand while the jurors were still leaving the jury box.

He shouted at Mason in a paroxysm of rage, "Why you . . . you . . . you dirty, despicable shyster! . . . I could kill you!"

Mason raised his voice. "No, no! Don't kill *me*, Mr. Bain! You wouldn't inherit a dime!"

A newspaper reporter roared with laughter.

Court attendants crowded forward to separate the two men, and the jury filed slowly and thoughtfully from the jury box.

20

PERRY MASON, Della Street and Paul Drake sat huddled
in conference in the little restaurant across the street from
the Hall of Justice. The proprietor, an old friend, had
ensconced them in a private dining-room and brought in
an extension telephone.

Mason, eating a baked ham sandwich and sipping a
glass of milk, said, "Hang it, Paul, I still can't get a clear
picture."

"Well, the jury have a clear picture," Drake said. "Of
course, you did a masterful job with Nathan Bain. You
may have won over some members of the jury *if* your
client can get on the stand and tell a decent story. But
you know she can't do it, Perry."

"Why not?"

"There's too much against her. Her finger-print on the
wrapper, the fact that she hurled that bottle out of the
window. She must have hurled it out of the window, and
there must have been some witness who saw her. You
can't believe that those men would have gone out and
started searching the grounds just on the strength of a
general investigation. Holcomb hasn't brains enough for
that."

"No," Mason conceded. "Some witness saw her throw
the bottle out of the window, or saw someone throw it
out of the window, that's a cinch."

"Well, there you are," Drake said. "She gets on the
stand and tries to tell a story, and then Hamilton Burger

jumps up and starts to cross-examine her, and by the time he gets done with her she'll be the greatest poisoner since Lucrezia Borgia."

Mason nodded glumly.

Drake said, "I've been watching that court-room, Perry; I've been talking with people who have listened to the evidence, and while you certainly made a magnificent job of stripping the mask off Nathan Bain, nevertheless your client is in a mess. That fit of hysterics put a noose around her neck."

"I'll say it did," Mason said wearily. "This business of getting into court representing a woman and then finding she's been holding out on you is tough on the nerves."

"Well, what would you have done under similar circumstances?" Della Street asked. "She thought her secret was safe. She knew that if she told you it would prevent you or any other reputable lawyer from taking the case."

"I suppose so," Mason agreed glumly, "but I still don't get the picture. Did you notice Nathan Bain's face when I asked him about the death of his first wife?"

Drake said, "You surely flabbergasted him."

"Why?" Mason asked.

"He'd been drilled and rehearsed on how to take your cross-examination; but this was an unexpected blow in a particularly vulnerable place."

"You agree with me it hit him hard?" Mason asked.

"He damn near fainted," Paul said.

Mason frowned thoughtfully, then, after a minute or two, asked, "You phoned Marta's parents?"

"The minute you made the point."

"How did they take it, Paul?"

"They're catching a plane, demanding the body be exhumed and raising hell generally."

Mason grinned.

"As I see it," Drake warned, "if the body *is* exhumed

and if she did die of arsenic poisoning, you may get a
hung jury *if* the defendant can tell a convincing story.
But if the body is exhumed and she didn't die of arsenic
poisoning, Perry, you're a gone goose. You'll have made
a martyr out of Nathan and a shyster out of yourself."

Mason nodded. "It's not a gamble I like, but it's a
gamble I have to take. A lawyer has to throw all his chips
out on the table when he gets in a situation like this."

"If your client could only explain that bottle of arsenic,"
Drake said.

"She can. She wanted it for a cat."

Drake shook his head. "The jury won't believe her,
Perry. Just wait until you hear Burger's argument to the
jury."

"Yes," Mason said sarcastically, "I can imagine Hamilton Burger saying, 'The murderess thought the wool had
been pulled over the eyes of everyone, and then when this
damning, this tell-tale piece of evidence, which her
Counsel is now trying to minimise, was brought into
Court, what did she do?—Ladies and gentlemen of the
jury, I don't ask you to accept *my* valuation of this damning bit of evidence. I ask you only to accept the valuation
which the defendant herself placed upon it.' . . . And
so and so on, ad infinitum."

"You make it sound damn convincing," Drake said.

"So will Hamilton Burger," Mason told him. "Call
your office, Paul. See if there's anything new."

Drake put through a call to his office and said, "I'm eating lunch. Anything new in the Bain case? . . . What? . . .
Let me have that again. . . . Hold the phone."

He turned to Mason and said, "A peculiar develop-
ment. We've been shadowing Nathan Bain, you know."

Mason nodded.

"Apparently Bain has no idea he's being tailed. Now I
told you that Bain, like all these men who have exploited

women by the exercise of irresistible charm, has a fatal weakness himself. As those fellows get older, they almost invariably fall for their own line. Some shrewd, selfish, scheming woman who is younger, is attractive, and on the make, gets them head-over-heels in love with them."

"Go ahead," Mason said. "What's the pitch, Paul?"

"Despite his attitude on the stand, Nathan Bain is absolutely nuts about Charlotte Moray. She's now back here in the Rapidex Apartments."

"Under what name?" Mason asked.

"Under her own name. She's been living there for months. Nathan Bain went to see her this morning just before he came to court."

Mason, pacing the floor, gave that matter thoughtful consideration.

"That should give you something to smear him with on further cross-examination," Drake said.

Again Mason nodded.

"Any instructions?" Drake asked.

Mason said suddenly, "Paul, I've got an idea."

"It's about time," Drake told him.

"Who will be in Nathan Bain's house this afternoon? Anyone?"

Drake said, "Let's see, Perry. I guess not. Bain and the housekeeper will both be in court and——"

Mason's interruption was sharp. "Paul, I want you to get a stake-out in some place near-by, where you can instal a recording machine. I want you to get into Bain's house and put a bug in the room that has the telephone."

Drake's face showed dismay. "Have a heart, Perry! You can't do that!"

Mason's face was hard as granite. "Paul, I'm gambling my reputation on this thing, and you're going to gamble right along with me. I want you to get a microphone in that room, a stake-out, and a complete recording device."

"Good Lord, Perry, he'll find the bug——"

"Put it where he won't find it."

"But he'll find it eventually, Perry. They'll be dusting or——"

"And by that time," Mason said, "they'll trace the wires and only find two loose, dangling ends."

Drake's face showed a glimmer of hope. "How long would we have to be on the job, Perry?"

Mason said, "Put two men on the house. I want to know when Bain comes in. I want to know who else comes in, and when they come in. Within an hour after Bain arrives he's going to get one telephone call. After that you can cut the wires, pick up your equipment and get out."

"It'll mean my licence if I get caught," Drake said.

"Then," Mason told him coldly, "don't get caught."

21

At the two o'clock session, Judge Howison addressed the crowded court-room.

"Somewhat against my better judgment," he said, "I have permitted the deputy sheriffs to admit spectators for whom there are no seats. These spectators will remain standing at the extreme edges of the court-room, along the walls, so as not to block the aisles. I wish to warn every spectator that his bearing must be compatible with the dignity of the Court. If there are untoward incidents I will clear the court-room.

"Mr. Nathan Bain was on the stand being cross-examined. You will resume the witness stand, Mr. Bain, and Mr. Mason will continue your cross-examination."

Nathan Bain had lost some of his assurance. Apparently the few questions Mason had asked him prior to the noon adjournment, and his loss of temper, had led him to realise that even the detailed coaching of Hamilton Burger was insufficient armour to protect him against Mason's thrusts.

Mason assumed a conversational tone of voice. "Mr. Bain," he said, "going back to your testimony concerning the use of this fluorescent powder. As I understand it, there had been persistent thefts from your house over a period of time?"

"Yes, sir."

"Coincident with the employment of Nellie Conway?"

"That's right, although I realise now that was merely a coincidence as far as time is concerned."

"Jewellery had been missing?"

"Yes, sir."

"And there had been no missing jewellery prior to the time Nellie Conway was employed?"

"No, sir."

"There had been no complaint from any member of the household as to things that were missing?"

"No, sir."

"Now, your wife kept her jewellery in a jewel case that was customarily locked in the desk in the living-room?"

"Yes, sir."

"And Nellie Conway, of course, was employed as a nurse to wait on your wife after the unfortunate accident which had damaged her spinal cord?"

"Yes, sir."

"And immediately after that accident, and at all times thereafter, your wife developed a feeling of bitterness toward you and would not permit you in the room?"

"My wife was nervous."

"Answer the question. *Did* your wife develop a bitterness of feeling toward you and would not allow you in the room?"

"Yes, sir."

"So you had no direct oral communication with your wife from the time of the accident until her death?"

"Unfortunately, that is right."

"Then you must have known prior to the accident that she had those incriminating papers secreted in her room."

"I did."

"How much prior to the accident?"

"I can't remember."

"Use your best recollection."

"Well, I . . ."

"Immediately before the accident, isn't that right?"

"Well, it may have been. She told me about those

papers on . . . let me see, the . . . the memory of the accident has, of course, obliterated so many things . . . it was such a shock. . . ."

"As a matter of fact, she told you on the very day of the accident that she had the goods on you, that she had the evidence of your infidelity, and she was going to divorce you, didn't she?"

"I . . ."

Mason opened his brief-case and whipped out a letter which had been sent to Victoria Braxton.

"Yes or no, Mr. Bain?" he asked sharply, jerking the letter out of the envelope and whipping it open dramatically.

"Yes," Nathan Bain admitted, shamefacedly.

"Now then," Mason said, "you're positive that items of jewellery had been missing from the house over a period of time after Nellie Conway was employed?"

"Yes, but I have repeatedly told you, and I wish to tell you again, that while you are using Nellie Conway's employment as referring to a measure of time, that is all it refers to. I am satisfied that Miss Conway had nothing to do with the loss of the jewellery."

"But it was disappearing?"

"Yes, sir."

Mason got up and faced him dramatically, standing with his eyes boring into those of the witness, until every person in the court-room felt the tension, then he asked in slow, level tones, "How—did—you—know?"

"How did I know what?"

"That your wife's jewellery was missing?"

"Why, I know generally what she had and——"

"You weren't communicating with your wife?"

"No."

"Therefore your wife couldn't have told you?"

"No."

"The jewel case was kept in the desk?"

"Yes."

"Your wife couldn't walk?"

"No."

"How did you know the jewellery was missing?"

Bain shifted his position uneasily on the witness stand.

"How did you know?" Mason thundered.

"Well," Nathan Bain began, "I . . . I just happened to notice that . . ."

"This desk was your wife's private writing desk, wasn't it?"

"Yes."

"But you had retained a duplicate key to that desk without her knowledge?"

"I had a key."

"The jewel case was kept locked?"

"Yes."

"And you had retained a duplicate key to that jewel box without her knowledge?"

"I explained that all to you once before, Mr. Mason."

"I am not asking for an explanation, I am asking for an answer. Did you or did you not retain a key to that jewel case without your wife's knowledge or consent?"

"Well, in a way, yes."

"Yes or no."

"I object to the question on the ground that it has already been asked and answered," Hamilton Burger said.

"Objection overruled!" Judge Howison snapped.

"Yes or no?" Mason asked.

"Yes," Nathan Bain said.

"Therefore," Mason said, "the only way for you to have known that items of jewellery had been missing *after* your wife's injury was for you to have surreptitiously opened that desk, surreptitiously opened her jewel box, and made a surreptitious inventory of the contents of the jewel box without her knowledge or consent, and without her specific permission. Isn't that right?"

"I was just checking up."

"Now then," Mason said, "what items of jewellery were missing from your wife's jewel case?"

"A diamond pendant. That is, an imitation——"

"I'm not talking about the items of synthetic jewellery that you placed there, but the items of genuine jewellery."

"I couldn't say."

"You didn't have an inventory of the contents?"

"No, sir, not of my wife's jewellery. Not a specific inventory."

"Then why did you go to the jewel case to make an inspection?"

"Just to check up."

"But if you didn't know what was in there how could you tell if anything was missing?"

"Well, I . . . I was just looking."

"And you can't tell us of any single specific item that is missing, or that was missing?"

"No, sir."

Once more Mason fixed Bain with accusing eyes.

"This girl friend of yours—with whom you had your affair, did you give her presents of jewellery?"

"Sir, do you mean to insinuate——"

"Did you give her presents of jewellery? Answer the question."

Bain ran his hand across his forehead.

"Yes or no?" Mason thundered.

"Yes."

"Thank you," Mason said sarcastically. "Now, were those presents of jewellery given to her in the boxes in which they came, or did you take them from your pocket and put them on her?"

"I can't remember."

"Can you remember any store where you bought any one, any single one of the articles of jewellery you gave her?"

"I . . . I mostly bought them at auctions."

"Do you have any single bill of sale for any one of those articles you now claim you purchased at auctions?"

"No, sir. I destroyed them."

Mason said, "I have been advised that the parents of Marta Bain, your first wife, wish to make an application to have the body exhumed. Would you have any objection?"

"Your Honour, Your Honour!" Hamilton Burger shouted. "I object to that question. It's argumentative. It's not proper cross-examination. It's foreign to the issues in this case. It's incompetent, irrelevant and immaterial and . . ."

"I think I will sustain the objection on the ground that it is argumentative," Judge Howison ruled. "However, I am disposed to allow Counsel for the defence a wide margin of cross-examination, particularly in view of the peculiar nature of the direct examination and the large amount of territory explored by you on direct."

"Are you willing to have Marta Bain's body exhumed?" Mason asked.

"Same objection."

"Same ruling."

Mason said, "Your Honour, I now ask that this case be adjourned until proceedings can be had for the exhumation of the body of Marta Bain, deceased. I feel that it is vital to the issues in this case to determine whether or not she met her death from arsenic poisoning."

"Oh, Your Honour," Hamilton Burger said, his tone showing an exasperation that indicated there was after all a limit to human endurance. "This is just a very adroit red herring drawn across the trail which is getting too hot to suit Counsel.

"If he had been so concerned about the death of Marta Bain, he could have made application for an adjournment before the case was tried. Now that we have a jury empanelled——"

"Nevertheless," Judge Howison interrupted, "the Court is inclined to think there may be something to the motion. I'm not going to rule on it immediately. I will take time to consider the matter and rule on it tomorrow morning. In the meantime, are you gentlemen prepared to proceed with the trial?"

Perry Mason shook his head. "Your Honour, the question of whether this motion is granted will effect my entire strategy in the trial. I do not care to go ahead until there has been a definite ruling."

"Very well." Judge Howison said, "I am going to reserve ruling until tomorrow morning at ten o'clock, and in the meantime Court will stand adjourned. The defendant is remanded to the custody of the sheriff, and the jury will remember the admonition of the Court not to converse among themselves or with any other person about the case, or permit it to be discussed in their presence; nor shall the jury reach any opinion as to the guilt or innocence of the defendant until the evidence is all in and the case has been finally submitted to it for decision.

"Court adjourned until ten o'cock tomorrow morning. In the meantime, I'm going to ask Counsel to cite any authorities they may have bearing on the question of the pertinency of an adjournment pending proceedings for the exhumation.

"Court's adjourned."

22

PAUL DRAKE'S tiny cubbyhole of an office was the nerve centre of the operations.

Mason and Della Street sat huddled around Drake's battle-scarred desk. The detective, with four or five telephones in front of him, reported operations from time to time as there were new developments.

"That early adjournment damn near wrecked us," he said. "If Nathan Bain had gone straight home he might have caught us. I certainly don't like this, Perry. It's taking last-minute, desperate chan——"

"They're taken now," Mason interrupted. "There's no use worrying about them. Where the deuce do you suppose Nathan Bain is?"

"He left Hamilton Berger's office half an hour ago," Drake said. "My shadow hasn't had a chance to report on him yet."

"If he should go to the Rapidex Apartments we're sunk," Mason said.

"Why?"

"I'll tell you after a while."

Drake said, "You're playing a desperate game. It's too filled with risk for you to let me know what it is. You're afraid that I'll refuse to ride along."

"No, that isn't it. You'll work better if you don't have your mind occupied with other stuff. Dammit, Paul, why don't you get an office that's big enough to walk around in?"

"Can't afford it."

"One would never suspect it from the bills you send. Quit worrying, Paul. A lawyer and detective who won't take chances for a client aren't worth their salt. Planting a bug isn't such a heinous offence."

"It isn't that," Drake said, "it's the chances you take getting in so you can plant the bug."

"I know," Mason sympathised. "But we can't pick and choose, Paul. We have to get certain information. We can't get it the easy way, so we have to get it the hard way. How did your man get in? With a pass key?"

"Sure."

"No one knows anything about it? No one saw him?"

"I don't think so. A neighbour *might* have noticed, but my man was carrying a basket of groceries, just as though he were a delivery boy."

"Where's your stake-out?"

"In a garage that we rented. I'm not too happy about that."

"Why not?"

"We had to rent it in too much of a hurry. I think the woman who owns the place thinks we're planning to hide stolen cars. I have a hunch she may notify the police."

Mason looked at his watch. "Well, we should be out of there within another hour anyway."

A telephone rang. Drake picked up the receiver, answered the phone, then nodded and said. "That's a lot better. Keep me posted. I want to know the minute anything happens."

He hung up the telephone, and turned to Mason. "All right, Perry, your trap's set, whatever it is. Nathan Bain and the housekeeper arrived at the house five minutes ago. My man tailed them there. This was his first opportunity to get to a telephone and make a report."

"There's someone else on duty?"

"Sure, sure," Drake said. "Don't worry about that. "That's all part of the routine. We have enough men on the job so we can let you know if anyone goes in or out, and keep you posted on developments."

Mason turned to Della Street. "Okay, Della, Do your stuff."

Della Street pulled a piece of paper from her pocket-book, spread it out on the desk and said, "I want an out-side line, Paul."

Drake threw a switch. "All right. That phone's con-nected. Dial your number."

Della Street's skilled fingers flew rapidly over the dial of the telephone.

"What's the number?" Drake asked, curiously.

"Nathan Bain," Mason said tersely.

Della Street sat with the receiver at her ear, waiting for an answer.

"Is it ringing?" Mason asked.

Della Street nodded.

Drake said in a low voice, "You do the damndest things, Perry. That letter that you pulled out of your brief-case and flashed in front of Nathan Bain, was that really a letter which Elizabeth wrote her sister, or was it——?"

"It was a recipe for a fruitcake," Mason said. "Dammit, Paul, you don't suppose they're not going to answer? Wouldn't your men——?"

He broke off as Della Street motioned for silence. Placing her mouth close to the telephone, she said in close, clipped, emotionless tones, "Mr. Nathan Bain? . . . Very well, please call him at once upon a matter of the greatest urgency. . . . Hello, is this Mr. Nathan Bain? Very well. This is the Receiving Hospital. A patient giving the name of Miss Charlotte Moray, residing at the Rapidex Apart-ments, has just arrived by ambulance and is being treated for arsenic poisoning. She claims this could only have come from eating chocolate creams which she received through the mail. She has asked us to notify you that she is being given emergency treatment, but suggests that if possible you come to see her at once."

Della Street waited a half-second, then in the same professional, efficient voice, "That is right. The name is Charlotte Moray. The address the Rapidex Apartments. Good-bye."

She hung up.

Drake looked at Mason with wide, incredulous eyes. "Of all the crazy, damn-fool things to do!"

Mason made an impatient gesture. "It's the only thing we can do, Paul. I have a theory. I have to find out whether it will hold water."

"But that isn't going to fool him," Drake said. "It will simply——"

Mason interrupted to say, "You keep your men on the job out there, recording any conversations that are heard over the microphone."

"But good heavens, Perry, you're not going to get anything that way."

"You can't tell," Mason told him.

They settled down for a period of anxious waiting.

After ten minutes, Mason said, "Hang it, Paul, I'll go crazy if I can't start moving around. How much longer do you suppose it will be before we get a report from your men in the stake-out?"

"Whenever they finish recording whatever there is to record. They're making regular routine reports every hour on the hour, but they'll report any developments that aren't routine."

"This won't be routine," Mason said. "It's like putting a camera out in the woods with a thread running to the flash-gun, coming back the next morning and seeing what's on the film. It may be a deer or it may be a skunk. You just have to wait until the film's developed to find out what tripped the shutter. That's the way it is with this stake-out."

"Perhaps it won't be the shutter that gets tripped," Drake said. "It may be a lawyer."

"It could be," Mason admitted.

"But, my gosh," Drake said, "the first thing he'll do will be to call Charlotte Moray."

"If he does, it will be interesting to know what he says to her."

Mason looked at his wrist watch and started drumming with the tips of his fingers on the desk.

Drake started to say something, then, after studying the expression on the lawyer's face, changed his mind and remained silent.

At the end of another five minutes Mason said anxiously, "How far would your men have to go to get to a telephone, Paul?"

"You mean the men who are watching the front of the Bain house?"

"No, no. The men who are on that stake-out."

"Not far, Perry. Just to a petrol station on the corner."

"How far in terms of minutes or seconds?"

"Two minutes at the outside."

Mason looked at his wrist watch again, then took a pencil from his pocket and nervously started sliding his finger tips up and down the pencil, reversing it with each operation.

"Just what are you expecting, Perry?" Drake asked.

Mason shook his head, said, "With every minute now I am expecting less and less. We should have heard before this."

Another five minutes passed.

Mason lit a cigarette, settled back in the chair with a sigh and said, "Well, Paul, I guess we've lost our gamble."

"It would help," Drake said, "if I knew what it was we'd bet on, how much we'd bet, and just how much we stand to lose."

Mason said impatiently, "Nathan Bain must have been in touch with Charlotte Moray and must have known that phone call was a plant."

"He didn't go out there," Drake said. "He and the housekeeper were at the District Attorney's office in conference with Hamilton Burger. When they came out they went directly home."

"Didn't stop anywhere and telephone?" Mason asked.

"I don't think so," Drake said. "I think my man would have reported it if they had. I told him to give me a report on everything they did, and he made that report fifteen or twenty minutes ago."

Mason wearily got up from his chair. "Then for some reason they must have called Charlotte Moray from the D.A.'s office. Now we'll have to figure something else. Tell your men at the first opportunity to cut the wires leading to the bug and go home. Clean out their equipment so the police won't find anything if they start following the wires."

"We'll cut the wires close to the house," Drake said. "And we'll do it just as soon as it gets dark."

"When will you be in touch with your men?"

"Within another twenty minutes. They report on the hour, even if nothing happens."

"All right," Mason said, "I guess that's it. He's probably suspicious."

The telephone, shattering the silence, caused Della Street to jump nervously.

"This may be it," Drake said, grabbing the telephone.

Mason stood poised and tense, waiting.

Drake said, "Hello . . . Yes, go ahead . . . What is it? . . Well, do the best you can. Give me a line on it.

You'll have to speak louder, I can't hear you. Get up closer to the telephone. . . ."

Suddenly Drake's face lightened. He looked up at Mason and nodded, said into the telephone, "Go ahead, keep feeding it into the line. Give me what you have."

Finally Drake said, "Hold the phone a minute. Wait there for instructions. Just hang on."

Drake pushed the palm of his hand over the mouthpiece of the telephone and said to Mason, "Bain and his housekeeper had a hell of a fight, standing right there by the telephone. Bain accused her of sending arsenic candy to Charlotte Moray. The housekeeper called him a liar and a bungler, pointed out how clumsy he'd been trying to kill his wife in that automobile accident . . . and then Bain evidently popped her one, and they started throwing mud back and forth. It came in perfectly."

"Does your man have all of it on the wax cylinders?" Mason asked.

"He's got it."

Mason grinned. "Tell him to sit out there for a while longer, then report again when it gets dark. Also let us know at once if anything new turns up."

Mason turned to Della Street, said, "Get Lieutenant Tragg at Homicide Squad, Della."

Della started dialling. Drake relayed Mason's instructions into the telephone.

A moment later Della Street nodded to Mason and the lawyer picked up the telephone, said, "Hello, Lieutenant. This is Perry Mason."

"What the hell do you want now?" Tragg asked.

"What makes you think I want anything, Tragg?"

"The tone of your voice. It's your polite act."

Mason laughed. "How grateful would you be if we gave you the solution of a couple of murders, all wrapped up with pink ribbon in a nice little package?"

"How grateful would I have to be?" Tragg asked cautiously.

Mason said, "A microphone would have to be police property."

"You mean that I'd planted it?"

"Yes."

"How certain are the solutions?"

"The cases are on ice."

"I guess it could be arranged," Tragg said, "but I wouldn't want to be a cat's paw. I'd want to be mighty certain I was playing a sure thing."

"You would be," Mason assured him. "Come on up to Paul Drake's office. By the time you get here we'll have everything ready."

"Okay, I'll ride along that far," Tragg told him. "This guy, Bain, doesn't look as good to me as he does to Holcomb and the D.A. . . . But, even so, you're going to have to show me."

Mason said, "Come on and be shown." He hung up the telephone, said to Della Street, "All right. Get Nathan Bain on the telephone."

"Nathan Bain!" Drake exclaimed. "Are you crazy?"

Mason shook his head.

Della Street's fingers were already busy with the manipulation of the dial.

"Hello," she said. "Hello . . . Mr. Bain? Just a moment, hold the line, please."

She passed the receiver to Mason.

Mason picked up the telephone, said, "Good afternoon, Mr. Bain. This is Perry Mason calling."

Bain said, "I have nothing to say to you, Mr. Mason. The District Attorney has promised me he's going to put a stop to your persecution of me. I'll see you in court tomorrow."

"Perhaps you won't."

"You're damn right I will!" Bain said angrily. "And when I do——"

"Just a moment," Mason interrupted, "before you make any definite appointments, Bain, you'd better look around the room and find the microphone. Good-bye."

Mason hung up the telephone.

Drake came all the way up out of the chair in startled protest. "Good Lord, Perry, do you know what you're doing? Do you realise——?"

"I think I do," Mason said, grinning. "Flight, you know, is an evidence of guilt. I think that within about ten minutes your man who's watching the house will report that Nathan Bain has dashed out and driven away in a hurry. I want Lieutenant Tragg to have a strong enough case so Hamilton Burger won't start punching holes in it."

23

THE garage had the dank, musty smell which seems to be spontaneously generated in buildings that are kept too long closed and where sunlight cannot penetrate.

It was cold and draughty. Paul Drake's men, bundled in overcoats, regulated the mechanism which turned the wax cylinders.

Lieutenant Tragg, flanked by Perry Mason and Della Street, leaned over the records, listening.

Paul Drake, nervously apprehensive, was standing slightly to one side, talking with one of his men.

The voices which were played back from the wax cylinder, amplified by a small loudspeaker, were sufficiently clear to be distinctly audible, although there was a slight distortion of the tones due to the amplification of the microphone.

At the end of some ten minutes, Tragg straightened as the voices on the end of the record ceased.

"Well, that's it," Mason said.

"How did you figure out what had happened, Mason?" Tragg asked.

"I was watching Bain's face when I accused him of having murdered his first wife. I saw that the thing hit him like a blow from a sledge-hammer. I thought at the moment it was because he was guilty, but later on I began to think about it and started putting two and two together.

"Of course, if his first wife had been poisoned by eating chocolate creams filled with arsenic, it stood to reason——"

"Wait a minute," Lieutenant Tragg said, "why didn't Nathan Bain get some of it if it was in the candy?"

"Because Bain doesn't eat chocolates. That's one thing he's allergic to. That narrows down the field. It had to be either Nathan Bain or the housekeeper.

"So then I started thinking. I wondered what would happen if the housekeeper had fallen in love with him, if she was one of those quiet, repressed, mousy women who would develop into a possessive——"

"Well, she was," Tragg said, "there's no question about it, now that I've listened to this conversation. They certainly are a pretty pair, and when they let go at each other hammer and tongs they told plenty."

"The housekeeper killed the first wife through jealousy. Then when she found she really was only one more woman as far as Nathan Bain was concerned, she still kept on in his employ just to be near him. Nathan Bain married money, and when he found he couldn't get hold of that money, he started trying to kill his wife. That guy sure has a way with women, and he sure played the field.

"It's interesting to hear the housekeeper on that record tell him what a clumsy, inefficient murderer he turned out to be, and how she had to step in and do the job, switching the arsenic tablets in place of the medicine the doctor had left when Nellie Conway, leaving the pill-box on the kitchen table, had moved over to the stove to warm up her coffee. That's when Bain popped her—a great pair they turned out to be."

Tragg suddenly turned to Drake. "What's the dope, Paul? What's happened over there? You have men watching the place."

Drake said, "Nathan Bain left in a hell of a hurry. He threw some stuff in a bag and was on his way. My man tried to tail him but there was absolutely no chance. Bain was hitting fifty miles an hour before he'd got to the end of the block."

"And the housekeeper hasn't shown?"

"No, she's still there."

Tragg smoked a thoughtful cigarette. "I guess it was pretty plain after all," he said. "Once you stop to figure it out, if the first wife was murdered and if Bain *didn't* do it, it almost *had* to be the housekeeper. It had to be someone who knew their intimate habits, who was in a position to slip poison into the candy, who knew that Nathan Bain was allergic to chocolate and wouldn't touch it. They're both of them a pretty kettle of fish. So Nathan Bain really did manipulate the accident that crushed his wife's spine, hoping he could kill her. What I don't see, Perry, is why he didn't get the housekeeper to give the sleeping medicine to his wife if they were that intimate."

"Don't you see," Mason pointed out, "that's the one thing that was the dead give away. He was afraid to let the housekeeper know what he was after, because the minute the housekeeper knew what he wanted *she* would have been the one to get those letters from Charlotte Moray. Bain had really fallen for the Moray woman, and he was afraid of what that crazy, insane, jealous housekeeper would have done to Charlotte Moray."

"I'm not too certain but what we'd better do something ourselves," Tragg said, "before she gets any ideas. I think I'll go over and pick this Imogene Ricker up. I'll want those records delivered down at headquarters."

"You'll have them," Drake promised.

Tragg looked at Drake thoughtfully and said, "You took a lot of chances on this thing, Paul."

Drake's eyes shifted.

"He was acting under my orders," Mason said.

Tragg cocked a quizzical eyebrow. "Okay, Perry, you

reached in your thumb and pulled out a plum. But one of these days the plum won't be there. You'll just get your thumb burnt and then it's going to be too damn bad."

"Oh, I don't know," Mason said. "I didn't take so many chances on this one. After all, it was almost a mathematical certainty, and the minute it became apparent that Nathan Bain was afraid to trust the housekeeper to get the purple letters written by Charlotte Moray——"

"Okay, you win," Tragg interrupted. "You don't have to explain when you've won. Winners never explain. Losers always do. I'm going over to pick up Imogene Ricker. You folks want to tag along behind?"

Mason nodded.

"I'll stay here," Drake said.

"You get those records down to headquarters," Tragg said, "and be damn certain nothing happens to them."

"Are you telling me," Drake said with feeling.

Tragg got in his police car. "It's only around the block, Perry, but I want my car there because I'll be taking that Ricker woman to headquarters. Do you want to drive your bus?"

"I think so, Lieutenant. I'll park right behind your car. If she should want to make a statement you can borrow Della Street to take it down in shorthand."

"I'd have to want that statement pretty damn bad to borrow your secretary," Tragg said. "I'm going to keep the Perry Mason angle out of this just as much as possible. The D.A. won't like it."

"To hell with the D.A.," Mason told him. "If you get a confession, call in the newspaper reporters and let the D.A. read about it in the headlines tomorrow."

"Are you," Tragg asked, "telling me how to run my business?"

"Sure," Mason said, grinning.

"Well, it won't work quite that way," Tragg admitted

"I'd get the D.A. on the phone and explain to him what it was all about and tell him he'd better come up to headquarters in a rush, but before he got there, somehow or other the newspaper men would have had a tip. They'd be phoning in the story about the time the D.A. arrived. . . . You give me about two minutes head start," Tragg went on, suddenly becoming crisply business-like, "then you can drive up to the house and see what the score is. And you fellows keep those records tuned in on that live microphone so that you hear everything. If she wants to get it off her chest, I'll see that she does the talking in the room by the telephone. Okay, let's go."

Tragg drove away. Mason gave him a two-minute start, then he and Della Street followed.

The police car was in front of the house. There was no sign of Lieutenant Tragg.

One of Paul Drake's men, who was shadowing the house, sauntered over to Mason's car. "Tragg just went in a few minutes ago," he said.

"I know," Mason told him. "Who let him in? The housekeeper?"

"No. The front door was unlatched. When he didn't get an answer, he opened it and walked in."

"Oh-oh!" Mason said.

At that moment, the door opened. Lieutenant Tragg beckoned.

The lawyer ran up the steps to the porch.

Tragg said, "Get your car, pick up Drake's men and get the hell out of here, Perry. I've just telephoned headquarters to send out the squad car."

"You mean," Mason asked, "that she——?"

"Evidently he throttled her . . . he was crazy in love with that Moray woman. When he and Imogene got to hurling verbal brick-bats at each other, he started choking her. Perhaps he only intended to make her lose consciousness so he could get away. . . . Anyway, it's a mess now, and I've got to play it my way. Remember, that's been my microphone all along. Round up Paul Drake's men. Tell them to get the hell out of here, and fast."

"How about Bain?" Mason asked apprehensively. "That Charlotte Moray woman may be in danger. If he should start for there and——"

"You don't have to keep telling me how to run my business," Lieutenant Tragg said. "Within sixty seconds a radio car will be staked out in front of the Rapidex Apartments. If Bain shows up they'll collar him. Shake a leg, Mason, get those agency men cleaned out of here."

Mason nodded, turned, took Della Street's arm, and started running down the porch stairs.

"Well," Della Street said, as Tragg gently closed the front door, "perhaps after all it was better that way, Chief. That poor housekeeper must have been about half-crazy. Don't you think it was better?"

"A hell of a lot better," Mason said grimly. "I'll chase Paul Drake's men out of here and then you go call up the hotel and get a nice airy room with a good, big bath."

Della Street raised her eyebrows. "What cooks?"

"Tell them," Mason explained, "that it's for Victoria Braxton, and that she'll be in sometime late this evening."